WILDERNESS THERAPY

Paul Cumbo

One Lane Bridge Publications
AMHERST, NEW YORK

One Lane Bridge Publications
Amherst, New York
www.paulcumbo.com

Publisher's Note: This is a work of fiction. All of the characters, organizations, and events portrayed in this novel are either products of the author's imagination or are used fictitiously.

Cover art by David M. Cumbo
On the web at www.dreamprismpress.com

Wilderness Therapy / Paul Cumbo. – 1st ed.
Hardcover ISBN 9780988208636
Paperback ISBN 9780988208650
eBook ISBN 9780988208643
Library of Congress Control Number (LCCN): 2020906344
YAF011000 Young Adult Fiction / Coming of Age

ALSO BY PAUL CUMBO

Boarding Pass
A Novel

Ten Stories
A Short Fiction Collection

Blue Doors: 150 Years of Jesuit Education
at Canisius High School, 1870–2020
A Sesquicentennial History

ON THE WEB AT PAULCUMBO.COM

PRAISE FOR WILDERNESS THERAPY

"Paul Cumbo has written a masterpiece that will grab you and hit you hard. This novel is about much more than 'wilderness therapy.' It's a great story, masterfully told."

Leonard Sax, MD, PhD, *New York Times* Bestselling Author of *Boys Adrift: The Five Factors Driving the Growing Epidemic of Unmotivated Boys and Underachieving Young Men*

"Powerful storytelling coupled with a spot-on portrayal of the teenage psyche. Cumbo's intricate, realistic characters, and the demons with which they wrestle, invite readers into the complex and often misunderstood emotional landscape of male adolescence."

Michael Gurian, *New York Times* Bestselling Author of *Saving Our Sons: A New Path for Raising Healthy and Resilient Boys*

"In *Wilderness Therapy*, Cumbo conjures an ensemble of sympathetic characters and offers a lovely map of how they might return from the wilderness of stereotypic, lonely boyhood. At a time of growing concern about the current generation of young males, this message from the trenches is affirming and inspiring: to know a boy, holding him close and accountable, is the ordinary magic of redemption."

Michael Reichert, PhD, Author of *How to Raise a Boy: The Power of Connection to Build Good Men*

"Cumbo's nuanced, intuitive understanding of adolescent boys is vividly displayed throughout *Wilderness Therapy,* a completely compelling novel."

James Power, EdD, Headmaster of St. Anselm Abbey School; Former Headmaster of Upper Canada College, Culver Academies, and Georgetown Preparatory School

"Cumbo's *Wilderness Therapy* is a tough and tender rendering of the human condition...a foray through the wilderness of wounded spirits and misguided solutions..."

Ann Holmquist, EdD, Vice President for Mission, Loyola High School of Los Angeles

"Cumbo offers readers a twisty psychological drama of loss, redemption, and trust... The mystery and thriller elements reveal themselves quietly, but then quickly take over the narrative, and the final 100 pages of the novel will have readers on the edges of their seats. The satisfying and complex conclusion adds further emotional depth without lapsing into bathos. A moving, slow-burn thriller..."

Kirkus Reviews

PRAISE FOR PAUL CUMBO

"Cumbo's stories are tender and well-crafted."

Publishers Weekly

"Excellently paced, thought-provoking fiction."

ForeWord Magazine

"Cumbo's tales feature a spectrum of sympathetic characters…this author provides ruminative, true-to-life fiction…Elegant writing…"

Kirkus Reviews

"Cumbo, at a very young age, shows himself to be a superior stylist, writing imagery that stays with the reader long after his book has been set aside."

Peter Johnson, Paterson-Prize-Winning Author of *The Life and Times of Benny Alvarez*

In Memory of Norman E. Gannon, Sr.

MARCH 5, 1925 – MARCH 26, 2016

"The light shines in the darkness, and the darkness has not overcome it."

JOHN 1:5

1

MIKE WHITTAKER'S FATHER always left for work before dawn, while the rest of them slept. So when Mike woke up, peered through the frosted panes of his bedroom window, and noticed his dad's pickup still in the driveway, he rubbed his eyes, pulled on a sweatshirt, and trudged downstairs to see what was up. *Maybe a snow day,* he thought, savoring the possibility of pancakes and a lazy morning of video games. But the kitchen was still, other than the low rumble of the furnace kicking on and the dripping faucet. No sign of pancakes. Instead, Mike found his dad sprawled at a weird angle on the front porch, clutching his keys. His thermal coffee mug lay on its side, still steaming, the dark liquid spreading into a pool of brown slush on the stone steps.

As he stood by the casket at the wake, people told him that everything happens for a reason. His voice cracked when he tried to thank them, his narrow shoulders hunched, sweating in a cheap, itchy suit next to Mom and Andrew. It was an endless line of tearful handshakes and hugs. Perfume and aftershave. Breath mints. His mother's mascara running down her cheeks, eyes red from crying.

Andrew leaned against her, clinging to her leg, neck craned to look up at the crying grownups.

Occasionally, Mike stole a glance at the casket. There was a piece of lint on his dad's shoe. He almost reached in to brush it off. But he couldn't quite do it. It would get buried, too.

He wondered what they had done with his father's defective heart. Did they take it out? Toss it somewhere? Incinerate it? Or was it still in there, seized up like a damaged engine, pumped full of embalming fluid? Mike decided he would never know. And as they buried his dad on the shortest day of the year, just before Christmas, his heart broke, too.

*

As the earth tilted, light grew steadily into the spring of his fourteenth year. Melting snow cascaded, plummeting in flumes and spray over ancient granite, and the primeval forest surrounding their small Adirondack town yawned, stretched, and hummed with new energy. Soon, the mill where his father had labored with other tough, northern men rumbled to life, and the air once again carried the clean, honest scent of cut timber. It had lingered always in his father's rugged flannel and his sap-stained boots. As the shock subsided and he began to accept his father's death, Mike embraced all that stuff about things happening for a reason. About life going on.

It was true. He drew strength from it. Life went on.

Until, three and a half years later, when that wisdom would abruptly cease to mean anything to Mike, and those who'd peddled such nonsense—himself among them—became so many fools.

2

H E COULDN'T SLEEP. Mike's face stung from the gash and the stitches, and a pulsing ache radiated from the back of his skull. His knuckles were shredded, and his arm throbbed under the thick bandages. Whether he closed or opened his eyes—even his *eyes* hurt—the images were there. Like grainy documentary footage. Some of it in motion, some of it still.

The weight of the revolver in his hand, the stock slippery from his sweating palm. The white-hot rage that catapulted him from that bench. The smell of grass and sweat and blood. Handcuffs gnawing at his wrists. The shocked faces as reflections of maple trees slid over the cruiser's tinted windows.

He shivered under a thin blanket. It was August, but the air-conditioned holding center was frigid, and the slender mattress did little to cushion the metal shelf that served as a bed. Across the dark corridor was another boy around his age, a heavily built kid with a shaved head, a mess of tattoos, and a nasty black eye. The deputies had dragged him in a few hours ago.

Now he was murmuring in a low, guttural voice. At first Mike thought it was directed at him. But the kid was talking to no one, or maybe everyone. Ugly, nonsensical stuff. Like an angry drunk in an alley. Sometimes it morphed into a rhythmic, wounded, warbling sigh that sounded almost...*canine*. Periodically, he swore loudly—abrupt, hard syllables that echoed in the concrete and metal of the cells—and it startled Mike each time. With each outburst, he clutched the pillow tighter, trying to cower into the dark corner. It went on for hours. When the other kid finally passed out, Mike could hear him breathing. Heavy, wet, and raspy, like a tranquilized animal.

A wounded dog.

No. That's no dog.

That's a wolf over there.

They keep wolves here.

He remembered the hot flash of the camera in booking. Then standing naked, his bloody clothes in a bin, pulling on the orange coveralls, the deputies watching. *Did they notice the cuts?* Not the ones from the fight. The other cuts. *They had to have.*

No phone. No wallet. No keys. Weightless, yet leaden.

The hours in this room.

His mother today, that questioning look in her eyes. The way she'd stared through him. Like a stranger.

He didn't realize he was crying until he felt a hot tear roll over his ravaged cheek. But he was. He was crying for Dad. For Andy. For Mom.

He was scared now. No denying that. Like so many times in the past, when things had been tough, he tried to think of his dad. To picture his face. What he'd say. The deep calm of his voice. But now, when he needed it, Mike had trouble remembering his father's face. That had never happened before. Then, in a moment, he could see him. He pushed Dad aside. He didn't want to connect Dad with...

With what he'd done today at school.

Oh Jesus, what have I done?

I haven't fixed anything.
I didn't make it any better.

He wept, covering his face with the thin, scratchy blanket, stifling the sobs, trying not to wake up the monster across the hall.

*

Uncle Dave was a mess. Unshaven, jacket off, tie loose. Sweat glistened on his forehead as he leaned in close, struggling to keep his voice low. "Mike, this was about protecting both of you. It worked. You don't go to prison. And your mom will have enough money for a fresh start."

"We should've fought—"

"Jesus, Mike. We've been through this. You almost *killed* the kid."

"But I didn't! And he's not the freakin' victim!"

"Cut the crap. You dodged prison. All you have to do is—"

"Some bullshit therapy program in the woods."

"Do you have any idea how lucky you are that this—"

"You think I'm lucky?"

Uncle Dave closed his eyes. His voice was low. "Mike, you need this. You need to...to work through things."

"You my psychologist now? Thought you were my lawyer. Which is it?"

Uncle Dave looked up at the ceiling and leaned back in the chair, shaking his head.

"Six weeks. It's run by former cops. A husband and wife. And yeah, she *is* a psychologist."

Mike shook his head, staring at the carpet.

"You'll be with other guys like you. Just a small group. Borderline cases. Maybe you can talk about...stuff." Uncle Dave's eyes narrowed. He hesitated and glanced at the scars on Mike's arms.

There was a loud buzz as a deputy opened the door. His mother came in.

She hugged him weakly, then pulled away. When he was little, she used to massage his forehead, cheekbones, and temples at naptime, lying next to him. He'd do the same, sometimes tickling her more than he meant to. Her skin had been smooth, soft. Now it was stretched and thin. She reached into her pocket. "This was your dad's." She placed the tiny, weathered silver cross on a chain in his hand. Her fingers felt brittle in his. "I was going to give it to you as a graduation present, but you should have it now." She pressed his hand. "Maybe…maybe you'll pray there, Mike."

Mike nodded. Yeah, he'd wear his dead father's cross and he'd tell her what she needed to hear. It was just another lie in the thick catalog of things he'd kept from his mother. She didn't deserve any more hurt. "I'll try." He unfurled the fine metal chain, lifting it around his neck.

His mom reached up to work the tiny clasp. "Me too." She straightened the cross and smoothed his collar. He shifted uncomfortably.

"Mom, I swear, when I'm back, we can move. Or whatever you want. Far away."

"I'll see you in six weeks, baby. Then we will. We'll start all over. Far away."

He looked at Uncle Dave. They shook hands first, but Dave pulled him into a hug. Mike whispered in his ear. "Take care of her, okay?"

His uncle nodded. "I will."

*

"Didn't think they put prisoners in first class," Mike muttered, toying with the latch on the tray table. The jet had just leveled out above the clouds, and his ears were still popping from takeoff. They were in the first row. Flight attendants busied themselves in the galley, preparing the drink cart.

Dietrich, the plainclothes State Trooper next to him in the aisle seat, was young, maybe thirty. He thumbed through a fitness magazine, then leaned over and whispered, "Normally we'd go in the very last row. But there are a lot of families on this flight, and the Captain wanted you up front, away from the kids. Anyway, better if you don't mention the whole prisoner thing. Makes people nervous."

"Good thing I'm out of the orange jumpsuit, then." Mike was plainclothes too, now. Just a regular lanky kid of seventeen, with a dirty blond buzz cut and nothing beyond peach fuzz for a beard. He had a runner's lean build and a ruddy complexion from his landscaping job. Grass stained jeans. On a normal day, he wouldn't attract a second glance. Just a clean-cut all-American teenager. But there was plenty to see now. The ragged, stitched-over scar on his cheekbone. The scabbed cuts and scrapes on his knuckles and elbows. The oversized bandage on his forearm.

Despite all this, Mike felt unexpectedly *light* since they'd taken off. At ease, somehow. Prone to making wisecracks. Like he used to, before everything happened. His dad had once called him "a board-certified wise-ass." Maybe it was the momentum of flight—the fact that he was, literally, hurtling away from what had happened at over five hundred miles per hour. Whatever it was, Mike welcomed the odd flutter of good humor. He ran his finger along the armrest. "Never been in first class before." He looked up at the cop. "Think they'd serve me a beer?"

Dietrich rolled his eyes. "I mean it, Whittaker." He reached into his bag and fished out a car magazine, tossing it in Mike's lap. "Just read the magazine or go to sleep."

Mike noticed Dietrich's wedding ring. "Been married long?"

Dietrich raised his eyebrows, shook his head, and continued paging through his magazine. He paused at an article about erectile dysfunction.

Mike smirked. "Aren't you a little young for that?"

"Shut up."

"No, I get it. They told us in health class it's happening to younger guys now. Too much…internet time."

"You always talk this much?"

Mike watched the flight attendant push past with the drink cart. "Got any kids?"

Dietrich sighed, closing the magazine. He turned and looked at Mike, his voice low. "Listen. You don't seem like a bad kid. But let's be clear: we're not buddies. I'm your police escort until I hand you off in Montana. You'll do plenty of talking where you're headed, believe me. In the meantime, it's not my job to chat with you. In fact, it's part of my job *not* to. And we're sure as shit not going to discuss my family."

Mike nodded, but he couldn't resist. "Or your, um, health. Got it." Across the aisle, an executive type glanced nervously at them before turning back to his newspaper.

"That's enough, kid," said Dietrich. "One word from me, and this little deal your lawyer worked out ends when we land. It's back to the jumpsuit and the cuffs." Mike's good mood dissolved like a sugar cube in hot coffee. Now the guy in the suit was really staring. Dietrich noticed, and flashed his badge with a subtle flick, keeping it out of sight of other passengers. He leaned across the aisle. "No need to be concerned, sir. Headed for rehab, not prison."

Mike looked up to see a little boy making his way clumsily up the aisle toward the bathroom, his mother holding his hand. The boy spotted him and stared with a guarded expression. Mike tried to smile, but then he caught the mother's eye. Her grip tightened, startling the boy. She glanced hurriedly away, nudging him forward. Mike blushed as heat rose to his ears.

He reclined his seat a little, crossed his arms, and turned to stare out at towering cumulus clouds. Above them, miles away, he saw the silver speck of another jet flying in the other direction. It was bright against the deep blue. Absently, he touched the small silver cross dangling from the chain around his neck.

3

DIETRICH SHOOK HIM AWAKE. Mike stretched and rubbed his eyes, then turned to the window. He took in the view of the Rockies outside Missoula. Yellow aspen leaves covered the midrange slopes, giving way to gradually thinning pine forests. Above the tree line, tendrils of snow extended like frozen rivers through the crevices amidst granite peaks. It was a captivating sight. Even though he'd lived in the mountains his whole life, the Adirondacks were just hills compared to this. Far below, in the hollow of a valley, he spotted a tiny, teardrop-shaped lake. It was a deep azure at first, and as they passed over and the angle shifted, it caught the sun for just a moment, shimmering like a puddle of mercury.

His ears were plugged again. The plane was descending.

Montana.

*

They walked through the small arrivals wing to the designated spot in front of a coffee shop. It was Dietrich's turn to be funny. "So, Whittaker, can you spot the retired cop in this crowd?"

Mike smirked. There was no doubt who the cop was, despite the bustling crowd. The military crew cut alone might have given it away, but it was the sheer size of the guy—well over six feet and built. Mike figured he was maybe ten years older than his own father would have been, somewhere in his early fifties. Dad jeans, boots, flannel button down, and gray fleece vest. Smartphone on a belt clip, and the bulge of what was probably a side holster under the vest.

Dietrich approached him, showing him the badge. "Jim Crane?"

"That's me, Trooper Dietrich. Thank you for the timely delivery." He was all cop, hard around the edges, except for something that Mike couldn't put his finger on. Something good-natured.

"Easy luggage," Dietrich said, clapping Mike on the shoulder and smiling. "A little turbulence, but nothing out of control."

"Well that's good. Michael, I'm Jim Crane. Glad to meet you." His grip was crushing. Jim's hands were nearly twice the size of his own.

"Uh, you too."

Crane turned to Dietrich. "So, you bouncing right back east or staying here for the night, Trooper?"

"Nah. My kid's got a little league game in the morning. I leave in an hour."

"Paperwork?"

"Right here. I need the verification code first."

Crane read a code off his own papers. "Got the right little con here?"

"Okay. He's all yours." Dietrich handed over a manila folder. "Good luck, Whittaker."

Mike nodded, his arms crossed. "Hope your kid wins. Oh…keep an eye on that health issue."

The trooper chuckled, shaking his head. "Good luck up on Mount Everest or wherever." He looked at Crane. "Watch out for the wit on this one, sir. Razor sharp."

*

Jim Crane's head was only inches from the ceiling of the pickup. It was a big crew-cab with Arizona plates, some kind of special edition. Leather seats, navigation system, nice speakers. It had all the trappings of a cop car, too, like the guy couldn't quite let go. Police scanner, dash light.

They pulled slowly around a row of cars, waiting to pay and exit the parking lot. Huge mountains loomed in the distance. Mike pointed at the scanner. "Thought you were retired."

"What's that?" Jim was paying the parking fee, distracted.

"I thought you were a retired cop."

"That's right."

"What's with the flashers?"

"Volunteer fire company." Jim cleared the parking lot and they pulled out onto the highway. Mike was used to mountains, but these were a hell of a lot bigger. The sky was bigger, too.

"Been out west before, Mike?"

"Nah. We were gonna go skiing out here someday. Never happened."

"You live in the Adirondacks, right?"

"Yeah." *What else do you know about me?*

"Pretty country. Spent some time there at a wedding in Lake Placid." Jim gestured at the road ahead. "Aren't you gonna ask me where we're going?"

"Aren't you gonna ask me what happened to my face?" Mike smirked, gently touching the stitched-over scar above his jawline.

"I know what happened to your face."

"You don't know the whole story." He watched a bird fly alongside them for a moment. It was big. Some kind of hawk.

Jim looked at him sidelong. "I never said I did. But that's why we're here, isn't it?"

Mike watched the blur of the gravel shoulder. There was a train track running alongside the road. "Truth is, Mr. Crane—"

"Call me Jim."

"Well, Jim, I know this was a better deal than prison. But as for why I'm *here*, I have no idea."

Jim turned to look at him. "You're here to start over, Mike."

Mike scoffed, then muttered, "You don't get to start over."

"What's that?"

"I said you don't get to start over."

"But you do, Mike." Jim nodded out at the mountains. "Out here. Up there. You do."

They rode silently for a few minutes.

"So where are we going?"

"Not much further. Just a place to spend the night before we fly out. You'll meet the rest of the group."

"How many of us are there?"

"There's gonna be eight. Six of you, my wife, and me."

Some chatter came over the scanner, and Crane reached to turn the volume down. Mike glanced at his hand. Some big college ring.

"What college is that?"

"Huh?"

Mike pointed. "Your ring."

"Oh. West Point."

"Really?"

"Yes sir."

"What did you do in the Army?"

"Armor."

"Armor?"

"Armored Cavalry. Tanks."

"Where?" Mike asked.

14

"Different places." Jim rubbed his neck.

"Combat?"

"Yes. Iraq. Round one, that is."

"What was that, 1990?"

"Ninety-one, ninety-two."

"Think we shoulda been there? Like, was it worth it?"

"What do you think?" Jim eyed him.

Mike hesitated to turn his head, but he did. They locked eyes. It made Mike feel small. "Dunno. I don't really know enough about it. My teacher said it solved one problem but created, like, ten more."

Jim looked back up at the road, adjusting the sun visor. "Did your teacher spend any time there?"

"Um, no. He's only, like, twenty-five."

Jim nodded. "Well, he might be right. Sometimes it was really clear why we were there. Sometimes it wasn't. Lot of things are like that."

"How long were you in the Army?"

Jim smiled. "You're a talker, Whittaker."

"I am?"

"You are. Usually I get the silent treatment. The other guys didn't talk much—other than Manny, he's a chatterbox."

"Sorry." Mike looked at the dashboard.

"Nah. Don't be. It's good to ask questions."

They turned onto a secondary road lined by spruce trees. In a way, it reminded Mike of that other road back home. The place where…*where it happened.* But wider. More open. No steep hill.

"Anyway," Jim continued, "to answer your question, I was active about eight years. I was a Major. Got out after Iraq."

"Then you were a cop?"

"For a while, yeah. Arizona State Police."

"But now you run this…this thing?"

"No. Liz—my wife—runs it. I just drive and follow orders." He chuckled quietly.

"You guys have kids?"

"No." With that, he reached for the radio and turned on a country station. It was a song his dad used to like.

*

"You've really got a knack for this, buddy." Dad stood with an arm around his shoulder as they looked up at the unfinished tree house. *"Never thought it would look this good."*

Mike had just turned twelve. It was mid-July, and hot. They were in the woods behind the back yard, both covered in sawdust and dirt. Treehouse construction was in "Phase Three." Mike had plotted the design in four phases on graph paper. The plans were meticulous, with right angles and tight, disciplined architectural lettering. He'd been on an architecture kick ever since visiting Uncle Dave in Manhattan.

Dad was helping him every afternoon, and full days on weekends. Andrew tagged along often, but he was only four and still taking naps depending on the day. Today was one of those days, and after a busy morning helping Mike, Andrew had just about passed out at the table halfway through his peanut butter and jelly sandwich. Mike wiped his face and carried him into the family room, and the kid had fallen asleep on Mike's shoulder before they even got to the couch. Mike lay him there next to mom, who was reading a magazine, and she smiled. "Thanks," she whispered, and brushed Andrew's hair from his eyes. Mike knew his little brother wasn't planned. He'd overheard his mother talking to one of her friends on the phone. "We thought Mike was it. Nothing for years. And then along came our happy little accident," she'd said through laughter, her voice low. Mike stuffed the rest of his second sandwich in his mouth and headed back outside, where Dad was waiting, tools in hand.

"Little guy passed out?"

"Like a rock."

The original tree house design was more ambitious—hexagonal, with two decks and four windows. Running water via hand pump. But Dad had talked him down a bit, assuring him that "sometimes simple is stronger." He'd settled for a square frame, and postponed the plumbing arrangements. The foundation, decking, and framing were finished. An aluminum ladder leaned against the trunk for temporary access; eventually Mike's design called for a pulley system—a sort of hand-over-hand elevator. When Dad encouraged a regular rope ladder, Mike had glared at him.

"It looks okay, doesn't it?"

"More than okay. A little off on your lumber estimate, though."

"Yeah." Mike glanced at the few remaining two-by-fours stacked nearby. "Need maybe six more. And another sheet of plywood." They both chuckled. The broken board lay on the ground. They'd dropped it from the tree that morning, leaving a giant splinter in Dad's hand where it slipped. He'd let loose a string of obscenities that sent them both giggling.

"Don't tell your mother what I said." He rubbed his hand. "Jesus, that hurts."

"Think we can get to the lumber yard today?"

"If we go now."

Mike loved the truck. It was his dad's one extravagance, a big, full size extended cab, loaded, with a moon roof and leather interior. He kept it immaculate, though traces of sawdust followed his dad home from the mill and showed up everywhere. Andrew's car seat was anchored in the back, which Mike found funny. A baby seat in such a badass truck. They cruised through town, headed out toward the lumber yard. Country music played. The sun was hot on his arm out the window.

"I really mean it. You're good at designing stuff. You still reading those architecture books?"

"I am."

"You used to build pretty impressive stuff with Legos."

"Remember that tower? The one with the elevator shaft? What was I, seven?"

"Yeah. But you had different plans for the future then. Jedi Knight."

"Gave up on that. Too complicated. Dark Side and all that."

Dad laughed. "I'm all for architect." They turned onto a dirt road. Dad raised the volume, tapping along on the steering wheel for a minute, but then abruptly reached for the knob again. "Hey, Mom's birthday's in a few weeks. Had an idea."

"Yeah?"

"We haven't been to the beach in years. We could surprise her with a trip to Cape Cod."

"Wow! Like, this summer?"

"Yeah. Next month." His dad looked at him, smiling. "Not excited, are ya?"

"But Dad," Mike looked out the window at the passing trees. "Can you take the time off?" Mike knew there wasn't a lot of money. There hadn't been, ever since Andrew was born. The happy little accident!

"We can't fly to Hawaii, but we can drive to the beach." He laughed. "Might have to stay somewhere, um, cozy, but at least we'll be near the ocean."

Mike grinned. "Hey. It'd be Andy's first time at the beach."

"Yeah. I wanted to wait until he was out of diapers. We took you when you were little. Let me tell you something. You ever have a kid, don't try changing diapers on the beach. Sand everywhere."

"I'll remember that. But I'll wait a while. One surprise kid is enough, right?"

His dad turned and looked at him. They pulled into the lot. Mike reached for the door.

"Hey, hold up a second." His dad shut off the engine and rolled down the windows. The smell of wood filled the truck. Pine sap, weather treatment, and varnish.

"What you just said. About…you know, surprises."

"Dad, I was just—"

"You're twelve now, and I guess if you've figured that out, then I should probably…there's stuff that dads are supposed to—"

Mike shrank into the seat and turned to look out the window. "Dad."

"What?"

"I already know."

"Hold on. I'm just…look. You're—"

"Dad. Like…I know already."

His dad grinned. "You do, huh?"

He blushed. "Yeah, Dad. We have health class."

"But the stuff they say at school, and the stuff…um…online, it's not…"

"Don't worry. I don't even have a girlfriend."

That sent his dad laughing. "Good. Wait a few years." he said, chuckling. But then Dad pursed his lips, nodding. Mike could see him out the corner of his eye, even though he was staring, intently, at the latch to the glove compartment. "Right, well. I just thought maybe it was time to talk about that. And if you ever have any questions—"

"I don't, really. Maybe I will when I'm older, but I don't right now."

"And I want you to stay off those websites."

"Yeah." Mike blushed and reached for the handle again.

"Mike, hold on." His dad was looking at him. His eyes were wet.

"What is it?"

"I love you."

"You too."

They hopped out of the truck into the hot sunshine.

*

Jim Crane slowed the truck, and they turned into a gravel driveway headed downhill. Forty or fifty yards ahead, clear of the trees, stood a tall chain-link security fence with barbed wire at the top.

There were a few nondescript steel buildings, beyond which lay a small lake, maybe half a mile across. The water was flat calm, a mirror image of the trees and distant mountains. They stopped at a kiosk, where Crane held a fob to a reader then entered a code. A motor whirred, and the gate rolled open.

"What is this, another holding center?"

"Does it look like a holding center?"

"Well, no. But I mean, with the fence and all that."

Crane smiled. "Airport. Montana style." As they turned around the corner of a corrugated blue building, Mike could see that the metal buildings were small aircraft hangars. A small radar tower rested atop the largest, studded with antennae and other instruments. A long concrete airstrip extended the length of them, and along the shore, a few brightly colored seaplanes sat docked at a wide wooden pier. Several large crates and fuel canisters were lined up next to it.

"Ever flown in a small plane?" Jim asked, pointing at one of the seaplanes.

"Nah. Not like that."

"Well it'll be a hell of a ride, then."

"Yeah." Mike looked to the end of the pier, where a few guys his age were seated at a picnic table, chowing down on what looked like hotdogs. They were all dressed the same, in some kind of uniform. A middle-aged woman—Jim's wife, Mike assumed—stood at a charcoal grill, tongs in her hands. She waved at the truck and Jim waved back. The boys all squinted in his direction, shielding their eyes from the sun.

"Am I the last one?"

"Second to last. A kid from Texas gets in late tonight. Hungry?"

"Starving. Gotta be honest. I wasn't expecting a lakeside barbecue."

"I'll help you unpack your luggage."

He started to say, "Um, I don't have—" and then caught the joke. "Right."

Crane put the truck in park and shut off the engine, smiling. "End of the line for today. Hop out, son."

Mike swung the door open and climbed down. It was hot. His shoes crunched on the dusty gravel.

Jim came around to his side, and handed him a canvas duffel bag and a pair of hiking boots. "Head over to that building. It's the bunkroom. You'll see a space set up for you. I want you to put these clothes on. Everything you're wearing now goes in the plastic garbage bag, which you can throw in the back of my truck on your way out. They told me size ten for the boots, right?"

"Um, yeah."

"Lemme know if they don't fit. Boots will be important." With that, Jim nodded toward the closest building, then turned and walked down toward the pier.

Oh yeah. Mike called after him. "Oh…uh, Jim?"

Crane turned around. "Yeah?"

"Can I wear my cross? It's just this." Mike held it up between his fingers.

Crane nodded. "Yes, Mike. Carry your cross."

Mike slung the duffel bag onto his shoulder and headed over to the building, the boots dangling by their laces from his other hand. It was cooler inside, and his eyes took a minute to adjust to the darkness. Only a small row of narrow windows near the ceiling—more like vents, really—let in daylight. He was in a sparsely furnished bunkroom with a concrete floor. Six cots were lined up, three each against opposite walls. He was immediately aware of the neatness and symmetry of everything in the room. Each cot had a mummy-shaped sleeping bag stretched out on top, an inflatable pillow at the head and a folded towel and washcloth at the foot. A small double shelf stood next to each cot, and a few items were on each, in exactly the same location. He saw a metal canteen water bottle, a cup, a toothbrush, three sticks of deodorant, a safety razor, a tube of shaving cream, and a few other toiletries. There was also a wool cap, a pair of nondescript sneakers, a pair of flip-flops, an LED headlamp, a package of pens and pencils, what looked like a blank hardcover notebook, and a copy of the *New American Bible*. Below that were several pairs of socks, some of them heavier hiking-style and others light cotton, a couple pairs of pants, underwear, t-shirts, and a gray sweatshirt. Everything—right down to the placement of the toothbrush on the edge of the shelf—was precisely the same for each cot. A strip of masking tape was attached to the foot of each cot, with names handwritten in flawlessly neat block letters with a permanent marker. He glanced at the names, beginning with his own:

WHITTAKER, MICHAEL
RODRIGUEZ, MANUEL
DAVIDSON, ALBERT
KOWALSKI, AIDAN
TUCKER, LIAM
ALLEN, TAYLOR

Army, alright. He set the duffel down on the bed. A door led to the bathroom. He flipped on the fluorescent light and took a leak. When he came back out, the lights in the bunkroom were on, and the woman he'd seen on the pier stood at the foot of his cot, looking down at a manila folder. She was short and powerfully built. Her bright green eyes narrowed when she looked up with a wide smile. She smelled like charcoal smoke and lighter fluid. Above her jeans, she wore a gray t-shirt emblazoned with "USAF," and she had a small pistol holstered on her belt.

"Hello, Michael."

Mike stepped forward and extended his hand. "Hi."

She closed the folder. "I'm Liz Crane. Pleasure to meet you. Welcome." Her grip was strong, like Jim's.

Mike glanced at the Air Force t-shirt, then pointed at the bunks. "Didn't know this thing was sponsored by the Defense Department."

"Old habits, Michael. Jim and I run a tight ship."

"I see that.

"It's part of—"

"—starting over?"

"Yes, exactly. It's part of starting over."

"Air Force?"

"Yes."

"A pilot?"

"Nope. Intelligence. I'm a psychologist. Did forensic and clinical work for a lot of years in Phoenix with the State Police after I got out. That's how I met Jim."

"They have psychologists in the Air Force?"

"I'm living proof." She nodded toward the cot. "Well, you'll have everything you need. Please get yourself changed into what's in the duffel and come down to meet the others in a few minutes."

"Is that my file?" he asked, looking at the folder.

"Yes, it is."

"Guess you pretty much know my story."

"Only the part that's been told."

"Don't suppose I get to see what's in there."

"Don't suppose you do, no. I'm glad you're here, Michael." She turned to go.

"Thanks." Then, after a second, "I noticed there's no locks on the doors."

"That's right."

"I thought there would be."

"There won't be." She pointed at the light switch. "Flip that off when you come down, please?"

"Sure."

Unzipping the duffel, he found a pair of khaki hiking pants made of a rugged fabric and a military-style nylon-webbing belt. There were some synthetic wool hiking socks—he knew the brand; he'd been hiking the Adirondacks his whole life—and a white t-shirt. A pair of gray wicking-fabric boxer-briefs. *Jesus. Uniform underwear, too?* He couldn't help laughing. He was a boxers guy, always had been. Eric swore by boxer-briefs. They'd had serious debates about it more than once.

He hadn't gotten to say goodbye to Eric, and it irked him. He'd probably tried to visit him at the holding center. They'd been friends since kindergarten, ever since slamming heads together in the bounce house at the lumber mill's company picnic. "Concussion buddies," his dad called them after that, always chuckling at the phrase. It was one of the many things that had been running through Mike's mind over the past few days: none of this was fair to Eric. Eric had always been there for him, and yet, for the past month, Mike had shut him out. For just a second, he felt an almost physical pang of guilt. *Jesus, man. I wish you were here with me.*

He pulled on the boxer briefs. It made him feel like he was getting ready to go running at cross-country practice in his compression shorts. He shimmied around, adjusting the fit. *Well, that's an adjustment. Starting over, right?*

He put on the rest of the clothes and laced up the boots. They felt good, like they were already broken in, despite being brand new. They were pricey, and it occurred to him the same was true for the sleeping bag, headlamp, and various other gear. *Expensive restart for six little convicts.* He pulled the last item from the duffel, a nondescript khaki baseball cap, and put the bag at the foot of his bed. He paused for a second, looking at how the others were arranged, neatly flattened with the shoulder strap tucked in. He did the same, then pulled on the cap. Stepping into the bathroom again, he looked at his reflection. *Jesus. You look like a goddamned mercenary.* He had a lot of scars. The jagged line on his face from the fight was rough, yeah. But the gash on his forearm—the one from the crash—that was the ugliest.

4

STRAIGHTENING HIS CAP, Mike stepped outside. The sun was blinding. He could hear laughter from the end of the pier and saw that the other boys had noticed him. He felt different in the new clothes and hiking boots. The boots were light but solid. He felt...ready. Ready for what, he wasn't sure. He continued down onto the dock, which swayed slightly. To his left, the seaplanes rocked in the breeze, pulling on their lines. They were bigger than they'd looked from the shore, and he saw several rows of seats inside one of them as he passed. A few yards away, the group of four boys was seated at the table, along with Liz. As he approached, all four of them looked up. They were dressed exactly like him. Jim was working the grill.

"Dogs will be ready in a minute, Mike," said Jim.

Liz walked over and stood next to him. "Okay guys, this is Mike. Introduce yourselves."

A tall, heavily built black kid who looked older than the rest stuffed the remainder of a hotdog in his mouth, then brushed his hands on his pants before extending one to Mike. He finished chewing. "Sorry. Taylor." His voice was deep, with an odd accent that

Mike couldn't place. He had a five 'o clock shadow. He smiled, but somehow, his eyes showed little expression. They seemed to look right past him.

Next was a small boy with a pale complexion and light blue eyes. His blond hair was close-cropped in layers, and he looked young enough to be a middle-schooler. His sunken chest and bony shoulders were adrift inside the t-shirt fabric, even though the sleeves extended only halfway down to the elbows of his long arms. His hands were shoved deep in his pockets. He had a nasty black eye. "I'm Aidan. From Chicago," he said, and sat down.

"I'm Manuel," said the third boy. "Call me Manny." Mike immediately noticed his eyes, which were a shade of light brown he'd never seen before—almost more like a dark blond. His head was clean-shaven, which made his eyes stand out even more. He raised his hand for a high-five instead of a handshake. Manny then pointed to the flag tattoo on his arm. "Dominican."

Taylor said, "Come on, Manny. Tell him the truth. You're from Queens." Aidan smirked.

Manny cocked his head and raised his eyebrows in a sidelong glance at Taylor and Aidan. He flexed his biceps, then, tapping the tattoo. "Yeah, I'm from Queens, but I'm *from* the Dominican Republic."

Taylor laughed. "You said you lived there 'til you were *three*, man."

Manny smiled. "And go back every summer, cabrón. I'm *Dominican.* Get it straight in your head."

Jim came over with a tray of hotdogs. Mike took one at first, then, reconsidering, took two, and thanked him. He turned to Taylor. "Where you from?"

"Backcountry Idaho, born and raised. On a ranch, no less."

"He wears flannel shirts and everything, man," said Manny, smiling. "He's got a shotgun. He's a dues-paying member in the NRA, man. He's more country than my abuelo, and that old man don't even have a toilet in his house down there in the D.R."

Taylor laughed. "Only cattle-ranching, flannel wearing, black kid in the American criminal justice system. And then there's this guy," he said, pointing at the fourth boy.

He was a muscular kid on the pudgy side, with a round, freckled face and a rust-colored brush cut. His food sat untouched on the plate in front of him, and he sipped from a can of Sprite. "I'm Albert," he said, his voice low and gravelly. "Michigan."

Manny chuckled. "Alberto here? Tan tranquilo. He don't say much."

Albert took a deep, heaving breath, crossed his arms, and looked out at the water. Liz passed Mike a can of soda and he sat down. Manny slid over, making more room. It was quiet for just a moment, but that didn't last. Manny pointed at Mike, talking through his food. "Okay. Nobody else gonna ask, so I'm gonna say it. Hombre, you got one kickass cut on your face. You look more beat-up than Aidan here. I'm wondering what the other guy looks like."

Mike looked around. They were all studying the nasty bruise. He could hear Jim flipping hotdogs on the sizzling grill. "Long story."

Aidan wiped his mouth. "Yeah, we all got long stories."

Taylor nodded. "Some longer than others, right Manny?"

"Damn right, campesino. Some *real* long stories." Manny laughed abruptly, his blond eyes lighting up. He pointed at Mike. "This beat up dude, he just shows up here, and he's all like, 'Whoa, what is this? I got this one crazy bald Latino gangbanger with tattoos and shit who never shuts up, a middle-schooler, a felon cattle farmer, some mysterious creepy quiet redhead from backwoods Michigan, a three-hundred pound badass-born-to-kill tank commander, and one scary lady shrink doctor packing heat and serving lunch! Boy's thinking like 'what *in the hell* am I doing here?' Right man? Sí?" Manny nearly choked laughing, clapping Mike on the arm.

29

Liz stood up. "While I may be 'the scary lady shrink doctor,' you can see that Manny does most of the talking."

"Yeah, uh, I guess so."

Manny shook his head, stuffing the last of another hotdog in his mouth. "And proud of it, Miguelito. Proud of it. See, in Queens everybody's always talking. Always some noise and shit. Sirens and dogs barking! Out here it's so quiet it makes me loco! Back home, it gets this quiet? Means somebody's either *been* shot or about to *get* shot, man."

"It's not so quiet now," said Albert, his broad, flat features creasing into what might pass for a smile, were it not for the complete monotone of his voice.

"Hey, hey!" Manny drummed on the table, pointing at Albert. "It can talk, ladies and gentlemen! Amigo mio tranquilo here can talk! And he found a sense of humor…sort of!"

Mike looked around the table. "How long you guys been here?" he asked.

Taylor answered. "Manny and I got here first, flew in on a red-eye. Those two earlier this afternoon. We've been waiting for you and this other kid, Liam. He's coming tonight."

"You guys seem like you've been together for weeks," Mike said. "Like one big happy family."

Manny laughed. "No, hombre. But we're gonna be, right? All close up and in each other's head, just about a hundred-twenty-eight miles due east of *nowhere*, man. That right, Liz?"

"That's right, Manny. You boys finish up. Take care of the trash and brush off that grill. We'll meet up in that gray building in a little while. Got some things to talk through." She and Jim headed up the pier, talking too low to hear. Jim got in the pickup and drove off. Liz disappeared into the gray building.

After they were gone, Manny leaned in closer. "We're gonna get real tight, real quick, chicos. One more muchacho coming tonight, then we all head up in that little plane with those two to start up this deep woods therapy shit. Get it *all* out there. Then we're gonna find out just how messed up each member of this happy little gang really is." He glanced up, and they followed his gaze. Now that Liz and Jim were gone, his voice was a little cooler. "I don't know 'bout you all, but I'm damn eager to find out what you've all done to win this little vacation, wherein the Lord Jesu Cristo has seen fit to place us together, side by effin' side. *Damn* eager, hermanos criminales."

Mike glanced around the table, uncomfortable. The rest of the guys avoided eye contact, looking down at their feet or off at the lake.

Except Taylor. "Manny, you're full of crap." He stood up and started cleaning the grill, the harsh, rhythmic scraping of the wire brush shaking the whole pier. "I'll get this. You guys clean up the garbage."

*

The gray building turned out to be another small aircraft hangar, one side of which was open to the airstrip with an extra-wide garage door. Inside, the equipment had been pushed to the walls, and a circle of eight folding chairs surrounded a small, nondescript table in the middle of the large space. A single fluorescent lamp humming overhead illuminated the space with a flat, neutral light that reminded Mike of the holding center, and the air had the stale odor of a garage. Around the periphery lay an assortment of aviation equipment—hoses, tool carts, some body panels, and various engine parts. Two cots, made with a now-familiar level of precision, were set up in the corner. Mike could feel the heat radiating downward from the metal roof.

He sat with the four other boys and Liz. She sipped tea from a steaming mug, one leg crossed over the other knee, reviewing something in a binder. No one talked. Aidan's boot tapped rhythmically on the concrete floor. Two chairs were empty, one next to Liz for Jim, and another for Liam, whom he'd gone to pick up at the airport. Outside, the light had turned golden, and the sudden arrival of a steady breeze kicked up some chop on the lake. The seaplanes bobbed on the pier, the fiberglass pontoons squeaking against the rubber bumpers. Liz paused in her reading periodically, glancing up at the group of boys and then at her phone. If she was unnerved by this circle of troubled teenagers, she didn't show it. The gun holstered on her belt might have had something to do with that. Mike had noticed that the other guys kept glancing at it, too. *Every guy in this room is trying to size her up.* She seemed mildly irritated that Jim wasn't back yet. From the occasional texts buzzing on her phone, Mike guessed that the inbound flight was delayed.

Who is this woman?

His thoughts were interrupted by the sound of the truck approaching on the gravel road. Two forms strode into view, silhouettes framed by the open hangar door. There was no mistaking Jim's tall, broad frame. Jim hit a button and the garage door closed. With it, the air became still again, the noise relegated to a steady rush and the occasional creak of the building's metal walls. As they came into the light of the overhead lamp, Mike saw more of the other figure: a boy of average height and build, with long, hockey-player hair that covered his ears and formed a chestnut-colored mane around dark eyes and an angular face. He was sharply dressed: chinos, leather cowboy boots, a braided leather belt clasped with a polished silver buckle, and a pastel green oxford with the sleeves rolled midway up his forearms. The empty seat was between Mike and Aidan, and after pausing briefly to look around the room, the new boy sat down quietly. No, it was beyond quiet: He made *no noise*, not even bumping the chair. His shoulders were relaxed, feet flat on the floor, no nervous shuffling. His hands were folded in his lap. As soon as he sat, Mike noticed a subtle scent about him. Aftershave, or cologne, maybe.

Who gets all dressed up for something like this?

The new guy noticed Mike looking at him and met his eyes with a slight, expressionless nod. Mike did the same. He looked considerably older than the rest of them. Mike could make out the scruff of a day's stubble across his face. The hair on his forearms was dark. But there was something else. Mike couldn't nail it down. But it was unsettling. His eyes darted around the room, trying to gauge the others' reactions. He could see it on all their faces.

A bigger wolf just walked into the room.

Jim worked his large frame into the small folding chair with considerable noise, scraping it against the concrete. Settled, he looked up at Liz and gave her a thumbs-up.

"Welcome," she said to the latest arrival, her hands now folded around her mug, the folders set to the side on the floor. "I'm Liz."

The new kid tilted his head slightly and gave a subtle nod to Liz. He looked around the circle with an unnerving slowness, pausing to meet each of their eyes. He cleared his throat. "Howdy." He uttered the two syllables in a calm, level tone, with an obvious southern drawl.

A few awkward seconds ticked by, and Jim broke the silence. "Guys, this is—"

"Name's Liam," he said, cutting Jim off. Mike and the others glanced at Jim, who looked slightly taken off guard. "From Texas."

"Only a vaquero from Texas can pull off cowboy boots," said Manny. His voice was quieter than before.

Liam smiled—just a slight turning up at the corners of his mouth. "Gracias."

"Okay," Liz interrupted, placing her mug on the ground next to her. "Now that we're all here, it's time to get started." Her voice was clear, strong, and measured. She spoke in a steady, almost rhythmic clip. "You're all here for different reasons. But in a way, you're all here for the same reason: to start over." She paused, looking around at each of them. "Each of you has done something that would normally land a young man in juvenile detention. Something that, in the arena of public opinion, marks you as...as dangerous." Mike shifted slightly in the seat.

"But none of you has a prior record. Not one of you has ever brushed up with the law at any point until your recent incident, and each of you has cleared a battery of legal and psychological evaluations. It's the opinion of the respective judges and various juvenile caseworkers that each of you will benefit from an alternative to incarceration." Liz stopped, reached for her mug, and took a sip before setting it back down.

"Jim and I have been running this program for two years now, with quite a lot of success. We're officially licensed to provide juvenile rehabilitation to young people who meet certain criteria, meaning we've been endorsed by both federal and state judiciary bodies to work with guys like you. I'm a licensed clinical psychologist. I've spent many years working with law enforcement agencies following a dozen years in the Air Force as an intelligence officer. Jim retired five years ago from the Arizona State Police. Before that, in the Army, he was an armored cavalry officer. He was a tank commander in the first Gulf War." She looked at Jim, smiling.

"You don't know each other's stories. But you will. It's our belief—our strongly held belief—that by sharing your stories, your experiences, and your struggles, each of you can make a fresh start." She paused, looking around the room. Mike could see the skeptical expressions on every face—but no one was saying anything.

"This program is only six weeks long. We're not under any illusions that you'll all come out of the mountains completely new people. What you've been through—the things you've done, and the things that have happened to you—aren't going to disappear or be forgotten. But if you work with us, and work with each other, we believe that at the end of six weeks you'll be ready to take your lives in new directions with continued help."

Jim took over. "It won't be easy. This isn't some summer camping trip. The place we're taking you is a completely isolated, private wilderness preserve. It's one of the most beautiful places in the world—great spot to work through stuff and get your head clear. But it's no resort. There's no internet access." He glanced quickly at Aidan, who was staring at the ground. "Not even cell service. Only way in and out is by seaplane, or one rugged, dangerous, two-week trek with technical climbing gear. We stay in touch with the overseeing court offices via satellite phone. You won't have any contact with the outside world, not even your families. Your parents and guardians have signed off on that. It's a geographic clean slate, so to speak. Nobody up there knows you or your past, except Liz and me." He nodded at Liz, who picked up the lecture.

"We have some rules," she said, her eyes narrowing. "We'll go over more particulars once we get up to the mountain. But let's start with 'The Big Three.' You guys are all, technically speaking, in legal detention here. If you fail to adhere to the rules, you will be returned to your local jurisdiction for juvenile detention. First off, no one leaves our direct supervision. Eventually, you guys will be spending time on your own and as a group. But in the first phase, you will almost always be within sight of one or both of us. If you break that rule, we have the authority to arrest you on behalf of the State of Montana. We will detain you until we can have you remanded to court custody."

Okay, so I don't think anybody's gonna mess with her.

"Same goes for your behavior with each other," Jim said, making a circular gesture with his hand. "That's Big Rule Number Two: Respect yourself, each other, and us. Any violence or threatening behavior will get you on the first flight out. I was in the Army for a lot of years. I know the difference between guys horsing around and real fighting. That's when the game changes."

"Let's face it," Liz said. "Each of you has at least one episode of aggression in your recent past, and that's why you're here. But your legal and psychological evaluations also indicate that each was anomalous in nature—a one-time thing, resulting from unusual circumstances."

Unusual circumstances. Understatement of the century, lady.

"Look," said Jim, spinning the West Point ring around on his finger. "Our team reviews every referral to this program. You've screwed up, but you're fundamentally good boys."

Liz nodded. "Last of the three main rules: Be honest. We're not going to accomplish anything up there if you don't. No bullshit."

This was the first time Liz had cursed, and apparently the other guys noticed it, too. Taylor glanced up at her, and Manny's eyebrows rose a bit. "When we talk as a group, when we ask you questions, you need to be real with yourself, with us, and with each other. We already know you're tough. Let's figure out what *else* you are."

The wind had died down now. Jim got up and reopened the garage door. The water lay flat again, reflecting the pastel wash of sunset. "As for tonight, I suggest you guys get some rest. Lights out in a half hour. We leave early in the morning. You'll be expected to be showered, dressed, and fully packed—everything that's in your bunk spaces, that is—by six. Meet down by the pier to help load the plane. When the work is done we'll have breakfast before we go. Anybody have any questions?"

The boys were all silent.

"Okay, then," Jim said, and he and Liz stood up. The group began to do the same, but then Taylor spoke up.

"Hold on. I do have one question."

Jim and Liz sat back down, followed by the rest.

"I want to know *why*."

"Why, what?" asked Jim.

Taylor turned to Liz. "I don't get it. Married couple. Both retired pretty young. Military pensions. You could be making serious bank somewhere."

Jim and Liz exchanged glances. Her voice was quiet. "We were wondering when someone would ask." She stared down into her tea cup. "And we'll tell you, eventually. Just not now."

Jim nodded. "Come on over here, you guys." He waved the group over to the open garage door. "I'll show you where we're going."

Mike followed the others. Outside, they could see the stars beginning to come out over the distant mountains. The sky had faded into midnight blue. Jim pointed up toward the mountains, roughly northeast from what Mike could tell. "Way up there, in the deepest part of the Bob Marshall Wilderness, there's an old hunting lodge on a small lake. Federally protected land. Completely undeveloped. You're going to one of the most beautiful places on the planet. Most people won't ever see it or even know it's there."

"So," said Manny. "Somebody just flies us up there in one of those things, drops us in the middle of the mountains, and that's that? We're on our own in the middle of nowhere?"

"Drops us off?" Jim asked, looking at him, puzzled. "Oh! No, Manny. The plane stays with us. I'm the pilot."

*

Every guy in this room is awake.

Mike was pretty sure of it. There wasn't a lot of chatter after Jim and Liz sent them to bed. Mike was exhausted, and not in the mood to talk. Even Manny had little to say. Just six guys going through normal nightly routines. Taking a leak. Brushing teeth and washing faces. They took turns in the small bathroom, politely deferring to each other for use of the sink. It was really all so ordinary.

Taylor asked if it was okay to kill the lights. After that, it was just the rush of light breeze, crickets, and water lapping against the shore. Inside now, there was just quiet breathing and the occasional swish of one of them shifting around in his sleeping bag. There was an odd range of smells in the room. The musty backdrop of the concrete floor. Nylon sleeping bags, new boot leather, the minty aftertaste of toothpaste, and, of course the familiar reek of body odor and sweaty clothes.

A dull, pulsing headache had bothered Mike since dinner, but it was fading as he lay quietly. He reached up and traced the scar on his face. It was rough, tender to the touch, and he could feel the frayed end of one of the stitches. He thought of his mom. Her hand slapping him, how much it had stung. But then, how tightly she'd clung to him in the holding center.

That was only this morning.

It really only has been a day.

He rolled over, did his best to scrunch into a ball, and closed his eyes.

*

Mike's truck had been a birthday gift from his grandparents last summer. They'd had a small party—just Mike, his mom, his grandparents, Andrew, and Eric. Besides Eric, friends had been pretty hard to come by after his dad died. He had buddies on the cross-country and swim teams, other kids he grew up with, but Mike had kept them all at an awkward distance throughout high school. Other than his brother, Eric was the only friend who mattered.

Andrew had helped him blow out the candles, hurriedly moving things along, itching to get to the presents. The kid had been so excited when they finished the cake, fidgety as all hell as Mike opened a couple small gifts. Finally, with a nod from their grandfather, Andy pulled him by the arm to the front window to show him the truck parked in the driveway. A bright red bow was affixed to the hood of a black full-size pickup, a nice rig maybe seven or eight years old. Andrew ran ahead, swung open the door, and leapt into the passenger seat, beaming, eager to take the first ride with his big brother. Mike stared in disbelief, trading glances with everyone. Eric grinned. "We going for a drive or what?" After saying thank you and giving a big hug to his grandparents, Mike jogged to the truck, keys in hand.

"Be careful!" his mother called out, hands on her hips. "Go slow on that hill! Andrew, you ride in the back seat! Seatbelts!"

Eric rode shotgun. Mike felt strong holding the wheel. It was a big truck—like his dad's had been. They listened to country as they cruised with the windows open. Cool, pine-scented summer air rushed through the cab. They drummed out the rhythm with their hands, singing along, off-key, laughing at how bad they sounded. They pulled over and stopped in a clearing at the top of a hill. It overlooked a wide valley of spruce trees. The three of them sat on the tailgate in their hooded sweatshirts, sipping from cans of soda in the reddish, slanting light of sunset.

Late that night, as Andrew snored in the tent behind them, Mike and Eric sat by a campfire near the tree house sharing a joint. They leaned against a log with their long legs outstretched, both wearing LAWSON XC hoodies. The truck's massive front grille loomed in the driveway, firelight reflecting on the chrome. The campout was a spontaneous idea—Andrew's, actually—but Mom was okay with it since it was Friday night. They had camped here all the time when they were younger. They used to sleep in the tree house, but it was too small for them now.

Mike took a deep drag, the familiar buzzy warmth radiating through him as he closed his eyes. Mike let the smoke go, smiling as it billowed in front of him. It made a thick, opaque cloud in the cold air. He passed the joint to Eric. "Last one, I think. Make it count."

"The truck is sick. Chick magnet. No more hitting on middle school girls." Eric finished it off, and tossed the butt into the fire.

"Screw you." They laughed. Back when they were freshmen, Mike had reluctantly gone to the middle-school semiformal with Nicole Wrafter. Their moms worked together, and she was nice enough, but Mike considered it a favor and nothing more. Eric never let him live it down. Of course, Eric didn't have much ground to stand on, since he'd never had a girlfriend, either.

Mike checked to make sure Andrew was still asleep. "Still got those beers?"

"Yeah." Eric reached over to his backpack and pulled two cans out. "Still kind of cold. Here. Happy birthday."

"What, no card?" Mike pulled the tab, and foam gurgled out. "Shit." He put it to his lips and slurped. "The hell, man? Shake these up enough?"

"Sorry. Rush job to get 'em out without my dad seeing." Eric threw another log on the fire and sat down, adjusting himself. "Between the beer and the weed we're gonna be in great shape for running this fall."

"Coach'll be pissed if we aren't faster this year."

"Yeah. Well, we've got time to practice. Preseason doesn't start for a month." Mike took another slug of beer.

Eric did too, belched loudly, and chuckled. Wiping his mouth, he nodded toward Andrew. "Think he's gonna start running?"

"I took him out with me last week. He got pretty winded, but I guess it wasn't bad for his age and no training. He did a mile in under nine."

Eric gestured toward the truck with his beer. "You shoulda seen him when he told me about the truck last week. He was ready to burst. Surprised he managed to keep the secret."

Mike smiled. "He's a pain the ass sometimes. Leans on me for everything. And Christ, if he doesn't learn to chew with his mouth closed, I'm gonna kill him. Drives me nuts."

"Hey. At least you don't have a pre-teen sister to deal with. Drama city."

Andrew muttered something in his sleep, and they turned to look at him. "I've noticed he's starting to look a lot like my dad. More than me." A log crumbled in the fire, and sparks hovered, rising. They nursed the beers quietly for a minute.

"Shit, you're not kidding. Now that you say it, he does."

Mike picked up a stick and prodded the fire. "I miss him a lot on birthdays."

"Sorry, man."

Mike chugged the rest of his beer. "Got another one?"

"Yeah." Eric opened the can slowly this time, letting the pressure fade. The foam trickled out onto the ground as he handed it over. "Happy birthday, buddy. Cheers." He tipped his beer, knocking it against Mike's.

Later, zipped into his sleeping bag in the tent, Eric and Andrew slept on either side of him. Mike stared up through the mesh window at the tree house, a dark silhouette against the starry sky.

5

IKE HAD NO IDEA what time it was when he woke with a start. It was raining—he could tell that much—but there was some other noise, too. Like footsteps on the gravel. It was dark, but he could see that two of the others—Taylor and Manny, he thought—were standing up on their cots, peering out through the narrow window at the top of the wall. Two others, maybe Liam and Aidan, were hunched up on their elbows in their sleeping bags, looking disoriented.

"What is it?" Mike asked, his voice hoarse.

Manny whispered. "Don't know, hombre. But somebody—oh, shit! It's Albert! He's running!"

Mike clambered up onto the cot between Taylor and Manny. Someone else elbowed his way next to him. He squinted, trying to see what was going on through the rain-splattered glass. He saw Albert wearing his rain jacket and backpack, crouched low, half-running across the tarmac, headed for the water.

"Where the hell does he think he's going? There's a twelve-foot security fence," muttered Taylor.

Mike looked where Albert was headed. "Must be going for the lake. Gonna swim out around it."

"Loco cabrón!" said Manny.

"Won't make it," said Liam, whom Mike realized had shouldered up next to him.

"How do you know?" replied Manny. "He's moving fast!"

Taylor was pulling on his boots. "We should stop him, guys."

"Don't bother," said Liam, yawning in his Texan drawl.

"Why?"

"Because *she* will."

"Oh, damn!" said Manny, bouncing on the cot. "Look at that lady run!"

Mike saw her then. Liz running—no, sprinting—after Albert, her boots digging hard and loud into the gravel. Jim followed behind. Albert spotted her over his shoulder and broke into a run, but there was no chance. In a single, fluid leap, Liz was airborne. She brought Albert—a boy almost twice her size—down in a painful crunch clearly audible over the distance and the rain. She had his face pinned in the mud, her knee on his neck, and in less than two seconds she'd torn the backpack off him. They saw the glint of metal as he cried out, his arms wrenched behind. Cuffs secured, Liz stood up, heaving, hands on her hips, catching her breath like a sprinter on the track. "Goddamnit!" she yelled.

Jim hoisted Albert, wriggling like a hooked fish, up off the ground with one arm. He braced him, immobile, against his chest. Liz picked up the backpack. Albert kicked uselessly, spitting out obscenities as Jim dragged him back to the hangar. As they neared the bunkhouse, Mike and the other boys moved to the door, opening it and stepping out onto the threshold, just out of the rain.

Liz looked up at them. She was soaked, and Mike couldn't help noticing how tightly her Air Force t-shirt clung to her body. She had a cut on her forehead and tendrils of blood on her face.

"Get back inside, boys. Go to bed."

"Yo, you okay, Liz?" Manny shouted over the rain.

"I'm fine. Stay inside."

"Damn," Manny muttered quietly. "Remind me never to mess with that lady."

Jim passed close by the door, just feet from them, as if to make sure they got a good look at the struggling prisoner. Albert was red in the face, his wet, rust-colored hair plastered to his head. He was wincing with each jerky step, soaked, blood and dirt all over his face and hair. Mike could feel the heat radiating off the two of them.

"The hell you lookin' at?" murmured Albert, glaring at the group of them, his voice guttural, before Jim pushed him forward. "You faggots go play in the woods."

Just before he rounded the corner out of sight, Jim stopped, jolting Albert to a halt. He looked back at them. "This changes *nothing* for you guys," he said. "Up, dressed, and ready to load that gear by six." Albert tried to kick Jim's shins. Jim rolled his eyes, irritated, and wrenched him tighter, causing the boy to whimper in pain. Jim shook his head, smirking. "Well, it does change *one* thing. Our payload just got about two hundred-fifty pounds lighter, and you guys are gonna have a little more space to spread out on that plane. And more to eat. Now get back to bed. Stay inside." He looked up at the dark sky, rain falling on his face, then down at Albert, who stood limply. "Clearly, environmental conditions have deteriorated out here." With that, he pushed Albert around the corner and their shuffling footsteps faded.

Minutes later, back in his sleeping bag, Mike saw red and blue light pulsing through the window as a car pulled up on the gravel.

"That little light-show look familiar to anyone else, boys?" It was Liam. "Sure does to me." Nobody laughed. Outside, there was some brief, low conversation, footsteps, and two car doors slamming. The lights faded as the cruiser pulled away. After that it was quiet, except for the rain on the metal roof.

Yeah, Liam.

That little light show looks familiar.

*

Mike had never been handcuffed before. He'd never been read his rights or escorted to the back of a cop car, either.

He hadn't been scared, though it occurred to him that he *should* be. The anger—no, the *rage*—that had surged with seismic force had subsided. He felt quite calm, but a funny sort of energy pulsed through him, like a low-voltage electric hum. The morning sun glanced off the police cruiser's window and sent tiny pinpricks of dazzling light scattering across the blacktop.

The ambulance carrying Joe DeAngelo had sped away, its sirens fading in the distance. A huge Sherriff's deputy held Mike's arm in an iron grip, wrenching his elbow painfully as the cuffs gnawed at his wrists. He could smell the cop's aftershave over the lingering odors and tastes of the fight: grass, dirt, and the copper of blood in his mouth. At least five other squad cars surrounded him, forming a barricade to the school entrance. Ambulances and fire trucks. He squinted as blue and red lights danced in his peripheral vision. The principal, trainer, and athletic director were out there, along with a handful of other coaches and teachers. Everyone else had been evacuated. He spotted some of them standing in rows a hundred yards away in the faculty parking lot, behind police barriers, texting and calling. The dull pulse of a helicopter reverberated overhead. Aside from that and the squawking radio chatter, it was oddly quiet. Most people just stared at him, unmoving, saying nothing.

The Principal stood talking with two Sherriff's deputies. A State Police detective wearing latex gloves squatted on the grass next to

Mike's gym bag. He lifted the small revolver, handling it gingerly as he unloaded it into an evidence bag. Coach Swanson stood to the left, whistle dangling from the lanyard around his neck. A few yards away he saw Eric, who looked right back at him, utterly dumbfounded.

6

THE RAIN HAD CLEARED by morning. Mike awakened to the sound of birds outside. Looking around the room, he saw that Liam was out of his bunk, but Manny, Aidan, and Taylor were still asleep. *We don't look too dangerous. Just a bunch of kids.* He swung his legs to the floor, unzipped the sleeping bag, and stretched. Making his way to the bathroom, he knocked on the door.

"Yeah," came the unmistakable Texas drawl.

"Hey, it's Mike. Alright if I come in?"

"Be my guest."

He stepped in, took care of business, and went to the sink to wash his hands. As he was brushing his teeth, Liam flipped off the water and his hand reached from the stall for the towel on the hook. A few seconds later, Liam stepped out, wrapped in the towel. The kid was ripped, with a hairy chest. He could be in his twenties.

"Sleep good?" Liam asked.

"Fine. You?"

"Best night of sleep I've had in a while."

What the hell is that supposed to mean?

"At least it was quiet. Eventually."

"Yeah. Well, that's probably gonna be the last hot shower for a while. Might want to enjoy it," Liam said, putting shaving cream onto his face. "Y'all done with the sink?"

"Yeah." Mike rinsed his toothbrush. "All yours."

Twenty minutes later, the five of them were dressed and headed down to the pier. A light fog hung on the lake, which the sun was burning off quickly. Standing in a row in their uniforms and caps, Mike thought they looked like a small cadre of soldiers. Jim was seated on a plastic crate, paging through what looked like a manifest. Nodding, he checked a final box and stood up.

"Good morning. Okay. I'm gonna stand next to the plane and you guys are gonna bring me these things, one at a time. I'll load them. It's important that the weight is distributed evenly. I want you to give me the heaviest things first, which is gonna be those two." He pointed at two large, rectangular crates. "From there, work your way from left to right, ending with that smaller stuff."

No mention of Albert.

"This is everything for six weeks?" asked Aidan.

"Sure is." Then, chuckling, "No. I've already made one cargo flight with most of our food and supplies."

They began loading.

"Jim?" asked Manny.

"Yeah?"

"Who pays for all this? I mean, this is expensive shit, right?"

"Yeah, it is."

"So, who pays?" They all paused, looking at Jim.

"People who think you're worth it," he replied. "Now get moving. I want us in the air before the midday winds pick up."

It only took a little while to get everything loaded. Liz, meanwhile, had set up a tray full of bananas, apples, and cereal bars at the table where they ate yesterday. There was a gallon of whole milk and some paper cups. They headed over to the table. Liz was wearing a tank top, and Mike noticed a bruise on her arm.

"Morning, boys," she said. "Everybody have a quiet night?"

"Yeah. Real quiet," Aidan mumbled. "What'll happen to him?"

"Exactly what we said would happen, Aidan." She shrugged, wincing a bit and rubbing the bruise. "But he's no longer your concern. He made a choice."

"How's that arm?" asked Manny. "Looks like you took a hard knock."

"I'll survive."

Liam swallowed a mouthful of apple. "I don't think Liz gets pushed around, Manuel."

Liz and Jim traded quick glances. "You saw what happened. Okay. Hydration is important," she said, unwrapping a package of paper cups. "Finish off this milk and fill up your water bottles before we go." She handed one to Liam first, and they locked eyes for a second. Their expressions were blank, but Mike was pretty sure something got communicated. He just wasn't sure what.

*

It was a sunny morning, and as the plane took off, the glare in front and to the right confirmed they were flying northeast. Jim and Liz wore aviators and headsets. Jim's amplified voice crackled over the intercom. "It's a fine clear morning, boys. Look out to the left, and you guys can see some of the peaks of Glacier National Park way off to the north. We're headed east into the Bob Marshall Wilderness. More than a million acres. One of the biggest tracts of undeveloped land in the lower forty-eight."

"Pretty far off the grid," said Liz. "No place better to start over."

Far below, Mike saw a vast expanse of rugged landscape. No roads. No trails. Only trees, steep planes of rock, and broad plateaus dotted by tiny lakes. As they continued to climb, he noticed the sheared, naked gash of an avalanche, an immense boulder field scattered about the base. It was like the one on the side of Mount Colden back home, but even bigger. He imagined the immensity of an event like that. A hundred thousand tons of rock thundering down the precipitous slope, crushing everything in its path.

Mike had lost track of exactly how long they'd been in the air, but it wasn't long before they began to descend. Mike gripped his armrests, and noticed the others doing the same. The pitch of the propellers changed, slowing and deepening. The craft shuddered a bit, buffeted by wind and thermal layers, and they were jounced from side to side. As the ground below drew nearer, the ruggedness of the terrain became even more apparent. There was no sign of a landing spot from the side windows, but he knew they were closing in on a small lake, just barely visible over Jim and Liz's shoulders. He craned his neck. It looked like they were flying into a spoon-shaped valley, making their way down into the handle, headed for the rounded ladle. There was a final, rapid drop—met with some involuntary gasps—and the lake's surface loomed. Seconds later, a jolt as the pontoons skidded. They slid along the surface, water roaring beneath them and engines whining, slowing to a near stop after a surprisingly short distance. Jim turned to the left, and the plane plunged toward the shore, rocking as it heaved over its own wake. Mike lowered his head, face pressed against the window, looking to the top of the slope around them. Far above, pine forests gave way to towering masses of rock. It was like a fortress. The v-shaped notch where they had flown in was hundreds of feet—maybe even a thousand—above the lake. In every other direction, the slope must have been twice as high. There was a narrow, rocky beach in some places, but in others, near-vertical granite walls rose directly from the water.

They idled, drifting at a steady clip toward a narrow wooden dock. Jim shut off the engines and Liz stepped outside onto the pontoon, securing a line to a cleat. Jim adjusted the stick and the breeze turned the plane neatly about within a few feet of the dock, the nose now facing the expanse of the lake. Liz leapt off the pontoon, the craft rocking from the movement as she pulled it in and secured first one line, then another. She gave a thumbs-up to Jim.

"Here we are, boys." Jim removed the headset and his sunglasses. "Take a real deep breath as soon as you step out. Most people never get to breathe air this clean."

They all clambered out onto the rickety wood planks, gazing around, silenced by the surroundings.

"Wow," says Manny. "Wow."

The air was rich with the scent of pine. There was a purity to it. Rocks and sunlight and water. Mike had a flashback then—a vivid one—to a hike with his dad along the shores of Avalanche Lake. The sun was just as hot on his shoulders, and a warm breeze blew across his face. He hadn't thought about that day in a long time. He reached up and felt the small cross through his t-shirt. *You'd love it here.*

The short pier crossed shallow, crystal-clear water to the gravel beach, which gave way to a grassy meadow. About thirty yards in stood a collection of small, stout, wooden buildings with shuttered windows.

"We call this place Freedom Lodge," said Liz.

Manny snickered. "Sorry. 'Freedom Lodge?' Really?"

Liz nodded. "Yeah. I know. But I think you'll get it in time. Freedom comes in many forms, Manuel."

Manny pursed his lips. "Yes ma'am. Sorry."

Jim opened up the cargo door. "Your bunks are in that building to the left. The kitchen and storeroom are in that larger one in the middle. In a minute, we'll have you unload. But first, you need to listen very carefully."

Out of one of the boxes, he pulled a large nylon gun holster and attached it to his belt. Next, he opened a waterproof gun case. Inside was a revolver and several bullets. It was the biggest handgun Mike had ever seen—the barrel was just short of a foot long. Jim placed the gun, along with several bullets, into the holster. "This is bear country. And I don't mean cute little black bears. I mean Canadian Brown Bears. Grizzlies. Now I've never seen one come near the lodge, and we do have a wire fence around the property. But that's really just designed to reduce critter traffic. Believe me, a fence is not going to stop a determined bear. And even if it were fifty feet high, there's no reason why they can't get in anyway, because they are excellent swimmers."

Mike looked around at the other guys. Their jaws were set as they stared directly at Jim's gun. Aidan, in particular, seemed decidedly freaked out. His eyes darted all around. Even Manny was quiet.

"Which is why," Jim continued, "Liz and I are going to be armed for the duration of this stay. We'll be carrying bear spray, along with these big babies—he tapped the huge revolver on his holster—because it's the only handgun that will slow down a pissed-off grizzly. We also keep a twelve-gauge with slug rounds in the safe. Obviously, if any of you come anywhere near these weapons, you'll be arrested immediately and we'll call in the state guys." He gave each of them a hard glare, eyes moving slowly from one to the next.

"Now, and this is of absolutely vital importance—no food gets left outside. *Nothing. Ever.* That includes garbage. You don't even leave your deodorant or toothpaste outside, understand? Critters will find it, including bears. Sometimes we'll be eating outside on the deck, but everything will come in. We burn garbage every night."

"Doors and gates always get closed and latched," said Liz. Her gun looked absolutely immense on her smaller frame. "That includes the perimeter fence. Every door and gate is spring loaded to close automatically, but you have to double-check that they close fully behind you. You get lax on that, you're gonna have visitors. Obviously, bears are the bigger concern, but you get some of the smaller critters inside and we've got different issues."

"You ever shoot a raccoon with that .500, Jim?" Taylor asked. "That's something I'd like to see."

"You know guns, Taylor?"

"Biggest handgun on the market. Helluva kick. My dad has one."

"Gopher stew," said Aidan, smiling for the first time since Mike had met him.

"Didn't know you could laugh, blondie," said Liam, smiling. Aidan looked down at the pier, smirking.

"Okay, guys. You see that circle of chairs over there?" Jim pointed down a path, off some ways from the buildings. Adirondack chairs surrounded a stone fire-ring. "That's where we'll be meeting each evening. Meantime, get all this stuff unloaded. Everything to the central building, in the kitchen. Just put it inside; Liz and I will sort it out. First, take your personal gear to the bunkhouse."

As they got closer to the buildings, Mike could see their age. They were solid old log cabins. Heavy shutters covered the windows, the ancient green paint chipped and weathered. A single solar panel was attached to the roof, and sunlight arced off of the glossy black surface. Mike noticed a similar building about fifty feet away, which Liz pointed out as the kitchen and meeting room. She removed a padlock on the front door and swung it open, noisily, on rusted hinges. "I'll go around and open the shutters. Don't forget to keep the doors closed and latched."

It was dark inside, with only slivers of sun coming through a few gaps in the shutters. The musty odor was what Mike expected—a combination of age, weather, and wood smoke, with just a slight hint of mildew. The plank floor creaked noisily. There was a pipe stove in the far corner. Four heavy bunk beds stood against the walls. A round blue area rug covered most of the floor, centered beneath an old-fashioned, single bulb lamp fixture hanging from a roof beam. The only furnishings other than the bunks were several low dressers and three couches surrounding a coffee table. The couches were the heavy, solid kind found in college dorms. A door led to what Mike assumed was the bathroom.

There was a single window on each wall, and Mike noticed that like the roof, the windows were pretty new compared to most of the bunkhouse. He remembered his dad installing new windows in their house when he was nine or ten. At some point, he'd explained to Mike the strength and insulating qualities of double-paned glass. Mounted near the ceiling in the corner was a metal utility box, labeled "CAUTION: SOLAR INVERTER SYSTEM. RISK OF ELECTRICAL SHOCK. KEEP CLOSED."

"Yo. I see four bunk beds and five of us. Somebody's gotta share," said Manny. "Who's gonna be the bitch?" he asked, chuckling.

"I'll take it," said Aidan. "Used to have one."

"A bitch?" asked Manny, now laughing harder.

"A bunk bed," Aidan mumbled.

"Alright then," said Liam, and strode across the room, throwing his duffel on one of the lower bunks. Mike, Taylor, and Manny did the same.

Aidan looked around briefly, then threw his bag up above Manny's. "Mind if I sleep up top?"

"It's cool, hermanito," said Manny.

Taylor opened the other door and looked inside. He shook his head, smiling. "Goddamnit. I was afraid of that."

"What?" asked Aidan.

"Come check this shit out."

They crowded into the small bathroom, which was missing a key feature. There was no toilet. Two lime-crusted showerheads protruded from one wall, and a small window provided light and a view out into the woods. A cracked ceramic sink was attached to the wall, and a low-wattage bulb hung above a mirror, which was cracked and cloudy in places. There was only a single knob for each shower. Taylor twisted one of the knobs, which squeaked as air hissed from the nozzles, sputtering for a few seconds until a weak stream of water poured out. It splashed noisily on the concrete floor, snaking toward the drain. Taylor held out his hand to test it. "Damn, that's cold."

"What the hell," muttered Aidan.

"We are *off* the grid, boys," said Liam, laughing. He elbowed Mike as he brushed past him back into the main room. "Told you to enjoy that hot water, eh?"

Taylor sighed. "Must be an outhouse somewhere."

"Goddamnit," muttered Aidan. "This is gonna suck so much."

"Get over it, blondie," Manny said, tousling his hair. "We're here to *start over*, remember?"

"Could you guys stop calling me blondie?" Aidan said, whipping his hair out of Manny's reach, his voice quavering.

Manny grinned. "Yeah. Sure, little guy."

Aidan shook his head and walked out, muttering.

"I'm kidding, I'm kidding. Jesus. Lighten up."

"Manny," Taylor said, "give it a rest, man."

Manny shrugged. "Kid's gotta learn to lighten up. We're here for *a while*, right, Miguelito?" He clapped Mike on the shoulder.

Liam appeared in the doorway, holding the cast-iron kettle from the stove, smirking. "Well, we can heat up about a half-gallon of water at a time."

"I hate this!" It was Aidan, up on the top bunk, lying face down, the pillow pulled tight over his head.

"Shit. Is he *crying*?" Manny whispered, pointing up.

Nobody said anything for a minute.

"Let's go get the rest of that stuff," said Taylor. They headed outside.

7

SEVERAL HOURS LATER, they sat in the circle of Adirondack chairs around a crackling fire. The sun was low enough that the valley lay in shadow, even as the top of the eastern ridge still glowed orange. The temperature had dropped quickly in the late afternoon, and when they'd stepped outside after eating dinner in the dining room, Mike noticed the chill immediately. It wasn't long before they all pulled on the gray fleece jackets and traded their baseball caps for the knit caps. *Now we look like a traveling ski team.*

Mike looked down at his notebook. Over the past hour, they'd been taking notes. "You'll write all this down," Liz had said, "because that's how your mind will remember it. And also," she'd continued, looking around at each of them, "because then there's no excuse for not knowing it."

"Okay," said Liz, throwing another log on the fire, which sent sparks rising. "So those are the nuts and bolts. But let's talk about what really matters." Mike noticed that everyone's posture changed, his included. They sat up a bit, setting the notebooks aside.

Jim shifted forward in his chair, his elbows resting on his knees, and looked around at each of them. "Guys, like we said last night, each of you is here because somebody—including us—believes that you deserve a second chance. That each of you is capable, with the right guidance, of facing up to what you've done. That each of you is strong enough to confront it, get stronger by confronting it, and eventually put it behind you."

Liz picked it up. "You guys are gonna get to know each other *really* well. Same goes for me and Jim, but you guys are each other's best resource. You have the greatest potential to help each other." She clasped her hands together. "The truth is, you have a fair amount in common. Let me lay a few things out there. First of all, you're all guys. It may be obvious, but it's important, right? No girls here to distract you. Secondly, you're all around the same age. Aidan's sixteen; the rest of you are seventeen. You're all smart. You've done well academically, in the top quarter of your classes throughout high school. And finally, each of you has recently been arrested."

Her voice softened. "But there's something else. Each of you has also lost somebody close." Mike felt a lump in his throat.

He glanced around the group. Manny was looking directly at Liz, nodding. Liam stared at the fire, unmoving. Taylor sat quietly, picking at a loose chip of paint on his chair. Aidan settled back into his chair, arms crossed. *That is one fidgety kid,* Mike thought. He'd noticed that Aidan kept reaching toward his pocket, like he was feeling for his phone. And when it wasn't there, the kid started tapping his heels or nervously picking at his fingernails. *Like an itch you can't scratch, brother.* Truth was, Mike had felt a little strange without his own phone, and he'd caught himself reaching for it, instinctively. But now that it had been a while, he'd pretty much gotten used to it. *Guess Aidan hasn't. Maybe he's one of those kids who's always plugged in. God, being here must suck.*

Liz continued. "If this is going to work…that is, if you're going to get anything out of this, you've got to talk to each other. Not just in our nightly sessions. You've got to challenge each other to share what's going on. Let the burdens you've been carrying fall on each other's shoulders."

Taylor sat up suddenly. "Alright. So, when does this start? I mean when do we get into it?"

"Aren't we 'getting into it,' fast enough, hermano?" Manny asked.

Mike looked at Taylor. The kid had a point. Mike did want to get into it, he realized. *Enough of this preliminary warm-up shit. Let's do this. Hard reset. Let's go.*

And then, before he could finish the thought, Taylor said it perfectly. "No offense, Liz, but enough of all this orientation shit. Okay? We get it. Close the doors and turn out the lights. Don't piss in the common areas. Color inside the friggin' lines. Fine. But let's get to the point, huh? I want to know who the hell you guys are. And you want to know who I am." His voice was level at first, but quickly rose as he pointed around the group. "I mean, we've been playing along, being polite, wearing our little uniforms. But nobody here, not one of us, has said a goddamned thing about why he's here! About what we did!" He was leaning way forward in his chair now, practically half-standing up, his eyes wide, looking around. A bead of sweat dripped down his forehead. He wiped it, settling back into his chair. "Time to get real. If I'm gonna bunk with you guys for six weeks, I wanna know who you are. So let's start this shit, huh?"

Liz and Jim sat quietly, relaxed in their chairs, apparently unmoved by the outburst. After a moment, Liz smiled. Her voice was quiet. "Well, you're on, then, Taylor."

Taylor took a deep breath, his nostrils flaring and chin lifted, glaring at Liz. The firelight glimmered on his wide, almond-shaped eyes. "Yeah. Yeah, okay. I'm on then." He paused again, hesitating. "I just about killed a horse and my dad in the same night."

Mike's gaze snapped up from the fire. "You what?"

Manny laughed. "This cabrón's more loco than I thought."

"We've got this horse. My dad's obsessed with him. Had him my whole life. Well, I got pissed at my dad, and I got real drunk, and I beat this horse with a two-by-four, and then I did the same thing to my dad." The fire crackled.

Aidan spoke next. "What the hell did he do? Your dad?"

"We grew up on a huge ranch in Idaho. When the crash happened, he got into trouble and couldn't hang onto it. Had to sell it. Still got to live there, but he was never the same. So he started getting drunk. Beat up on my mom, and my brother, and me. This one night, I was doing a shift with the volunteer fire department—I was taking EMT classes. Anyway, I get home from that shift and he's real drunk. I took it back to him."

"But why the horse?" Manny asked.

Taylor shot back. "You got a good reason for everything you did, Manny?"

"Nah, but a horse, man?"

Liz put her hand on Manny's arm. "Taylor, thanks."

Taylor nodded at Liz, then took a deep breath, shaking his head as he looked at Manny. "Obviously, there's more to it. But you wanted to know why I'm here. Screw it. That's why I'm here."

As if on cue, a log disintegrated, crackling loudly as a flurry of sparks rose into the darkness. It was completely dark, now, and Mike could see a night sky full of stars. More than he'd ever seen. Nobody said anything. He glanced out at the lake, which was flat calm. Not even a ripple of breeze now. Taylor's words echoed in his head. *So is that how it works? Do we just start spilling it?* Where would he begin?

But he didn't have to. At least not just yet, because Manny did.

8

"I GOT CAUGHT UP in some shit with my hermano. My bro. He was in with a gang in Queens. Some real bad guys came lookin' for him. Anyway, I wound up hurting a guy—it was an accident, but it was bad. We were running from these guys, and we end up in the kitchen of this restaurant. I almost killed the owner. I was scared as shit. He's got, like, little kids, and his wife is there, screaming an' shit. Being honest? I almost tried coke that afternoon. I didn't, but I did have it on me. That's the...what you call it again, when it's like, a weird coincidence, but like, a bad one?"

"You mean irony," said Liam.

"That's it, Tejas. That's the irony of it. My brother? He's in jail. He's done some bad shit, believe me. But, anyway, this judge, he says I got things to figure out. Cabrón says I gotta learn to, like, control my anger better. Work shit out. And not, like, blame myself for everything that ain't worked out in my life. Which is mostly bullshit, right, because a lot of it's my fault. But a lot of it isn't. Anyway, this deal's better than jail, comprende?"

*

Jim leaned in toward the fire. "Okay. It's safe to say the ball is rolling. But I think that's enough for tonight, guys. Taylor, Manny, thank you for telling your stories. That took guts to get right into it. You guys should—"

"No," said Liam, his voice quiet but firm.

"Excuse me?" Jim said, looking up at Liam.

"I said no. Those two told their stories. I want to hear the rest." He looked around the group. "They tell, we all tell. Tonight. Agreed?"

Liam was right. What would they do otherwise? Go back to their bunkhouse? Talk about the weather and football and girls or something? Mike was tired. Exhausted. They all must have been. But in a strange way, he was amped. Suddenly, the prospect of telling these guys the story was more appealing than he'd ever thought it could be. He didn't understand it. But it was contagious. Like there was something in the air after Taylor and Manny. Something that was pushing him to do the same. To be like them. To join them in this.

He knew he couldn't say everything. *You can't ruin the deal.* But it was like...like he had a craving to tell it. To unload it. And for a second he panicked. Trying to sort out what he could and couldn't say. He thought back to the conference room. About what Uncle Dave had said. About the arrangement. *Be careful. You tell all, the whole deal for Mom goes south, idiot. Doesn't matter that you're in the middle of nowhere. Remember, these two are cops. Or sorta cops. Ex cops. Whatever.* But he did want to talk. He wanted to tell them about his father. He wanted to tell them about Andrew. He wanted...*God, I want to tell them all of it. Maybe even the truck.* His mind was racing.

"I'm with Liam," he said. "I think it's only fair."

Aidan just shrugged.

Liz put another log on the fire. She looked around at each of their faces. "Well, we asked you guys to step up. You are. Not gonna stop you now. So, who's next?"

*

"Guess I'm up," said Liam, stretching his arms. "I messed up my soccer coach. My friend died in an accident around Christmas. We went to this boarding school. Anyway, this guy and I were tight. We were roommates. We were both national team prospects, actually. But then he was drinking and he fell off this embankment, and...shit." Liam paused, staring at the fire. "He died."

"Few months later my coach just said the wrong thing at the wrong time—and I beat hell out of him in the locker room. Put him in the hospital. And I had drugs in my bag. So here y'all are, and here I am with y'all."

Liam stood up abruptly, then, which startled Mike, and the others as well, apparently, as they all shifted in their seats. Jim and Liz—on reflex, it seemed—reached for their holstered guns, bracing for a moment before the tension subsided. All of them noticed, and Liam raised his hands, surrender-style. "Whoa, whoa, whoa...sorry...y'all a little *jumpy* or what?" He stretched, twisting his hips. "Just stretching."

Manny chuckled nervously. "Better watch it with the sudden moves 'round here, gringo."

"Guess our little sharing session has everyone on edge," Taylor said.

"Why don't you sit down, Liam?" Liz's voice was level. She straightened her fleece, relaxing her posture, hands folded once again in her lap.

Liam, eyebrows raised, sat down slowly. "No sudden moves. Got it." Mike found himself staring at Liam. *Something is definitely off with him.* And then, almost as if he'd said it out loud, Liam looked up, directly at him, and they locked eyes. When they did, a jolt of…something…coursed through Mike. *What the hell was that?* But he knew. *It's fear. Instinct.*

Jim interrupted his thoughts. "Mike, you next?"

"Hmm?" He looked to Jim.

"Would you like to tell your story next?"

"Oh." He sat up straight in the chair. He realized now that his heart was pounding. "Yeah, sure." He glanced to the side, just for a second, long enough to see Liam was still looking at him. He looked around at the others, all focused on him now. He turned to the small, withdrawn boy to his left. He needed a way to stall, to regain his composure. "Unless…Unless Aidan wants to go first."

Aidan sat up taller, taken off-guard by the sudden attention. "Nope. No," he shook his head rapidly, and then bit his knuckle. "I mean, thanks," his voice slowed. "I'll go last. Um…go ahead." Aidan's hand was trembling.

The others probably weren't close enough to notice. But Mike looked at Liz.

She noticed.

*

"I brought a gun to school." Saying it out loud felt strange, but there was something oddly liberating, too. Again, he felt that tight, pulsing, nervous energy that had become so familiar over the past month. That tingling, fluttering current of edgy, electric warmth. It rose in his chest and radiated to his fingertips. He was looking deep into the heart of the fire, at the shifting palette of wavering heat among the glowing embers.

"My little brother drowned in the town pool. He was nine."

Manny's voice was barely a whisper. "Lo siento, man. Sorry."

"There were two lifeguards—twin brothers. They were both in my class. I...I hurt one of 'em. Bad."

Manny nodded. "Man, if my brother drowned on some cabrón's watch like that, I'd—"

"Y'all ever shut up, man?" Liam asked, his Texan drawl thick. "Let him finish."

"I brought the gun to school. Preseason practice. The guy was on the football team. I'm a runner. I...I just lost it one morning and I decided he had to pay for it."

Manny's eyes widened. "Wait, you mean you *shot* the bastard?"

"Manny." Liz's voice was level, but forceful.

"Sorry."

Mike looked at Manny. "No. I had the gun in my hand. But when I saw him, I just...I dunno. I dropped it. I just beat him. I was wearing steel-toed boots." He turned back to the fire. "They said I almost killed him."

*

They sat there, listening to the sounds of the fire, no one speaking. "That's a lot of stars." Manny's voice broke the silence. "You never see anything like that in New York. Down on the island. You see them there. Especially when the power goes out at night."

"You get down there a lot, Manny? To the Dominican Republic?" Taylor asked.

"Used to. Not in a few years now. Miss it. It's better there in a lot of ways."

Jim shuffled forward in his seat, poking at the fire with a stick. Sparks rose as the flames rekindled. "How about you, Aidan? Ever seen stars like this?"

The small boy brushed his hair aside. Mike had noticed that Aidan had a habit of doing that. His hair was long enough to hang over his eyes. "No. Never have. Haven't really been out of Chicago too much. Well, not even Chicago. Just the cozy little suburb outside the city. Anyway, I don't do outdoor stuff. I didn't even know there *were* this many stars, to be honest."

Mike was sure this was an invitation from Jim for Aidan to share his story, but the kid didn't bite. Instead, he shoved his hands deep in the pockets of the fleece jacket and looked back up at the sky. Half a minute passed in awkward silence.

It was Liam who spoke up next. "Spill it, Aidan. We're tired."

Aidan shrank further into the chair, his shoulders somehow curling in even more than they already were. "I don't—" his voice cracked like a seventh grader, and he stopped abruptly, wincing, obviously embarrassed. Clearing his throat, he started again. "I don't want to do this tonight." He started to stand up. "I mean, we're all wiped out. Maybe we could just get to sleep." No one else moved, though, and he settled back into the chair, exhaling loudly.

"No offense, shorty," Liam cracked his knuckles loudly, "but I'm afraid you can't pull that. Not after the rest of us have laid it out."

Manny nodded in agreement. "He's right, man. You can't hold out on us now. Not if we're all gonna go sleep in that cabin together after telling each other all that shit. No way. You know our dirt, man. What's yours?"

Aidan looked at Jim, then Liz, with a pleading expression on his face. She smiled at him. "How about just the basics, Aidan? Just the general idea."

Aidan hunched up, bringing his knees to his chest, and clasped them with his arms. "My story…it's not like you guys. It's different. I just…"

"Aidan." It was Liz, her voice clear and level. "Tell them."

He buried his head in his knees for a moment. He looked up, and took a deep breath. "Okay. Okay. It's…well, I didn't really *do* anything, okay? I just…sort of…*facilitated* something." His brow was furrowed now, and he was staring at the flames. It seemed like he wasn't going to say anything else.

"Facilitated what?" asked Mike.

Aidan was startled by the question, and his eyes darted to Mike's. "Oh. Umm. It's all online. I'm into coding and app design. This friend and I made this website that…well, it's a long story. It started out pretty innocent, like, for trading homework and stuff. We started making a lot of money off it but then it got bad. Like, it caused a lot of trouble."

Taylor's voice was tinged with humor. "You're here 'cause you made a *website?*" He glanced over at Mike, and then around to the rest, a questioning look in his eyes.

"Yeah." Aidan absently nibbled his thumbnail. "But it got…bad."

"How bad could it—"

"Bad. FBI was involved. And one kid's in jail. Another was in the ICU for weeks. Almost got killed over it."

"Some website," Liam muttered. "What the hell was it? You some kind of pervert?"

Aidan shook his head rapidly. "No! No…I mean, it wasn't like that…Look, it's complicated. I'm not proud of it, and I—"

Liz cut him off. "Aidan, that's enough for tonight. Thank you for what you shared. We're going to have a lot of time together."

"Okay. Goodnight." Aidan stood and headed up the path to the cabin. The rest followed, one by one. No one said anything.

As he stepped away from the fire, Mike felt just how much the temperature had dropped, and how dark it was outside the circle of light. He looked at the stars again. They were even brighter than before.

9

THE CABIN WAS ONLY a few degrees warmer than outside, and light from the single, low-wattage bulb barely reached the edges of the room. Aidan stood in front of the window, looking out at the stars. Liam was shuffling through his bag, pulling out his toothbrush.

Mike shivered. "Cold in here."

"Could make a fire in that stove," said Liam, on his way into the bathroom. Mike could hear him rinsing his toothbrush. And then, garbled through a mouthful of toothpaste: "Gonna be a *long* six weeks, amigos."

Taylor came in from outside. "Damn. Thought it might be warmer in here."

"Let's get that thing going," said Manny, nodding toward the cast-iron stove. "Might as well get used to it." He went to the stove, and opened the doors. "Ah, shit. We don't have any wood." He looked at Taylor.

"Why you lookin' at me?"

"'Cause you're, like, a firefighter," Manny said.

"So?"

"So, you know about fires and shit, right?"

"So I gotta haul the firewood? Screw you." He stared at Manny, his arms raised, looking somewhere between pissed off and amused. After a moment, they both laughed.

Each of them carried armfuls from the woodpile until there was a good supply, at least for a couple of nights. It took a few tries to get the fire started. There was some debate about the best way to go—log cabin or teepee. Mike smiled. It was the same argument he used to have with Eric when they went camping. Maybe the same argument any group of guys has when it comes to building a fire. He looked around at them, and felt...*okay*. Like he used to, before everything went bad. And it was confusing. Because he knew he shouldn't feel good. After all, he was in a cabin in the middle of nowhere with a handful of strangers who—except—*that's it.*

As he glanced around at them—this collection of oddballs, each with his own crazy story—he realized that maybe they weren't strangers now.

Bullshit. You've known them less than forty-eight hours.

You don't know anything about them.

They don't know anything about you.

They don't know half your story, and you don't know half of theirs.

Who knows if any of that shit they said was even true?

But as he handed the scraps of firewood to Taylor, the voices of doubt subsided.

Mike brushed his teeth and looked in the scuffed mirror. The scar on his face looked a little better. He was amazed how much it had healed in the past few days.

Manny came in. "Helluva a story, hermano." He shoved his toothbrush in his mouth. "Thought I was the most loco hombre here."

"Doubt it," said Mike.

Taylor had the fire going, and Mike could already feel the heat radiating when he stepped back into the main room. After a couple minutes, they were all in their bunks.

There was a knock at the door, and Jim stepped in. "Everybody here?" He glanced around the room, counting them. "Looks good." He flipped out the light. "Sleep well." He stepped out, and the door clicked shut behind him.

Mike lay there, hands behind his head. Firelight danced on the ceiling. He could hear the rest of them breathing. No one talked. The fire crackled.

He thought about the drowning. About Andy.

*

His little brother's death was an accident. Everyone knew that. Mike knew that. He was used to unpredictable, cruel, arbitrary stuff. Like when his dad had died. Life was just shit sometimes. They were a Catholic family, but to Mike, it was hard to find meaning and faith in God's Greater Plan when the plan seemed to suck.

As for the drowning, the events had been told and retold. On the news. In the paper. To the cops. Even at the funeral reception. Andy had been swimming with his friends. They were horsing around like kids do. Swimming underwater, holding their breath, jumping in and out of the water, doing somersaults. He'd drowned. Nothing suspicious. No one had held Andrew underwater. He hadn't hit his head on the bottom. He was just a nine-year-old boy who drowned in the goddamn pool. The coroner looked for some cause: head trauma, a stroke, an aortic aneurysm, an allergic reaction—*anything* to explain how it could happen so quickly. There was no indication of anything, though, other than drowning.

Witnesses said the young lifeguards—the DeAngelo twins, Joe and Alex—did everything they could. They did CPR until the paramedics from the Lawson Volunteer Fire Department arrived within six minutes. But Andy died anyway.

Back when Mike's dad died of a heart attack at forty-one (cruel, arbitrary, but Part of God's Plan) three and a half years ago, his mom had been a pillar of strength. Mike's father's life insurance policy was small, and his mom didn't make much as the Principal's secretary at Lawson Elementary. Things were tight, but she'd made it work.

But Karen Whittaker was no longer a pillar. Three days after Andy drowned, she needed to be hospitalized. She'd stopped eating. A couple years following dad's death, they'd finally begun to joke that their house was haunted with his ghost when odd things happened. But now it wasn't funny. The place was haunted by four ghosts now: a father, a husband, a son, and a brother.

It took his mother nearly two weeks to use the word "lawsuit." Mike sat at the kitchen table, listening in as she talked to Uncle Dave—her brother and the family lawyer, by default—in the living room. Uncle Dave told it like it was: it would be a difficult case. Andrew's death was tragic, but there wasn't anything to suggest negligence. The lifeguards had done their duty, by all accounts. The medics from the volunteer fire department had arrived as quickly as humanly possible. Without anything to suggest any wrong moves, Uncle Dave said, there just wasn't much of a case.

The DeAngelo twins were the lifeguards. Everyone in town knew them. They were the great grandsons of Giuseppe DeAngelo, founder of DeAngelo & Sons Lumber Company. The mill was the lifeblood of the town, employing close to half the adults, including Mike's dad before he died. Joe was a linebacker and co-captain of the varsity football squad. Alex was a swimmer and the yearbook editor.

Alex had broken down at Andrew's funeral, but Joe had stood stone faced and pale, staring at the floor. Neither one would look at Mike. Both disappeared quickly after the service. No one heard much from them. The assumption around town was they'd gone to Lake Placid, where the DeAngelos owned a vacation home.

It had taken Mike a few days to work up any anger toward the DeAngelo boys. Hell, it had taken him time to work up *any* feelings after the numbness of the initial shock. The anger grew, but there was nothing to say. Nothing to do. But their—what was it? Their silence. They hadn't so much as come over to Mike and his mom at the funeral. They wouldn't even look at him. They were *cowards*.

But even then, he knew it wasn't on them. It was on him.

He should have taken his brother swimming. That's the real reason he didn't like the happy pills that the psychologist had recommended. Because he needed the guilt. No, he needed *more* than the guilt. The pills had created a fuzzy dullness in his mind, like all the hard edges were softened. He didn't like it.

About a week after they buried Andrew, he was back to work landscaping. He was pulling weeds—fighting a really stubborn cluster of thorny vines that was strangling a sapling behind one of the old Victorians on Lancaster Street—when one of the thorns pierced his glove. The pain was shockingly intense, and he swore aloud. But he realized something. Pain. The physical pain. It was so clear. So intense. And it felt...fair. He discovered he didn't want the pain to end. No. He wanted it to last. Yes, he thought, that's what you deserve! To hurt. He took a rake to the rest of the vines, ripping them out violently. The pain in his hand throbbed.

Later that night, Mike had climbed out of bed, careful not to wake his mother, and gone into the bathroom. First, he flushed the antidepressant pill down the toilet. *Not gonna numb it anymore. I'm gonna feel this all the way.* Then he undressed, and unfolded the tiny blade of his small pocketknife. He looked at it in the cool fluorescent light. He chose a spot in on his thigh—up high, where people wouldn't see it—and cut with the tiny, cold blade. He kept it shallow, maybe just half an inch long. He winced, and his toes curled

75

with the sting. Repulsed and fascinated, he dropped the knife and looked at the slow trickle of blood on his leg. That's when the tears came.

And he sat naked, shivering on the cold tile floor with his knees hugged to his chest, his mother sleeping in the next room, his brother dead, his father dead. He wept quietly, alone, with the pain and the truth and the fury of it all screaming inside him.

10

IT WAS DARK when Mike woke up, and surprisingly cold. The fire in the stove had long since gone out, with just a few wisps of smoke rising from barely glowing embers. He thought he was the first one awake, until he saw that Liam was missing from his bunk. The rest were asleep. Manny snored loudly.

He slid out of the sleeping bag, unzipping it just enough to get out, trying to be quiet. The wood floor creaked. He stretched, reaching for the LED headlamp he'd left out on the small headboard shelf. Slinging it around his head, he shuffled into the bathroom.

Shit. Except you don't go to the bathroom to go to the bathroom here at Camp Badass. You go out into the freezing effing cold.

He traded the headlamp for the wool cap. He put on his flip-flops and the fleece jacket, stepping outside as quietly as possible as he pushed the door closed behind him. There was just the slightest light in the sky; a shade of indigo instead of black, and the stars had faded. The looming cliffs and mountains around him stood in dark relief, and he could smell the rich aroma of the forest and the cold stone of the lake. He shivered. His feet were freezing in the open-toed sandals.

Something in the corner of his eye caught his attention, near the lake. Squinting, he could make out Jim, the glow of a cigarette brightening for a moment as he inhaled, then dimming. Jim saw him too, and waved. Mike threw him a casual salute and continued shuffling toward the outhouse.

When he rounded the corner of the kitchen cabin, he saw Liam on a damp, grassy patch of ground, shirtless, in sweatpants, grunting and straining as he worked through a rapid series of pushups. His movement was fast but fluid, his clearly defined triceps working like pistons as he rose and fell with mechanical efficiency in concert with his rapid breathing. Steam rose off of him from a film of sweat. Just in the space of maybe five seconds before he noticed Mike, he worked through at least a dozen. When he did see him, he paused just long enough to nod and mutter "hey" before starting up again. A tattoo of a soccer ball bent and flexed across his upper back.

Mike's voice broke the stillness of dawn. "Ambitious."

Liam laughed, the sound barely audible between grunts. "Habit."

"Ambitious habit."

"Should join me." Three more pushups. "Stay strong." He kept going.

"Maybe tomorrow."

"I'll wake you up." Three more. "If you want."

Mike ducked into the outhouse, swinging the door shut. It smelled better than the ones he'd used on the Adirondack trails, where throngs of hikers left plenty of evidence. Gaps on all four sides let in the steady breeze off the lake and the scent of pines. He was in the middle of his business when he noticed the lack of toilet paper.

Damn.

"Hey, Liam?"

Liam had moved onto crunches. He didn't stop. "Huh?"

"Help me out with some toilet paper? Forgot it."

"Yeah. Just a second." He cranked through what sounded like twenty or thirty more crunches, then jogged off toward the cabin. After a minute, he came sauntering back, tossing a roll through the opening at the top. "Let's leave that out here, yeah?" He was breathing hard.

"Will do."

"We better get the rest of them up. Looks like Liz and Jim are almost ready, and our pals are still sleeping. I guess you and I are the early risers."

"Guess so. I'm used to morning cross-country workouts. Same with soccer?"

"Every day."

Mike stepped out of the outhouse and switched off the headlamp. "Been in there yet?" He pointed behind him with his thumb as they began walking back toward the cabin.

"No. Probly will before we set off though. Sounds like a trek today."

"You hike much?"

"Nah. Soccer, soccer, and more soccer. Haven't really hiked since I lived in Texas."

"Well, I don't think you'll struggle too much. You're pretty ripped, bro."

"Y'all hittin' on me, Mikey-boy?"

Mike laughed. "Sorry. Maybe after a few more weeks up here."

"Six weeks in the woods could change a guy in all kinds of ways, eh?" Liam smirked and clapped Mike on the back.

They walked back to the bunk house. The steps creaked as they climbed up onto the small porch. Liam pulled on his shirt, which he'd left hanging on the railing. "Looks like a clear morning. Hey, check that out," he said, nodding toward the far side of the lake, off to the right. Even though they couldn't see the sun itself—it was still out of sight from their vantage point in the deep valley—it caught the very top of the western ridge. With the rest of the valley still in shadow, it looked like a brilliant flame. The light expanded as they watched, sliding down the rock face in slow motion. They heard a noise off to the left. It was Liz, seated in a chair on the porch of the kitchen cabin, a steaming mug of coffee in her hands. She smiled and gestured with the cup toward the western ridge. "Worth getting up for, isn't it?"

Mike nodded, then looked back up at the broadening plane of light.

Liam stretched his shoulders. Mike could smell the sweat on him as he leaned in close, whispering, glancing sidelong toward Liz. "Hey. Does she creep you out at all?"

Mike's voice was low. "Liz?"

"No, the other 'she' up here with us, dude." Liam rolled his eyes.

"I dunno. I mean, I guess she gets in your head a little, huh? But that's her job."

"In your head a little. Yeah. Good way of putting it." Liam cracked his knuckles again and leaned in close, whispering. "Well, between us, I think she's kinda hot."

Mike was surprised by how uncomfortable the comment made him feel. "Um. Let's go wake up the others."

*

"Sixteen hundred ninety-four vertical feet," said Jim, looking at his handheld GPS. He was breathing hard. "Good job, guys. We made it."

They'd just pushed through the last hundred feet of climbing, well above the tree line, and stood now at the top of the slight dip in the western ridge. To the north and south, the granite slopes rose dramatically several hundred more feet, but from here they'd earned their first view beyond the wall of the ridge. To the west, along the path they took flying in, it dropped more gradually, flattening somewhat before rising again to another ridge several miles away. Beyond that, it was rugged mountains as far as Mike could see on this clear morning. Behind him lay the bowl-shaped valley, with the teardrop lake glistening far below. The camp was just a narrow strip of land between the water and the thick forest.

The climb had been steady and challenging. Manny, characteristically, had talked incessantly at the start, but after the first ten minutes, he'd shut up. They'd hiked the last couple hours mostly in silence, other than the occasional stilted conversation during water breaks. After last night's deluge of self-revelatory information, Mike enjoyed the quiet. Besides, it would have been too hard to keep up a conversation during the climb. Jim and Liz tossed out reminders about sunscreen and water, along with occasional geological trivia. They were armed with their .500's, and both had a set of cuffs and two canisters of bear spray clipped to their belts.

Reminder: this ain't summer camp.

Now, sucking air at the top, Mike and the others were soaked with sweat. The steady breeze coming over the ridge felt good—they'd had full sun at their backs since breaking the tree line. The chill of the early morning was a distant memory. Liz pointed to a flat area in the shade of a large boulder. "Let's take a seat over there. We'll break out some snacks."

They made their way over. Mike dropped his pack. It couldn't have weighed more than ten or twelve pounds, but it was a relief to set it down. He leaned against the boulder and sipped from his water bottle, arms resting on his hunched-up knees. The others seemed just as happy to sit down. They each took out the plastic bags of pre-packed food they'd been assigned to carry, and a collection of rations lay scattered before them like a survivalist's feast: beef jerky, nuts, granola, crackers, sliced cheese, and pepperoni. Digging in, Mike found himself remarkably satisfied with the simple food. He was starving.

Liz took off her sunglasses and perched on a rock. "We've climbed up here for a few reasons. First of all, the exercise is good. We'll be doing something like this every day. Don't worry—it won't always be this intense. But we're also up here because it's beautiful. Might sound sappy to you guys, but as Jim and I said before, we chose this place for its isolation and beauty.

"So, unlike last night, you guys won't do a lot of talking up here. I'm gonna guide you through something like a meditation, and then the rule is no talking during the hike down. This is a time for silent reflection." She took a deep swig of her water bottle. "Now listen. The key to effective meditation is to center yourself. We're gonna take a pretty simple approach to it. So finish up eating whatever you have, and then make yourself comfortable without lying down. No falling asleep. Just lean against a rock, or whatever, but keep yourself upright." They shifted around, rearranging legs and arms and backpacks.

"Okay. Close your eyes." Liz paused. "No, really, I mean it. Liam. Manny. Close 'em."

Mike took a deep breath and did it. For a second, he squinted around to see what the others were doing, but then he closed them all the way.

Liz spoke in a quiet, level voice. "Become aware of your breathing. Try to slow it down. Inhale through your nose...okay, hold it a second...now exhale through your mouth. Good. Again...in through the nose, hold it a second...out through the mouth. Keep that up." She paused again while they took a few breaths. "Feel the way the air fills your lungs, and the way they empty when you exhale. Feel it, like fluid." Her voice was slow, calm, monotone.

As she continued, Mike felt oddly calm. Whatever Liz was doing was really working somehow. As she went on, rambling about feeling their breathing and their heartbeats and their fingertips and the texture of the rocks and the tingle of the breeze on their scalps, it was *working*. Of course, he wasn't sure what *it* was. Only that whatever it was, it was making him feel a calmness that had become so rare as to be totally foreign now. It was almost intoxicating. At one point, as Liz continued, Mike realized he was smiling. Not at *what* she was saying, but because of the way he felt. *Joyful. Alive.* He noticed he'd been rubbing the scar on his arm, gently tracing it. And now that he realized it, he mapped the geography of the wound. The indentations and the ridges. But unlike before, he wasn't angry at it. He wasn't angry *about* it. He wasn't…he wasn't *anything* about it. It was just there. It was just part of him, connected to every other part of him.

And as he breathed, as he felt all these things and none of these things, he became aware that he'd stopped listening to Liz. Sure, he could hear her, but he wasn't listening anymore. He wasn't even sure what she was saying. Instead, a vivid picture of his brother had come into focus. It started with just his face, but quickly it became an animated memory—a three-dimensional, virtual reality of recollection—and he was with Andrew in the backyard—Andrew just two or three—and Mike was pushing him on the tire swing, his mop of chestnut hair at crazy angles as he leaned back, giggling—and Mike could hear him. He could swear he actually *heard* him. He smelled grass and sunscreen. Mike could feel the gentle impact, the texture of the tire as he pushed, the creak of the rope and the hinges and the pendulum motion of it all so real.

"…and the face of that person," Liz was saying. "Tell that person what you want to say to him or her…"

And then the memory faded.

"Now slowly open your eyes…don't speak…just open them."

When he did, his vision was blurred, and he reached up to feel his face wet with tears. His impulse was to wipe them away, to brush away this evidence of feeling, but he didn't. Instead, he looked past the circle of wolf-boys, past Liz and her voice, at the horizon of distant mountains, at the vast and infinite and unforgiving and frighteningly beautiful landscape before him, and he let the tears continue to run down his face. He felt them drip onto his hand, but he still didn't move. It was only when he felt a hand on his shoulder that he turned and saw that Manny's eyes, too, were wet. And then he saw, as he looked around, that the same was true for the others. Except he couldn't see Liam's eyes, because he'd stepped away, leaning against the boulder, his back to them. If there was any emotion on his face, no one could see it.

After a few moments, Liz and Jim stood up. Silently, the rest arose, shouldering their packs, and began the hike back down. No one talked. As they descended, the walls of the valley rose up around them and the lake gradually grew closer. The sky was clear, and the sun was hot on their faces for much of the hike. Breezes came in waves, like cool fluid, giving reprieve from the heat. Mike's thoughts were the same: they flowed, one after another, seeming to arrive effortlessly, then faded. He thought about his mom, and what she might be doing right now. He thought about his dad. He thought about Eric and the other guys on the cross-country team back at school, about Coach Swanson. He *didn't* think about the town pool. He didn't think about cutting himself. Or that day in the truck. Or about Joe DeAngelo, or the gun he'd almost killed him with. He didn't think about complicated legal decisions. He ignored the rhythmic pain in his legs and the burning of his feet and the bright sun that was directly above them.

Mike ignored it all, because in his mind there was only one thing now: a still frame of his little brother on that swing, clutching the rope, leaning back, hair flying, his face frozen in the middle of a broad, giggling smile.

11

THE SUN BEAT DOWN from a cloudless afternoon sky. As they came down off the trail, the lake stretched out before them, the azure water still and inviting. Liam asked about swimming. Jim said the water would be so cold they'd re-think that pretty quickly, but they were welcome to try. Liam took off his shirt, sprinted to the end of the dock, and did a cannonball. Half a second later, he popped back to the surface, sputtering, and heaved himself out of the water.

"Jesus Christ! Holy shit!" He was bouncing on the dock, hugging himself. He grabbed his t-shirt and used it as a towel. "Well," he said, his teeth chattering, "it *was* refreshing, y'all." Mike was tempted, but not enough to try it.

Liz stood on the shore, arms crossed, looking amused. "I would personally appreciate it if you'd hold off until you're done with this afternoon's work duties, then get cleaned up for real. Like, with soap. I can smell you guys from here."

After lunch, Jim divided them into groups. Manny and Aidan started on firewood duty. Mike, Taylor, and Liam were assigned to gather rocks from the perimeter of the camp, then haul them in a wheelbarrow to a few different places. They shored up the pier, built up the fire ring, reinforced the posts holding up the anti-critter fence, and repaired a few of the stone pathways between buildings. After a while, Jim handed them a wood saw along with rakes and spades for a couple hours of raking up debris, trimming trees, and other odd landscaping jobs. Mike shook his head: *what I wouldn't give to smoke one of those end-of-the-day joints with Eric right now.* And with the thought, another pang of guilt.

They wrapped up their work as the light began to fade, sunbeams illuminating the east ridge as the sky took on its evening hues. Finally, the tools put away in the shed, they rested for a few minutes, sipping water, not talking. Mike was absolutely wiped. He was soaked again with sweat; they all were. Their clothes and faces were caked with salt, dirt, and pine sap. His hands were bleeding in a few places. He was sore, but not as sore as he knew he'd be the next day. He smelled like a sweaty animal.

Before they could go to dinner, it was time for the inaugural cold shower. Jim called in through the window. "Ten minutes, then I want you over at the kitchen cabin. No messing around. It's got to be an early night, so get a move on it. And hey, remember—cold water builds character, guys." He laughed as he walked away.

Mike thought back to the first morning cross country practice freshman year, and how nervous he'd been about the open showers. After their cool-down stretch at the end of practice, Coach Swanson pulled the new guys aside in the locker room. "Okay, listen. This is high school. You clean up after practice." A few seniors paraded by in nothing but flip-flops, carrying towels, chatting casually. "It's only weird if you make it weird."

Now they stood in the doorway of the bathroom, wondering who was supposed to go first. Breaking the silence, Manny said, "Well, enjoy the show, chicos." He stripped down and, with only a second's hesitation, twisted the knob and let cold water pour over his head, his face registering shock. "Shit!" Squinting, he reached for the soap. "Dios mio, hace frio!" He laughed. In the middle of scrubbing himself, he looked up at the rest of them still standing there awkwardly. He smiled, doing an exaggerated, effeminate pose. "You like what you see, amigos?"

"Shut up, Manny." Taylor pulled off his shirt. "Okay. Since the drill sergeant has the clock ticking, I'll take one for the team and join this clown." Mike, Liam, and Aidan stepped back out to the main room, unpacking their stuff, listening to the splashing water and the expletives that accompanied it.

Manny came out a few minutes later, wrapped in a towel. "Not bad, locos. Pretty refreshing."

Taylor was rinsing off as Mike walked in and hung his towel. "Not that bad once you get used to it."

Mike got in, and after a series of hesitant, shivering attempts, he did it. The water felt so cold on his back, it made him hyperventilate for a moment until he got a little used to it. Aidan came in and stood by the sink wrapped in a towel, absently picking at his thumbnail, shoulders hunched, staring at the floor.

Aidan probably hadn't had a Coach Swanson talk.

Just go for some humor. The great equalizer. "Yo. Aidan. I'm not gonna bite you, man."

Aidan looked up, lingering maybe just a little on Mike, then his eyes darted quickly to some spot on the wall. "Um, I'll just wait 'til you're done."

Pretty sure he just checked me out.

Just then, a memory. Mike was ten. Dad was driving him and Eric home from a movie, and they were trading wisecracks about a kid in the eighth grade who'd come out of the closet online. Dad had pulled the truck over and schooled them both about respect. It had made Mike pretty uncomfortable at the time, and he and Eric rode quietly the rest of the way. Later, Dad had explained that Uncle

Dave was gay. It was a revelation. Mike had always been pretty tolerant since.

Liam came in and stood in the doorframe, wrapped in a towel, smirking. "Y'all good in here?"

"Everything's fine." Mike grabbed his towel off the hook, drying off, and pushed past him into the main room. "All yours, Aidan."

Mike went over to his bed, finished toweling off, and started to get dressed. Manny and Taylor had paused to watch Liam, who was still standing in the doorway with his back to them.

"Hey, Liam," Mike said.

Liam looked over his shoulder back into the main room. "What?"

"What are you doing, man?"

"What am I *doing*?"

Mike lowered his voice and mouthed the words. "He's…uncomfortable. Can't you just give him a minute alone?"

Liam smiled and rolled his eyes. He took off his towel and continued into the bathroom. "Hey buddy," they heard him say to Aidan, his voice artificially chipper. "Mind if I join y'all?"

Mike looked at Taylor and Manny. Both were shaking their heads. "Cabrón," mouthed Manny.

Taylor rolled his eyes. "Yeah," he said, quiet enough to keep it among the three of them. "Blondie's a little out of his element."

A few seconds later, Aidan rushed out, still soaking wet, his towel wrapped tightly around him. He still had some soap on his narrow, bony shoulders. He made his way to the dresser, avoiding eye contact with the other guys as he put on deodorant, shivering.

"Hey amigo," said Manny, "still got some soap on you."

"Oh." Aidan looked up at him, pulling on his t-shirt anyway. "Yeah." He finished dressing with rushed, jerky movements, his back to them.

After a moment, Liam strutted out, no towel in sight. He shook his head like a dog, throwing droplets around the room. "Whew!

That's gonna take some getting used to, what y'all think?" He looked down at himself, and pointed. "Damn. I shrank."

"Dude," Taylor said, "You done showing off now? We get it. You're a god among men. Even in the cold. Come on. Put some clothes on."

"Y'all got a problem, cowboy?" Liam was still smirking as he put on deodorant. He shook his head, then started getting dressed. "Listen. Let's get something straight. If I'm gonna be stuck in this shack with y'all for the next six weeks, I'm sure as shit not gonna worry about who sees my junk. It's all good, right, blondie?" He clapped Aidan on the shoulder as he shuffled past, and the smaller boy winced.

Manny glared at Liam. "You're a different kind of guy, Tejas."

Yeah, Mike thought. *That got weird.*

*

The dinner menu was nothing to write home about, but after the physical exertion of the day, all of them were ravenous and eager to get the meal ready. Up until then, Jim and Liz had taken care of meals, mostly using items they'd prepared in advance. The duty would switch to the boys now, and Jim had posted a meal assignment schedule. He oversaw the kitchen, pointing out the various supplies and showing them some techniques for chopping potatoes and properly rehydrating and cooking the freeze-dried meat.

Jim took them outside to show them the water apparatus. A hundred-gallon plastic cistern tank rested on an elevated platform at roof level, providing gravity-driven running water with a microbe filter and a solar purification system. A similar drum stood atop their bunkhouse, although the capacity was smaller. Jim showed them how to fill the tanks with buckets from the lake, accessing the hatches via stepladders on the side of the cabins. Aidan mentioned that maybe they could boil some water and pour it into the bunk-house supply to heat it up for their showers, or rig up some kind of electric heating element to wrap around the water pipe. The others looked at each other, eyebrows raised.

Liam nodded approvingly. "Got an engineer's mind, eh blondie?"

Aidan blushed. "Wouldn't be that hard."

"I think you'd electrocute us, hermanito. Don't be doin' that shit, okay? I don't want to die naked. Well, unless I'm in bed with—"

"That's enough, Manny," said Jim.

The kitchen was equipped with a two-burner propane stove, and the larger solar panels allowed for better lighting than the bunk house. Over dinner—rehydrated chicken stew with diced potatoes and carrots—Liam seemed distracted. More than once, Mike noticed him staring out the window or absently at some spot on the table, mindlessly nodding to the conversation. If the others saw it, they didn't let on. Except maybe Aidan, who had seated himself as far from Liam as possible, and avoided eye contact with him.

When they were finished with dinner, Liz brought out some cookies and hot chocolate. Jim spread out a topographical map on the table to show them the route they'd taken. Mike knew topo maps. While Jim rambled on about the elevation gain from the lake to the pass, Mike looked at the surrounding area. It was clear that even moving quickly, it would be at least a three or four-day hike—and a treacherous one—just to reach the closest marked trail, and then another two, maybe three or four, to the nearest road or ranger station. The pass they'd climbed appeared to be the only viable way in or out of this valley without technical equipment and skill, but it would definitely take technical climbing to go any further west. He realized how isolated they really were. They all took an enthusiastic curiosity in the map, maybe for no other reason than because it proved the difficulty of what they'd accomplished.

But Mike was pretty sure that Liam had a different sort of interest in the map.

He's studying it.

Liz sees it.

She was subtle about it, but she was watching Liam, too. She clenched and unclenched her jaw, her head cocked slightly and eyes narrowed. Liz glanced over at Mike.

Shit. Mike looked down as quickly as he could, but not quick enough.

After dinner, he was glad to be on dishwashing duty with Taylor. The others left, leaving the two of them working at the sink, scrubbing the pots and plates. It was hard to wash dishes with cold water, and he scrubbed hard.

Taylor rinsed a cup. "You think every day's gonna be like this? This much work, I mean?"

"Hope not. I'm wrecked."

"Must be part of the program. Keep us too wiped out to cause any real trouble, huh?" Taylor laughed, squirting more dish soap onto his sponge. "It'll get us in mean shape, though."

"True." Mike paused drying a plate, and glanced quickly around. In a lower voice: "What do you make of our pal from Texas?"

Taylor hesitated, then resumed scrubbing. "I dunno. He's alright."

Mike shook his head. "Not cool the way he messes with Aidan. Aidan isn't like the rest of us. He's…"

Taylor interrupted. "He's weak. I mean, he's not…you know, *tough.*"

"Yeah. I can't help it. I know he's only a year younger, but he's just, like…"

"Like such a little kid?" Taylor asked.

"Yeah."

Taylor gestured with a sponge. "We all know guys like Liam. He's a jock."

Mike chuckled. "Yeah. He sure likes to be naked."

Taylor laughed. "I would too, if I were built like that."

Mike decided to press the matter. "But seriously, you don't feel like there's something else just…*off* about Liam?"

"I don't really see it, man. I mean, he's different, but I don't get that bad a vibe from him."

"Hm. I guess." Mike went back to drying the plate. "What do you think about Manny?"

"Dunno," said Taylor. "Seems alright. Just can't keep his mouth shut. Jesus, Mike. You interrogate the other guys about me, too?"

"No! No. I just…"

Taylor shut off the water and wiped his hands on his pants. "Give it a rest, man. You'll drive yourself nuts up here."

They heard someone on the steps, and peered out the window. It was Liz. She opened the door, leaning in.

"You guys almost finished?"

"Yeah," said Mike.

"We're waiting by the fire. Tonight, you get to tell your stories in more depth. Manny's going first. No surprise there, right?"

12

"MANUEL ALEJANDRO SANTA ROSA RODRIGUEZ," Manny said, his Dominican accent coming through unrestrained. "That's my name. But nobody ever called me Manuel except my father. He still lives in Santo Domingo. Never seen him much. Always been Manny to everybody else, including my mother. Sometimes Manuelito, but never Manuel. She only called me Manuel in the hospital. There she was, lying there on that hospital bed, barely able to breathe. And she's holding my hand between both of hers, holding it real tight, like, with her rosary all wrapped around my fingers, and she whispers so quiet. 'Manuel,' she says, and it surprises me, because she's never called me that. 'Manuel, baby boy, take care of your big brother before he gets lost.' That's the last thing she says to me, then she dies. Right there, my hand inside hers." He paused, staring at the fire. He scratched his temple. "Oh yeah. Cancer. She had breast cancer."

"Sorry," Liam said.

Manny nodded at him, then continued. "My brother Andres is twenty-one. He wasn't there. No, he was out doing what Andres does. It was ten p.m., so I could tell you exactly what street corner he was working when Mami died. Later that night he comes in to see her. And I'm still sitting there holding that rosary. The doctors and nurses left us alone. Machines were all off. No more beeping. I was praying for her. Andres comes in, hair slick, in his leather jacket and shit. I can tell he's high even though he's trying to act normal. He's always using, even when he's dealing. So, he's all, like, a *mess* when he sees her. Starts crying and shouting and carrying on, my mother lying there peaceful as an angel and he's shouting at the doctors. He's all out of control, man. I just keep thinking about the last thing she said to me. But Andres is already lost. Right then I don't want to take care of him. So I take that rosary and I run out of there. I run all the way to the subway station. I ride that train the rest of the night. Andres, he keeps callin' my cell, but I don't answer."

Manny got up from his chair and squatted in front of the fire, stoking some of the logs. He talked into the fire, not looking at any of them. "I can't sleep, so I'm just riding around on the train for a few hours. Finally, I get off, and I'm down near the water when the sky starts to get a little light. I go home then. Andres is all messed up when I get there. The apartment, it's a mess. All full of people and shit. We don't have too many relatives here, just one uncle and aunt and some cousins. But a lot of the guys Andres runs with are there. People crying and quiet and everything, but the guys trying to act all tough. Machismos. So when I walk in, everybody's staring at me. Andres runs up, he's hugging me so hard like he's gonna crush me, punching me and hugging me all at once, crying like a little baby. And then we both cry, then everybody's crying, even the tough guys." Manny threw the stick in the fire, sending sparks upward. "You ain't seen shit 'til you've seen a room full of hardcore dudes crying, man. All these tattoos and earrings and shit—I mean these are tough muchachos, you know.

"Well, like a month after the funeral, I start getting caught up in Andres' shit. I'd always steered clear of it, for Mami. Andres had kept me out of it. He wanted me to stay with her. Little Manny, home with Mami, keeping everything okay. But after she's dead, all these guys are around a lot more, 'cause now it's Andres' place. So it doesn't take long 'til I'm running with him. 'Til I'm dealing. I never used. Never once. Mami made me promise not to touch that shit, and I never did. Believe me, I've seen what happens. Anyway, Andres respects that. He, like, *honors* that."

Manny laughed, shaking his head. "So he keeps me 'clean of it,' like Mami always told me to stay. 'Stay clean of that business, Manny,' she'd say. 'That's trabajo susio y peligroso your brother's in.' Dirty and dangerous work. But everybody on the street knows I'm Andres' brother. I try to keep my head down. I try to go live with our tia in New Jersey. But she's gotta clear out a room for me, so that's taking a while. I'm even thinking maybe I'll go back to the Dominican Republic and find my father. He wasn't there for the funeral. He couldn't make it. Well, I don't know if he couldn't or he *wouldn't*. I tried talking to my grandmother on his side, but she doesn't know where he is either. So I don't end up going anywhere, and I'm there in that apartment with Andres, and we don't even know if our father *cares* she's dead, right?

"It's summer, so there's no school. One night I'm home alone. It's hot as hell—the power's out, so no air conditioning—and I'm sitting by a window, trying to get cool. Whole block, the power's out, so it's a little quieter than usual, but the city's never quiet. It's dark, though, just headlights and candles in people's windows. We're on the seventh floor. I'm sitting out there on the windowsill, and I hear some commotion. I look down. It's Andres arguing with somebody. Then the voices pick up, and I can tell it's going bad. Sounds like it's gonna be a fight. I go running down the stairs. When I get outside there's this scuffle going on, a few guys involved now. Dudes saying all kinds of shit, then there's punches. Andres, he's a mean boxer, man. He's solid. I'm okay, but he's a pro. Ain't nobody messes with

Andres in a fight. So he decks this guy, and what do you think is next, right? The guns come out. So now everybody's running and hiding and shit. I'm just standing there like a tool, so I duck back inside. Nobody shoots, but the cops are coming now—we can hear 'em. Andres gets taken in for fighting. They push him into the car, and I'm arguing with the cops to take me with him, but they take off. So there I am, standing there, some cop trying to ask me all kinds of questions, everybody talking at once."

He looked around, the firelight dancing on his face. "Sorry. I should get to the point, right? So anyway, I'm alone in the apartment that night. I don't call nobody. I should call my aunt. All the neighbor ladies, they're all up in my business, knocking on the door, everybody talking super-fast-old-Dominican-lady Spanish, everybody worried about little Manuelito. This one lady, Mrs. Portes, she was friends with my mother, she's persistent like crazy. But I keep the door closed and I sit there in the dark until I fall asleep, trying to ignore all of them. In the morning there's this knock. It's Child Protective Services. They take me downtown. I go meet Andres. He's in lockup. Tells me he'll be out soon. CPS tells me I can't stay in the apartment alone, being a minor. So I tell them about my tia. But she's in Jersey, so there's some paperwork they gotta do to have me go to a different state. Meantime I gotta go stay with some neighbors. Everybody signs some papers and some shit, and there I am, moved in with the Portes family. They're buena gente, but I don't know them that well, and it's weird. 'Specially since I think they're the ones that called CPS in the first place, maybe."

"Manny," Liz said, interrupting him.

"Yeah?" He looked up, his eyes wide, the firelight gleaming on his shaved head.

"Manny, try not to get off track, okay?"

He looked at her, his features softening. "Yeah. Yeah, okay. I'll cut to the chase. So a few weeks go by and Andres gets out. 'Cause it turns out he hasn't actually done anything. He didn't have a gun on him, believe it or not. He must have ditched what he was carrying before the cops got there. Andres is smart. He comes home. Well, then all kinds of messed up stuff happens. I'll skip over it. It doesn't matter.

"Point is, pretty soon some bad dudes are coming for Andres. He's alone in that apartment one night—I'm still staying with the Portes family—and he comes running across the hallway, banging on the door. He got a tip some guys were coming for him. But Mr. Portes, he doesn't want Andres coming in, no way; he won't let him in. So I get pissed, and I tell him if he won't let Andres in, I'm leaving. Mr. Portes won't budge, so I'm out. Now, remember, that was the day I almost tried coke. Like I said, I didn't do that shit, but I did have it on me. Anyway, Andres and I are running now, like, down the fire escape. That's when I remember I have the drugs, so I drop them. Good thing. I guess if I hadn't, things woulda gone pretty different later on. But Andres didn't drop whatever he was carrying. Anyway, so now some guys are chasing us down the street. We end up in this Korean restaurant. It's late at night so it ain't open. There's just an open door off the back alley, and we go in there to hide in the kitchen. These guys don't let up. They catch up. But this time Andres has a gun. These guys come in and Andres shoots. Takes one down. He's bleeding right there in this kitchen. There's two more coming at us. I'm friggin' scared now, man. I box with Andres and at this gym near us, but I've never been in a real fight in my life. Not one like this. Anyway, I grab this knife. This guy comes at me from behind, and I lash out with that knife. Turns out I cut an artery. Except, problem is, it's not one of the bad guys. Shit, no. It's the guy who owns the restaurant. Now the cops are there. The bad guys are gone. Now Andres is done for. He's in cuffs, And so am I. And the EMTs are all over the guy he shot and the restaurant guy I slashed, and I'm screaming that I'm sorry, I'm sorry, and this guy's wife and his kid now, they've come downstairs, 'cause they live above the restaurant. They're screaming at me in Korean, cops holding them back." Manny was sweating now, his voice even more rapid. He stopped, and when he started again, his voice had slowed down.

"He survives, this Korean guy. Mr. Park. He's okay. I didn't kill him or nothing. But he's in surgery for like, hours. And my brother, he's big time put away. He had drugs on him. I don't get to see him anymore after that. My uncle tries to call. I talk to him, like, twice, but I'm locked up tight now, too. So I'm in holding for like three nights before they send in whoever they send in. I'm scared, man. I don't know what's happening, and I just keep thinking, shit, Mami is up there watching all this. Finally they send in somebody to talk to me. Like some high-up CPS lady. I tell the whole story. I mean the *whole* story. I figure I'm headed for juvie, right? I don't get to tell Andres nothing. So my uncle, and Mr. Portes, they talk to this CPS lady. Next thing I know I got these head doctors talkin' to me, doing the whole psych evaluation thing, and I get this lecture from this lady about fresh starts and second chances and being a good kid in a bad situation and a week later I'm on a plane to Montana. And now here I am with you gringos."

Manny finally stopped—to breathe, it seemed to Mike—and sat back down in his chair. "I hurt somebody bad. It was an accident, but it was my fault, you know? But I got nothing back home. My father? He doesn't even exist, my mother's in the ground, and my brother's locked up so tight I couldn't even say goodbye." His eyes were wet now. He pulled his knees up, hugging them to his chest. "I got *nothing* back there, man. I got nothing else."

After a full minute of silence, he looked at Taylor. He wiped his eyes. "Guess I started some shit tonight, huh, vaqueros?" He laughed weakly.

Liz nodded. "This has to happen, Manny."

Taylor cleared his throat. "I'll go next."

*

"It started with my dad." He paused, and leaned forward in his chair. "I'm not gonna tell you guys everything 'cause it doesn't matter. What matters is my dad did everything right my whole childhood. People admired us. We stood out. The 'good black family,'" he said with a low chuckle. "I mean, you don't see too many black people in Idaho, guys. Especially ranchers. My mom and dad raised me and my sister Claire right. Made us study hard and read a lot. Dad taught us to ride and care for animals and use the land. We listened to country, not rap. 'None of that gangster garbage,' he'd say. They sent us to a good private school. We were happy, man. Dad was my hero. He grew up on that ranch. It had belonged to his dad. Lots of livestock. Over a thousand acres. Every day Claire and I would get up at dawn with him—our whole life, up at dawn, working the ranch with him before school. Damn, we were happy.

"But a few years ago, things got bad money wise, and he had to sell it off. We still lived there and all, but he didn't *own* it anymore. It happened so fast we couldn't even understand it." Taylor paused, rubbing his neck. "All of a sudden, he was drinking every day. He stopped doing stuff he always did. Know how I said I was with the volunteer fire department? He was too. He was a volunteer paramedic. It was something we did together, and he helped teach the EMT classes I was taking. But that fell apart. The chief picked up on the drinking and told him to stop coming. I was pissed. I kept going.

"Got worse from there. Soon he started beating on my mom, and then even a little on Claire and me. It came out of nowhere. He'd never even had a temper, man. Sometimes I think it wouldn't have been so bad if he'd always been a drinker. If he'd *always* been screwed up, ya know?

"One day everything went to hell. I get home from working out after school and my mom and Claire are gone. He started beating up on Mom, so they left. She left a voicemail on my phone. Told me where they were, to take my dad's truck and meet her. But I don't go. She keeps calling, but I turn my phone off. Instead, I go look for my dad. He's out there in the barn. He says some shit, and what do I do? I still don't get it. I'd never done anything violent before. But something snapped right then, and it came out of nowhere. Maybe you guys can relate." He stopped and looked around. Everyone was watching him. Everyone but Liam, who just stared at the fire.

"I hit him over the head with his bottle of whiskey, knock him out. I drink the rest of it. Now, I don't drink much. So I don't know why the hell I chugged that bottle, sobbing. It was nuts. Anyway, I get mad drunk real quick and pass out for a while. I wake up puking on the barn floor. I see him there on the ground next to me. You'd think I'd have calmed down. But no. Well, he gets up, too. He comes at me. I deck him in the face, and we're down and fighting. He gets me in a headlock. I slam him against the pillar. I break his arm. He's crying, screaming at me, saying the most ignorant, awful shit you can imagine. Stuff that the guy who used to be my dad wouldn't ever say. *Couldn't* ever say.

"And then something else snapped. Now I'm on this rampage, right there in the barn. He has this one horse he loves. Calls it Zippo. Like the lighter. He's taken care of Zippo for years. Me and Claire, too. All of us loved to ride that horse. Beautiful horse. The color on it…like cream. Well that horse is freakin' out, going all crazy in the stall, making this annoying high-pitched noise, and I'm so pissed, I grab this board lying there, and I'm about to hit my dad with it, but instead I slam Zippo in the face. I mean *hard*, man. Right across the eye, and set it bleeding. That horse is freakin' out now, and my dad's lying on the ground, moaning at me to stop, but I don't stop. I hit that horse again. And again. He's on the ground and I hit him again. I'm screaming and crying. I break his leg. By now I can hear sirens—cops come roaring down the road into the driveway. But I just kept hitting him and hitting him and hitting him. And that was it. Zippo stopped moving. And my dad was lying there, crying. And Zippo was bleeding, whimpering. I ran out of there, went sprinting down the driveway, and run right into the cops. They see all the blood, they see what happened, and they throw the cuffs on me. I hear one of the cops put Zippo down with the shotgun."

Taylor stopped for a moment, looking into the fire, his eyes full of tears. "I loved that horse. I love my dad."

13

THE THIRD DAY was all about work. Painting, fixing the siding, repairing the fence, and dredging the area around the dock to clear it of debris. They spent the day working silently. Mike was deep in his own thoughts, periodically mulling over Manny and Taylor's stories, and he guessed the same was true for the others. The evening brought rain, and they were grateful to have an early night with no evening session.

The following day began with another hike, although they were allowed to sleep in a little later—until seven. It wasn't exactly a leisurely morning, but Mike appreciated the rest. Like the first hike, this one took them back into the forest, through the perimeter fence, and then to a heavily wooded trail. This time they turned east instead of west, however, and traveled parallel to the shoreline for roughly a mile, circling to the far south side of the lake. As they hiked, the cliff face loomed over them, growing closer as the shoreline narrowed. Eventually, they could go no further. The bank petered out to nothing, and the sheer cliff rose hundreds of feet directly from the deep blue water. Just before that point, however, a narrow crevice opened, maybe four feet at the widest. The ground inside it ran steeply up, basically running straight *into* the cliff face. Jim led the way, and for fifteen minutes they trudged upward, sometimes on all fours. It was shaded and therefore cool, but they were all drenched with the exertion of climbing. The sound of their labored breathing and heavy footfalls echoed, and he could smell their sweat in the motionless air. It didn't seem like they were in there for more than ten minutes, but when they emerged onto level ground, Mike was surprised to see they'd climbed at least a couple hundred feet. They were on a narrow, rocky shelf, perhaps fifteen feet wide and twice as long. The lake was far below them, almost straight down; above them, the cliff rose at ninety degrees. There was no way to climb any higher.

While they caught their breath and drank some water, Liz explained that they couldn't stay long, especially given last night's rain. If there were any change in the weather, they'd be trapped. Rain would bring a flash flood, transforming the crevice into a whitewater flume in seconds. That image must have made an impression on all of them, because their pace on the way down was swift. Mike found himself glancing up frequently to check the sky. Thankfully, there wasn't a cloud in sight. Jim checked his thermometer. "Ninety-three, boys. This valley can really cook on a clear day. Stay hydrated."

This time, no one hesitated to jump in the ice-cold lake. As the dock came into sight, Liam dropped his pack and set off running. Within seconds, they all tossed their packs on the ground and sprinted after him, tearing shirts off. The shock of icy water was enough to knock the breath out of Mike, but he felt great sprawled on the warm dock, sun beating on his chest. They lay there, dripping dry, before Jim hustled them back for their morning assignment: more work on the perimeter fence. They had a half-hour of downtime after lunch, and they all napped. It was too hot in the bunkhouse, so they slept in the shade by the lake.

As Mike lay there, fading toward sleep, he heard a scratching sound. It was a chipmunk, busily nibbling on something held between its tiny paws. When Mike shifted, it froze, tiny whiskers trembling, and looked at him.

*

"Look how he's nibbling it, Mikey!" Andrew put his face right up to the glass of the tiny terrarium, fogging it with each breath. He was six.

"That's one hungry mouse." Mike smiled, watching the fascination in his little brother's eyes. Inside the five-gallon tank where Mike used to keep guppies, a miniscule brown field mouse was hunched over a bit of carrot. The oversized ears quivered. They'd slept in the treehouse, and the mouse appeared in the morning, peering out from the cold fire pit, a remnant of graham cracker in its little paws. Mike surprised himself when he was able to catch it, and they'd brought it inside and put it in the aquarium-turned-mouse-habitat.

"You think Mom will lemme keep him?" Andrew asked, his eyes getting bigger with wonder.

"Maybe. But you'll have to make sure he doesn't get out. And only for a while. He'll die if he stays there too long."

Andrew contemplated this, head cocked, and counted silently with his fingers. "A month. I'll keep him just a month, then we'll let him go."

Mike laughed. "I think Mom's gonna say just a few days, buddy."

"Maybe. Hmm." He frowned, then quickly lit up with a new suggestion. "Hey! Can you help me build him a little house? We can build it out of Lincoln Logs."

"You're gonna build a log cabin for your mouse?"

"Yeah! With a chimney! Will you help me, Mike?"

"You know you're a weird kid?"

Andrew's smile faded. "What? No, I'm not."

"You're a little bit weird, Andy. Normal people don't build log cabins for rodents."

His look darkened. "Am I really weird, Mike?"

Mike felt a hollowness in his stomach then, as he realized Andrew was taking him seriously. "No. I'm just kidding. Don't worry. I was just messing with you."

And then Andrew, in the way he always had, seemed to forget about everything else, and before Mike could resist, threw his arms around his shoulders in a bear hug. "I love you," he said loudly, not a hint of self-consciousness in his voice. Mike could smell the campfire smoke in Andrew's hair.

"I love you too, buddy."

*

Dinner had gone a little later, and so it was already dark when the evening session began. The fire crackled and hissed. Mike slumped in the Adirondack chair, his hands shoved into the pockets of his fleece jacket. His notebook rested on his leg. He looked around. The orange glow danced on their faces, and it was pretty clear no one felt like doing this tonight. Jim sat on the edge of his chair, leaning forward, elbows on his knees. His voice was quiet when he spoke.

"You guys ever been hungry? I mean *really* hungry?" His eyes moved slowly from one to the other. Nobody spoke for a few seconds.

"Hiking," said Taylor. "Went on a six-day backpacking trip in Colorado. I was distracted when we stopped for lunch, and I didn't even notice how hungry I was until dinner. I think I ate four bowls of whatever dehydrated stew we had."

"That ain't hungry, hermano. I've been hungry," said Manny. He shook his head. "You *chose* that backpacking shit. This one time, back on the island when I was little, we had, like, nothing but yucca for a week. It was a bad time, and we had no money. My dad grew yucca, so we had that. Boiled yucca. You guys ever had boiled yucca? It's okay, if it's like, fried up with onions and salt and all, but by itself? After like, five days? It's like—"

"Manny!" Jim was laughing. "Okay. We get it."

Manny looked sheepish. "Sorry. Yeah. I've been hungry."

Jim reached for a stick and stoked the fire. Flames danced. "I'm asking you guys about hunger because we want to talk about that a little bit tonight. We want to look at the idea of hunger, and what satisfies it, okay? Let's start with this. What does hunger feel like? Like, when you haven't eaten in a while and you've been working really hard. I dunno, like maybe…climbing a mountain ridge or something. In just one word. Tell us what hunger feels like."

"Empty," said Aidan.

"Drained," said Mike.

"Slow," said Manny.

Taylor picked at something on the bottom of his boot. "Weak."

Liam cracked his knuckles. "Motivated."

"Motivated?" asked Liz.

"Yeah. Like, motivated to get food."

"Okay," said Jim. "So, we have 'empty,' 'drained,' 'slow,' 'weak,' and 'motivated.' All good words to describe hunger. What we want you guys to think about tonight is how you take care of hunger."

Liz sat forward in her chair. "I want you to think about how you felt on our big climb. When we got to the top. Pretty drained, right? And then we broke out snacks. Crackers. Pepperoni. Cheese. Some trail mix with chocolate in it. How'd it feel?"

"It was a rush of energy," said Mike. "I mean I could physically feel it, like, waking me up."

"Same," said Aidan.

"Yeah," Taylor said, as the others nodded.

"Right," Liz continued. "It was enough to tide you over. But you were hungry again by the time we got back down. You guys ate a ton at dinner. Why is that?"

"Wasn't a real meal," said Taylor. "It was, like, just a snack."

"True," Liz said. "But it was a lot of calories. I mean, that trail mix is loaded with calories. And pepperoni? Loaded. Might have been a six-hundred calorie snack, easy."

"Still wasn't a real meal," Taylor repeated. "Not like dinner."

"Not like dinner," Liz said. "It was enough to stave off your hunger for a while. Give you a boost. But not for a long time. It wasn't really *nutritious*. I mean, you wouldn't be too healthy if you just ate that every few hours for six weeks."

"Alright," said Liam. "Can y'all get to the point?"

Liz eyed Liam for a moment. "The point, Liam, is that the snack was only a temporary fix. It made you feel okay, and it gave you what you needed right then, but it wouldn't be a sustainable way to fuel your body. Tonight we want to look at temporary fixes versus real solutions. And how we sometimes confuse those things." She turned to Mike. "Mike, are you hungry right now?"

"Me? No. We just had dinner."

"Right. Okay. But we'll do another hike tomorrow. So, if I offered you some extra food right now, would you take it?"

"I guess."

"Okay. Two choices. You can have two bananas or a candy bar. But whichever you choose, you get every night. So you can choose to have two fresh bananas or a candy bar *every* night. Whaddya want?"

Mike chuckled. "Candy."

"Of course. Sounds a lot better, especially after dinner. Except the bananas would be a better investment in your nutrition, right? They'd provide a lot more vitamins for the next six weeks."

"Better than yucca, anyway," Manny quipped.

"Okay. I think we get it," said Taylor. "We choose what we want, not what we need. Is that what this is about?"

"Yes and no."

Manny threw a stick in the fire. "Knew she'd say that!"

"I mean 'yes and no' because, yes: usually we choose what we *think* we want, and often that's not what we need. But is what we *think* we want, what we *really* desire?"

"Lady, I don't mean no disrespect, but you're losing me," said Manny. "She losing you guys?" He looked around, eyebrows raised.

"Do you know what you really want?"

"What, like, a candy bar?" Manny asked.

"Jesus, Manny," Liam said, shaking his head. Aidan laughed.

Liz nodded. Her voice became more serious. "I'm asking something bigger, Manny. I'm asking each of you if you know what you want in life. What you really hunger for." She leaned in closer, rubbing her hands near the fire. "Because a lot of people don't figure that out. And because of that, they spend most of their lives trying to satisfy one craving after another. Just a long series of false hungers. It's pretty sad, but it's more common than you might think."

Cravings. Mike knew those. *Not weed.* No, that's not what he thought of.

Pain. Revenge. Maybe she's right. Maybe they really are quick fixes.

But it was confusing, because as he thought about it, he still wanted revenge. He still wanted...

Do I?

"Quick fixes don't last," continued Jim. "Tonight, we want you guys to think about the difference between your real hungers and your cravings. Because if you don't figure that out, then it's hard to know how to satisfy the hungers that really matter. That's part of why we've come here. To strip down life. No phones, for example. No internet. That makes a big difference, right? Being away from those distractions?"

Manny smirked. "You gimme my phone back, I'll show you what distraction I'm craving. Pretty sure I speak for the group, jefe." They all laughed.

Liam cracked his knuckles. "Alright, so Jim, you're gettin' philosophical now. Y'all want us to figure out the meaning of life, right here around this fire, eh?"

Liz spoke first. "No, Liam. Nobody's asking you to figure out the meaning of life. We're asking you to figure out your most authentic desires."

"Authentic desires," Liam muttered. "Okay."

"You guys have those notebooks, right? Everybody have a pen?" Liz asked. "Okay. I want you guys to make two columns. At the top of one, write 'Cravings.' At the top of the other, write 'Authentic Desires.'" She gave them a moment to write. Mike heard the scratch of pens on paper. "Now before you start writing stuff down, I want you to remember something: This isn't just about material things. You could list qualities, or feelings, or relationships. Okay. You guys understand what you're doing?"

Mike nodded, and the others did the same. Aidan and Taylor were already writing. Liam rolled his eyes, then started scribbling, too. Mike looked down at the notebook on his lap. He hunched forward, and began to write:

Cravings	Authentic Desires
more money	not be in trouble anymore
hot girlfriend	mom not be effed up
my phone	get the hell out of here
have sex	revenge for Andy
smoke weed	

He looked around. The others were all still writing. He read what he'd written. *Let's cut the shit.* He made a new list.

Authentic Desires
never cut again
miss dad but be okay without him
miss Andy but be okay without him
be able to move on
mom be okay
mom stop drinking
start over far away from Lawson
be cool with Eric again
have other real friends
have a real girlfriend (like really in love)
get back in shape
stop smoking weed

Yeah, that's a little more honest. When he looked up, he saw that everyone was looking at him. They were already done. "Oh. Sorry. Took me a while."

"No problem, hermano," said Manny. "Long list there." He nodded, pointing his chin at Mike's notebook.

"Um. Yeah." Mike pulled the notebook closer.

Liz spoke up. "Okay, so you guys all have two lists. What I'd like you to do now is look at the two columns, and try to see which column involves other people more."

Mike looked at his lists.

She continued. "I think what you'll find is that the 'authentic' column involves other people more. Is that true for anyone?" They all nodded. "That's because so many of our most authentic desires involve the people who matter in our lives. Sometimes breaking it down like this—making a list on paper—can remind us of what matters." She paused and stoked the fire. "Okay. What we'd like you to do over the next day or so is to reflect on your lists. We want you to make sure you're being honest. Think hard and decide if there's anything on there that isn't real, or if you've left something out. Or if maybe you've put something in the wrong column."

Mike closed his notebook and stuck the pen in his pocket.

"That it for the night?" asked Taylor. They all started to get up.

Liz didn't move. "Not so fast. It's someone's turn to tell his story. Who's up?" She looked at Mike.

*

"My brother drowned." He looked up from the fire, following the smoke, seeing how it made the stars above him shimmer. And with that, the pressure built inside him, like a locomotive pushing him to spill it all, to let loose every goddamned detail, the whole story. *No. Not everything.* He glanced at Liz. *But she'll know I'm hiding something.* He was sure of it, and the pulsing heat inside him changed for a moment, shifting from that locomotive driving force to just...to just a motionless, burning shame. A feeling so obscure he couldn't process it. He felt it in the cuts. In the gash on his face. In all the self-inflicted miserable failures that marked his tired, wounded body.

She'll know. She'll know. She'll know.

Stop. He gripped the armrests, pulling himself more upright in the chair. *Start over.*

"I dropped him off at the pool. He wanted me to swim. I was too tired. I worked landscaping all week."

Mike swallowed. "God, it's a long story." He looked around, desperate now for a way out of this. Liz was nodding. Even Aidan, who'd been avoiding eye contact all night, was watching him. He took a deep breath.

"When Andrew died, everything fell apart. See, you gotta understand a few things. My dad—our dad—died a few years back, too. I was thirteen."

"Holy shit, man!" Manny was wide-eyed. "Your bro *and* your padre?" He inched away from Mike. "Man, you got the fuku! That's Dominican for a curse, man. That's, like, serious shit!"

Taylor kicked Manny's boot. "Shut up."

Mike continued. "My mom held us together. I held us together. But then…but then with Andrew gone, it was like there was nothing all of a sudden. Like it was all…it was all just…*nothing*, okay?" He gripped the chair harder. He glanced at Liz. Her eyes were directly on his. Hands folded in her lap. Motionless. Listening.

"I started…I started to…to cut myself." He looked up. *Still staring at me.* "Not like, to kill myself. No. They put me on these pills but they made me numb. And I hated that I couldn't feel what…Anyway, when I cut, I could feel…"

What the hell did you feel?

"I could feel the pain of it. It was something I could control. Something I could make happen. So I could actually *feel* how much I missed my brother." Tears were coming now.

He wiped them angrily. The other guys looked down. Except Liam. Liam kept staring at him, nodding, so he found himself looking Liam right in the eyes. He shuddered. "The hurt felt…I dunno. It felt *fair*, you know? I mean I wasn't out of control. I wasn't doing it every day, so nobody really noticed. Just a few times. Here," he lifted his sleeve roughly, pulling it up past his elbow, and pointed to a narrow trace of a scar just above his elbow. The other guys looked. Liz and Jim, the same. "And here," he said, louder now, as he grabbed the lower cuff of his pants, exposing his calf, where another faint, tiny scar traced the angular muscle. "And here," even louder as he stood up, his legs unsteady, shaking. He lifted his shirt, his fingers jabbing cruelly, carelessly, at a mark on his side. "And…here," he said, in barely a whisper now, pointing to the bandage over that deepest gash along his arm, the one he'd carved with that filthy, rusted thing in the moments before…

Before I…

No.

I'm not going to tell you that part.

He took a deep breath, pausing to regroup. "I hated everything." He sat back down, slumping into the chair. *Get back on track.* "I hated myself for not taking Andrew swimming. He asked me to. But I just dropped him off. And he drowned. And I hated those lifeguards—well, one of them more than the other. I hated Joe. He didn't even…" He caught himself.

Stop. You have to watch it.

Mike took a deep breath. "Anyway, everything was falling apart. My mom, she…she'd always been so strong. When our dad died, she got stronger, not weaker. But this…Andrew…it killed her, too.

"She drank and I cut. And I smoked almost every day. Lawson has a good pipeline of weed if you know where to find it. But my real drug was pain." *Okay. Back on track. You're back in control. Drive the story. Hands on the wheel.* The tears were slowing, and he shuddered in relief, knowing that the rush of whatever just happened was subsiding. He was regaining composure. His voice still quavered, but it was coming back to normal.

"It was getting real bad until one day…just a few weeks back…I was driving my truck. I'm doing like sixty, and I come around a downhill curve, and there's this goddamned buck in the road in front of me. I spun out, almost rolled over. Not sure how I didn't. Killed the damn thing but came out with just a few bumps and bruises. Anyway, I was just sitting there after that, on the side of the road, smoking a joint…and it's like *everything* changed. Something clicked. I didn't want to cut anymore. Things became real clear. Clearer than ever. Like hitting that thing snapped something in my head." He looked up at Liz, meeting her eyes, which had narrowed a bit.

You can see it, can't you?

"So...umm, I began thinking about him, you know? Andrew? And the lifeguards. I was staring at that dead buck. Its glassy eye was looking up at me, and...I dunno. I just suddenly felt something really clear. Like, things weren't pointless anymore. Like I had a job to do. A duty. Those kids—the twins—they still owed something. To Andrew. To my mom. To me. It had cost them nothing, okay? Their family practically owns the town. Long story, hard to explain. But they...it didn't cost them anything. They weren't paying for it. They let my brother drown. And then they just kept...living. Alex at least...I could tell he cared. But Joe? No. Joe just went to football practice. Went to SAT prep class. Like my brother's death was just...was just something that happened. So I walked away from that wreck feeling really sure about it. It needed to cost them something. Joe—it needed to cost Joe everything. Because it cost Andrew everything. It cost my mother everything. It cost me everything. And I knew what I was going to do.

There. It worked. You told them about the truck. Like an accident.

"I got out the gun. My dad always kept it in the closet. My parents didn't think I knew about it, but I did. After he died, I hid it in my closet. My mom must have forgotten about it somehow, or thought he'd gotten rid of it. Anyway, I put the gun in my duffel bag and went to practice that morning. And then...outside the field house. I just waited on a bench. When he came out, I..."

The memories flipped through his mind again. The blue sky, the smell of the grass, the arcing glare of sunlight bouncing off the glass doors of the field house as Joe pushed them open, the sound of the duffel bag dropping to the ground as he'd leapt to his feet, the give of the grassy earth under his work boots as he'd sprinted. His hair had been wet, just out of the shower, still dripping.

"I don't know what happened. I had the gun. It was loaded. I meant to use it. I'd sat there on that bench with it in my hand, hidden inside the duffel bag on my lap. When Joe stepped out of the field house, it was like…" Mike sat up, looking around at all of them staring at him intently. "It was like Taylor said. Like a switch flipped and I wasn't in control. I just jumped up, dropped that bag, and tackled him. I had the steel-toed boots from my landscaping job. Like…I'd gotten dressed for my landscaping job, even knowing I was gonna do this. Crazy, right?" He caught himself on the edge of laughter, but pushed it away, his eyes darting nervously to Liz.

"Anyway, no, I didn't shoot him. In fact, I guess I dropped the gun while I was running at him, because they found it in the grass a few feet from where we fought. It's like, I didn't even notice it or think about it. I just attacked him like an animal and kicked the living shit out of him. I barely remember it, except I had this weird tunnel vision. He got one good right hook with his school ring. That's where this comes from," he said, tracing the gash on his face.

"So, no, I didn't shoot anybody. But as my uncle the lawyer said, 'I brought a gun to school.' And I guess that's all that really matters, right? I had no prior record. Decent grades. Nice kid with tough life and all that. So here I am."

His heart was pounding, but it wasn't panic anymore. It was a weird sort of pride. Pride for having regained his composure. For keeping his hands on the wheel. For staying on the road this time, for gently applying the brakes, for slowing himself to a gentle, controlled stop, no worse for wear.

You did it. They're satisfied. They know enough.

*

Liz's voice was soft. "Thank you, Mike." He nodded. He didn't want to look at Liz. They sat quietly, listening to the fire.

After a moment, Jim stood up. "Okay. Be ready to hike at 6:30. It's back up to the ridge, tomorrow, but this time we're gonna work on improving the trail. Pickaxes and shovels. Bring an extra water bottle and your work gloves. Supposed to be hot."

They began to get up, but Jim stopped them. "Oh. One more thing." He reached behind him and grabbed a plastic grocery bag. "Here."

He tossed them each a chocolate bar. They tore them open and dug in. Mike shoved his notebook deep into his pocket.

No one did much talking at bedtime. Liam stood next to him as they both brushed their teeth, and clapped him on the shoulder. The others kept quiet, too, but they nodded at him when he passed. No one had the energy to build a fire in the stove, and despite the chilly temperatures, Mike was plenty warm in his sleeping bag. He was barely awake by the time Jim did bed check.

*

He was with Andy, back at home. They were lying side by side on Mike's bed, arms folded, staring at the ceiling. Andy was still in his Little League uniform from the game that evening. He was seven. Mike could smell the grass stains. Andy's team won, and they'd gone out for pizza with Mom. She'd already gone to bed.

"Mike, do you think Daddy's in heaven?" Andy asked.

"I know what they say in church."

"Do you believe that?" Andrew turned, his head propped on his elbow, and looked at Mike. He had little kid breath. Kool-Aid and nachos.

"I think I do." Mike sat up, and pulled some fuzz off of his sock.

Andrew was lost in thought. He looked at his baseball trophies, the newest one from today. The marble base was bluish in the moonlight.

Andrew whispered. "You think he can see everything we do? Like, if I do something bad?"

"Well, shit, I hope not." Mike chuckled. At fifteen, he hoped sincerely that his father hadn't been watching everything.

Andrew laughed. "You said 'shit.' Hey Mike? If you die before me, will ya make sure Dad doesn't see me doing bad stuff?"

"Yeah, I'll make sure. But that means I'd have to know when you're doing bad stuff, right?"

"That's okay. You can know. Just not Dad."

"Got it. But you know what, buddy? I don't think it matters."

"Why?"

"I guess up there, they love us no matter what."

Andrew furrowed his brow. "But what if heaven isn't there? Does that mean Dad just…disappeared?"

Mike put an arm around Andy. "Okay. You've got like, zillions of people on Earth. And they all die. And they always have."

"Yeah, so what?"

"So," Mike continued, "so there's got to be some point. I mean, why would we be here if it was all pointless?"

"Not fair. All you did was ask me another question."

"You wanna know what death is like?" Mike leapt off the bed and grabbed the pillow, holding it over his head, ready to bring it down on Andy. But his attempt at a glare gave way to a grin, and he dropped the pillow, laughing. "Get outta that uniform and brush your teeth."

Once Andy was ready for bed, Mike tousled his hair. "Goodnight, buddy. Try not to worry about it, okay?" He gave him a hug.

"Night-night." Andy nestled into the bed. And then, in a serious voice that sounded older than seven, "Thanks for the advice."

"Sure."

Mike paused in the hallway. There was a photo of them from a couple years earlier, hiking in the mountains. Dad had his arms around all of them: Mike, Mom, and Andrew. Not a cloud in the sky. He remembered Dad fumbling around, trying to balance the camera on a rock, setting the timer, and running to get into the picture.

He wondered if maybe Dad was watching. He looked up at the ceiling, half expecting, somehow, to get an answer.

14

IT WAS MIKE'S TURN to do laundry. It took a long time, and his hands were raw from scrubbing against the old-fashioned washboards. The soap residue made his arms itchy in the hot sun as he hung dripping clothes on the line strung between trees across the sunny, open bank. Finally, after clipping the last pair of pants to the line, he stretched aching shoulders, took off his shirt, and sat on the ground. It was a quiet afternoon, and he could hear the breeze on the water. The others were already back at the bunkhouse, cleaning up before dinner.

Mike looked out across the lake, absently toying with his dad's cross. He lay on the ground, propping his head against a tree root, looking up at the swaying branches. Here in the shade, cool breeze dried his sweat. He heard someone coming and hunched up on his elbows to see Liz. He started to get up.

"No need to get up, Mike."

He brushed dirt from his back and elbows, and reached for his shirt. "Sorry. I should get—"

"Relax," she said, and sat down on a rock a few feet away. "Nice out here in the shade."

"Yeah. It is." He leaned back against the tree and threw the t-shirt back on the grass. "What's up?"

"I saw you down here alone. Thought maybe we could chat a little."

"Okay." *About what?*

Liz looked out over the lake, squinting at the glare. "You know, Mike, I've worked with a lot of people in grief counseling over the years. And I have to say I'm impressed by you." She turned to him, her eyebrows raised.

"Impressed? Why?"

"You don't seem bitter."

Mike almost laughed. *Lady, you have no idea.* "Well," he said through a smile, "I don't know if that's really true."

She nodded. "I know what you did. But I'm not talking about that, Mike. I'm talking about your...your *affect*."

"My affect?"

"The way you talk to people. Carry yourself. You don't strike me as a particularly bitter kid."

Mike looked at the ground. "Well, I guess you're seeing, like, the calm after the storm."

"Makes sense." She looked back out across the water. "Still, that's a heck of a lot to go through as a teenager. First your dad and then your brother. Hardly seems fair."

This time Mike did laugh out loud. "I gave up on fair a long time ago."

"Yeah?"

Mike nodded. "Yeah. I just thought of something. Math class, freshman year. Our teacher was talking to us about probability. I was only half paying attention, but then somebody started talking about low-probability stuff like lightning strikes or shark attacks. Anyway, the teacher started going off about how people worry about low-probability events a lot more than high-probability ones."

Liz nodded. "Like worrying more about a plane crash than a car crash."

Mike sat up further. "Right. He was saying people worry about stuff that's more sensational. Like, there are tons of car accidents every day and hardly any plane crashes."

"Sure," said Liz. "Although, to be fair, there are a lot more cars on the road than planes in the air. And when a plane does crash, most of the people on it don't survive. But a lot of people survive car crashes." She tilted her head, looking right at him. "I mean, you did, right?"

Mike hesitated, glancing quickly at her and then back out toward the water. "Um. Yeah, I guess that's true. Anyway, one of the guys says something about going on vacation and being scared of shark attacks, and the teacher said that he was a lot more likely to die of a heart attack than a shark attack."

"Morbid teacher," Liz chuckled. "But yes, that's true."

"Sure it is. Except, the thing is, he was new that year, and he didn't know that my dad died of a heart attack. So he's up there, drawing diagrams and graphs and stuff, really having a field day with it, comparing the probability of a man dying from a heart attack to the chances of getting killed by a shark. One by one all the other kids started to look at me."

"I'll bet," said Liz, a sympathetic smile on her face. "So, what happened?"

"Nothing. I can tell you I thought a lot about probability that night. Anyway, like I said, I gave up on 'fair.'"

"Can't blame you."

"Right, 'cause what's the probability of losing your dad and your brother in the space of three and half years?"

Liz gave him a serious look. "I don't know, Mike."

"Yeah. Me neither."

They were silent for a long moment. Liz's voice was quiet. "But isn't that why you cut yourself, though? Because it was fair?"

Mike sat up, tensing his shoulders, and glared at her. "What?"

"Last night." She was looking right back at him. "You said, 'the hurt felt fair.'"

And here I thought we were just having a nice conversation. No. Of course not. This is a session. Everything's a session. Mike's heart pounded. He could feel it in his temples. The pinpricks on his neck and face. It didn't feel cool anymore. "Yeah, I said that." He rubbed a finger across the scar on his arm—then abruptly realized he was doing it, and stopped.

"It's okay, Mike."

"I don't..." He stood up, crossing his arms. He looked out at the water, then down at the ground. *Get out of my head!* "I don't do it anymore. It's over. I just...stopped."

"After the truck accident, right?"

He glanced back at her. *Stop. Stop looking...through me.* "Yeah. After that." The tears were coming now. *Damn. Stop. Don't cry.*

Don't.

You.

Cry.

He shuddered, and sniffled. He wiped his nose with a quick swipe of his arm. "It was just like it all stopped then, because..." *Cover story.* "It was like I realized, all it takes is one little accident and I could have...and then my mom, she'd be, like...I don't even know how it happened, I mean, I was just driving along and I must have been going faster than—"

"Mike." She gripped his arm, startling him. She was strong. She held him right where the scar was.

"Huh?" He looked down at her hand, then up at her eyes. They had welled up, too.

"Mike, it's okay."

"But I…I tried…"

"Shh." She looked out over the water. "It's okay, Michael. Scars are good. Scars are where we heal…even stronger than we were before." She let go of his arm.

He pulled his arm away quickly, then wiped his face again. He looked over his shoulder at the main cabin. The others were already there, getting dinner ready. "I should go get cleaned up for dinner."

"Yes, you should."

"Liz? Could we just keep that part—"

"Of course, Mike. That's only fair, right?" She turned and walked toward the main cabin. He looked back out over the water, tracing the ridge on his arm, and remembered.

*

The crash wasn't an accident.

After that first night, he'd cut a few more times. Just tiny, shallow, harder-to-see incisions he'd been making in the dark hours with his pocketknife, alone in his room, or in the woods. Places no one would see. Then again, who would notice? There was no girlfriend. Once preseason started, he'd be in the locker room after practice, but it's not like the guys would notice. Besides, they looked like little nicks that any kid might have on his hands, knees, or elbows. Especially working landscaping. It went on like that for a couple weeks.

But then.

It'd been a tough work day. One of the car dealerships along the county road had ordered stone pavers hauled in, and his crew had spent almost eight hours positioning the molded concrete bricks along hundreds of feet of beds and shrubs. They picked up a pizza after, which they ate behind the storage barn of the garden center. Like most days at the end of the shift, they broke into the well-hidden cooler of beer that they kept in the back of the truck under a pile of tarps. Mike scarfed down a few slices and chugged a cold beer, but he didn't hang around. He didn't feel like talking. Besides, they were all so goddamned *weird* around him since Andy's funeral, so cautious, as though saying the wrong thing would make him disintegrate or melt into a puddle. That's pretty much why he couldn't stand anyone these days, even Grandpa, even mom. So he'd left, picked up a gallon of milk for his mom, dropped it off at home, then he'd gone out driving. His mom didn't ask where he was going. She was parked in front of the television with the same vacant, glazed look she'd had since they put Andrew in the ground next to Dad. She had a drink in her hands, some show rambling on. So Mike found his way to the woods, up one of the logging roads. Killed the engine. Looked at his phone. Four texts from Eric:

6:13 P.M. : r u ok?

7:20 P.M. : dude call me

7:52 P.M. : the guys went home. wanna talk 2u.

8:19 P.M. : wtf just gonna ignore me?

He turned the phone off and got out of the truck. The evening was cool. He could hear water running in a nearby stream. The pine smell was strong. Must have done a recent logging cut nearby. Lawson: lumber and wood chips. Every resident of this town must have at least a few pounds of sawdust permanently caked to the lungs, he thought. He sat on the tailgate and lit a joint. He didn't have much weed left. Eric was his usual supplier. The dwindling remains had kept him in check over the past few days, enough to get through work, to listen to the bullshit and put up with the customers, to ignore the sympathetic, awkward silence that followed him around like an invisible force field in the small town where *everyone* knew *everyone*. The weed made him numb.

But right now, all of a sudden, he needed to *hurt*.

He looked around on the ground, spotted a piece of old barbed wire, and without hesitating, carved a bloody gash into his arm. It was a rusted, dirty thing that ripped and tore his flesh and maybe even a little bit of muscle in an unclean way as he dragged it across the top of his left arm, from near his elbow halfway to the wrist, twisting, digging hard and deep. Nowhere near the artery, though. He was that careful. He'd barely managed to contain the scream this time, biting down on a stick, panting, absorbing the pain and making it his own, channeling it and consuming it, letting it strangle something inside him.

But the truth was, he couldn't keep this up. No. The pain gave him clarity. It was time to finish it. Enough with the cutting shit. Enough with *everything*.

He wanted *out*.

He'd been pondering it for a few days now. If he did it, it was going to look like an accident. He'd decided on that right away, for his mother. So, bleeding and crying, he got back into the truck.

North Aspen road was a fifty-five mile-per-hour county highway a few miles outside the Lawson town limits. But it dropped to forty-five, then down to thirty-five, in anticipation of the sharp, insufficiently-banked right turn that lay at the bottom of a mile-long downgrade. At least five signs warned drivers of the rollover danger. A racecar couldn't take that turn much above fifty without losing control, so a speeding pickup didn't stand a chance. It would slide, roll, catapult over the low guardrail, and sail at least a hundred feet before slamming into the boulder-field below. It wouldn't be the first time this turn had killed a driver. There had been accidents here almost every year.

Now he had the accelerator pushed hard to the floor, his calf flexed painfully, every muscle tensed as he gripped the wheel with both arms. His seatbelt was off. The truck's V8 was furious, the machine redlining, screaming. He'd never heard it like that before.

But then, he'd never pushed it this hard, either. He hoped the balding tires would hold long enough to reach the curve before they lost their grip on the blacktop—long enough to achieve enough velocity to extinguish his life and his agony. It'll be a shame to destroy the truck, he thought for a moment. *What a waste*, he thought.

Mike hurtled toward his own voluntary obliteration. Above the truck's raging engine, a pulsing rush coursed through his head, echoing inside his skull. Somewhere on the periphery of his consciousness, there was music. He couldn't make it out over the roar, though, could only feel the reverberant bass alternating with the pounding in his chest. His eyes and face were wet, both from the steady tears and the sweat. His iron grip on the wheel wrought more blood from the grotesque laceration, and the dark, venous stuff oozed freely. He felt it dripping from his elbows.

It occurred to him, out of nowhere, maybe from the same place that all his many random, selfish thoughts did, that he was going to die a virgin.

The truck was barely under control—it might even be airborne already, for all he could tell—and he knew it was going to come soon. He could see the curve below him, no more than a quarter mile now, far too close and tight for a two-ton pickup to maneuver at this kind of speed.

As the turn approached, yawning toward him in a widening, bending plane of black, he became aware of the blur of tall spruce and pine on either side of him, and in the fading light, it was like a tunnel. The sky was blood red above him. It was probably another beautiful sunset, but that was impossible to see from this claustrophobic valley road.

He was going to die now.

He wasn't afraid.

This time I'll stay with you, buddy. He couldn't tell if the words actually came out, but they were clear in his head despite all the thunderous noise.

It's time.

But then a buck the size of a small horse was in the road. Instinctively, he slammed the brakes, sending the truck into a frantic fishtail, swerving with a violence so dizzying that for a moment he had no idea where the road was, his insides heaving as they might at the apex of a terrifying carnival ride. The animal hit the passenger side, a collision of crumpling panels and crushing bone. It was something Mike *felt,* but it was completely inaudible over the deafening shriek of the tires dragging, shredding and eventually bursting as the truck continued its spin, the steel buckling and glass cracking.

When he could see again, the haze of smoke and steam in the cabin was thick. He could taste the explosive, alkaline residue of the airbags, now deflating slowly like spent holiday balloons. The one in front of him, draped over the steering column, was marked with an oddly clear handprint, bright red with his blood. The windshield was a crystalline puzzle, still in place but shattered by the twisting force. The truck lay tilted at a crazy angle, nearly perpendicular to the road. It was face-down in the drainage ditch, the hood crumpled where it had come to a stop after tearing into the soil.

He pulled on the latch, fighting the door and pushing it open, a bent panel resisting and then giving in with a pained cracking sound. He vomited then, vertigo lifting and spinning him, throwing him to the ground. The acidic mess splashed on his arm, burning as it mixed with the bloody cut.

Standing again, holding to the fender for support, he could smell burned rubber and leaking gasoline. The dead engine hissed and ticked, shimmering heat fading into the cooling summer night. He made his way to the deer carcass. The animal's abdomen was ruptured like the tires on the truck, and the ruins of its antlers lay shattered beside sightless eyes. He glanced around, got his bearings. In the fading light, he could make out a mess of tire marks extending hundreds of feet up the hill, mapping the truck's swerving, skidding, uncontrolled trajectory. He'd plowed into the ditch just a few yards from the start of the curve. He was shaking and crying, but that was only adrenaline. No, the crash hadn't injured him in the slightest. All the blood was from before.

Mike began walking home as if nothing had happened. He pulled up the hood on his navy LAWSON KODIACS XC sweatshirt, and shoved his hands deep in his jeans. He sauntered up the hill, almost as if nothing had happened.

But it *had*, of course. He'd actually tried to do it. *Would* have done it.

It was an odd, cathartic moment, walking up this hill. Just like that, it was over and the suicidal impulse was gone. It occurred to him that even if he had to walk the whole way into town, he'd be home in time for dinner. But he should call the cops about the accident. Report the deer in the road. *Accident. Right.* For all anyone will ever know, that's what caused the wreck.

The *Buck of Fate*, he thought, beginning to laugh, somehow, through the tears, blurring his vision now as he dialed the cops. *The Buck of Fate saved me. Andy would laugh his little nine-year-old butt off about that.* They'd throw puns back and forth.

What the BUCK just happened?
Got distracted by the RACK on that one, huh?
Eight POINTS for Mike!
Oh DEER!
The BUCK STOPS HERE!

He was laughing again when the cops answered. He reported the wreck. Of course they knew him. *Everyone* knew the Whittakers.

There was just enough time for another joint before the Trooper or the deputy would show up. To calm down. There was enough time to get rid of it before they'd get there. He sat on the side of the road, smoking, his arm going from aching to numb. He wiped off some of the blood on the grass, and pulled his sleeves down further to cover the wound. This one would need stitches. But at least this one would be easy to explain.

Wrecked my truck. Could've been killed. Got out with a scrape!

It didn't escape him that if he'd actually succeeded in throwing himself through the windshield and wrapping himself around a spruce tree, his mother would be completely alone, her husband and two sons lost to separate tragedies in the space of just a few years.

Dad gone.

Andy gone.

Mike gone.

And Eric. What would it do to Eric? The one decent guy who'd stuck with him, who'd tried over and over for the past three weeks— no, the past three *years*—to be his friend. How had *he* held up through all this, watching Mike fall apart? Apparently, Mike didn't care.

Because you're a selfish bastard.

An hour later, his mother was holding him, hugging him for dear life, sobbing in a way she hadn't since the day after the funeral.

My God, she used to be strong. You would have destroyed her.

But Mike didn't cry. He was still numb. Maybe it was the weed. He could feel her bony shoulders with his arms. She'd lost at least twenty pounds, maybe more. She had a gameshow on in the corner. *Seriously*, he thought with half a sardonic grin, *it's bad. You would have destroyed her.* Suddenly his mind formed a clear picture of the Buck of Fate in the recliner, sipping a beer, watching the stupid show, nodding to confirm the point: *Yeah, you would have destroyed her along with yourself.* He held back a laugh. *Yeah. Must be the weed.*

No doubt she can smell it on me, right?

He was sure the cop had smelled it, too. But it was Chuck Merrin, the same deputy that had gotten to the pool first. So no, Deputy Merrin hadn't said anything about the weed. Just took Mike home. Arranged for a tow truck. Didn't ask too many questions, especially not after seeing the smashed-up deer. Eric called again while Mike rode home in the squad car. He ignored it; let it go to voicemail.

Mike's mother finished crying. It turned on and off like a faucet these days. She sat back down heavily in the recliner. She shook her head, took another drink, and just looked at him, a thousand unanswerable questions in her eyes. His mother didn't have much to say about the accident. His mother didn't have much to say at all anymore. She looked hollow.

She *is* hollow, he thought.

Just like me.

He'd left her sleeping in the living room, and headed upstairs. Lying on his bed, he thumbed through the texts from Eric. And one from Uncle Dave:

9:46 P.M. : Hey bud. Your mom told me about the accident. Let's talk. Call me.

Mike turned the phone off again, went downstairs, and retrieved the bottle of bourbon his mother had been drinking. She was snoring, and he shook her shoulder, waking her. He saw his dad's wedding ring, which she wore on a necklace, glinting in the lamplight. He half carried her to bed and covered her with a blanket. Brought the bottle upstairs. There were about six ounces left. He took a heavy swig, maybe half of it, and winced.

Time to toss a pill. He opened the bottle of antidepressants. The ones he was supposed to be taking. And just like every night for the past two weeks, he jiggled one out into his palm, reclosed the pill bottle, walked across the hall to the bathroom, and tossed the medicine into the toilet. He undressed, turned off the light, and lay down.

He reached for the bourbon and drained it, at once savoring and hating the burn.

*

"Hey Mike!" Liam's voice, calling from a distance, snapped him back to the present.

"Yeah?"

Mike looked up to see Liam walking toward him. "We've been looking for you, killer. Time to get cleaned up for dinner."

The breeze had picked up and it was cooler now. Mike realized he was shivering. He pulled on his shirt. "Sorry."

"You been down here this whole time?"

"I was talking to Liz."

"Yeah, I saw that. But that was like a half hour ago, man."

"It was?"

"You zoned out, brother. Thinkin' deep thoughts. Dangerous around here, ya know?" He laughed.

"Yeah. I know what you mean." He reached up and felt the cross on his chest.

"Anyway, come on. Dinner's almost ready. You probably have just enough time to take a cold shower. Everybody else is done. You'll have it all to yourself, so don't take too long. You'll raise suspicions."

They laughed and headed back up the hill.

15

THE NEXT DAY WAS BRUTAL. Jim came into the bunkhouse early—well before sunrise—and flipped on the light. Mike heard a chorus of groans and muttered expletives. He hunched up on his elbow and rubbed the sleep from his eyes. Jim threw a cereal bar at him.

"Morning, sunshine. Get powered up and be ready in five minutes. Fill your water bottles and put on your work gloves."

"The hell," Manny said under his breath, stretching as he swung his legs down to the floor. "What the hell we doing today, jefe?"

"It's trail maintenance day." Jim opened the door and stepped outside.

"Yesterday was trail maintenance day," Liam muttered.

"So much trail maintenance, so little time. Five minutes. Eat the bars. You'll need 'em." Jim pulled the door shut behind him.

Aidan clambered down from his bunk. "This sounds bad."

"It sounds real bad," Taylor said.

Mike got up, stretched, and stuffed half the cereal bar in his mouth. Liam shuffled past, scratching himself through his boxers and shaking his head. "Guy's messin' with my workout routine. I was just about to go."

Mike pulled on his pants and did his belt clasp. "Somehow, I think we're gonna get a good enough workout today."

*

Jim repeated his lecture about how to go at the trail with picks and shovels, removing roots and re-arranging rocks to level the switchbacks. He reviewed positioning and digging sluices to allow water runoff. After that, he paired them up and assigned them sections of the trail.

A few hours later, Mike and Liam were near exhaustion. It had been cool all morning, but once the sun rose high enough to hit the valley directly, it got warm. They'd started with their hats and sweatshirts on, but had peeled off layers as the morning wore on. Now they worked shirtless, bathed in sweat and caked with dust and mud. They'd settled into an alternating rhythm, trading shifts on the pickaxe and shovel.

It was Liam's turn with the pick. He swung it hard overhead, his muscles tensing as his core twisted, building momentum and driving the flat end home to break up a stubborn clump of roots. He jerked hard on the handle to release it, swearing as he nearly lost his balance. "Shit, man. How much longer 'til lunch?"

"Can't be too much longer. It's almost noon. Here. Take a break." Mike tossed him his water bottle.

"Thanks." Liam sat down heavily, leaning back against a stump. He gulped the water greedily and wiped his mouth. Mike drank from his own bottle.

Liam looked around, then scampered over and sat down close to Mike. He was so close that Mike could feel the heat rising off him.

"Liam, what the?" He shifted over a few inches.

Liam nudged his arm and leaned in even closer. "While we're alone, I wanna ask you something."

He swiped his forearm across his brow. Sweat droplets flew, some landing on Mike.

"Jesus." Mike reached for his crumpled, filthy t-shirt and mopped his face. "What is it?"

"Okay. You know how you told us that story? About your brother and all, and the accident you had, and the lifeguards and all that?" Liam was looking right at him.

"Yeah." *What the hell is this?*

"So, there's something I don't get."

"What?" Mike darted his eyes away, looked down, and absently began picking dirt from his boot.

"I still don't get it. Why you did it. Why you brought the gun. I *get* you were pissed at the one brother...what was his name?"

"J-," but the name sticks in Mike's throat. He clears it. "Joe. Joe DeAngelo."

"Right. How did y'all go from just being pissed to wanting to actually *kill* him?"

"I told you. It was after I...after I got in the accident. Like something snapped."

Liam took another swig from his bottle. "Mike, sorry, but y'all are what people call a 'nice guy.' So I'm thinking there's gotta be more to it." He cocked his head to one side, squinting. He nudged Mike's arm, leaving a dirty splotch. Liam leaned in even closer still, and Mike could smell his breath now. His voice was quieter. "Look. I know what it's like to be pissed. To want to keep it all in. My parents...everyone...I know what it's like to want to just..."

"To just disappear."

"Yeah."

Mike looked at him, hesitating. *You really want to know?* He looked around. They were still alone. He could hear Aidan and

Manny jabbering, but they were at least a few hundred feet up the trail. He swatted a mosquito. "Maybe there is. But I don't wanna talk about it, Liam. Not now."

Liam shrugged and stood up. "No sweat. Guess we've got nothing but time, right?" He flashed a smirk before swinging the pick, arcing it hard over his shoulder into the tough ground. It kicked up a spray of dirt.

Maybe another time. Maybe another time Mike would tell the whole story of what had tipped the balance. About what he'd overheard.

*

Coach Swanson had started preseason practices. Mike was eager to run after a half a week lying low while his arm healed up. He'd been on antibiotics for the lacerations. He told the doctor he'd had rusty garden shears lying on the back seat of the truck, and they'd flown forward when he crashed. Apparently, it was plausible enough. Even with well-done stitches, the doctor told him as he administered a tetanus shot, he'd be left with a permanent scar.

He had to work right after practice, so his bag was packed with his boots and work clothes. His mother would drop him off on her way to work. She didn't think he should go, after everything that had happened. She'd sobered up now, and he knew she wanted to ask him about it. The fact that he wasn't too badly hurt—and the fuzziness of how drunk she'd been when he'd gotten home—was enough to keep her concern under control, at least for now. But she hadn't seen the wreck yet. Maybe once she did, she'd freak out. Hard to tell. His mom took so many meds lately—randomly, it seemed—that her mood was impossible to predict. Sometimes she'd be manic, screaming, and completely irrational. Sometimes nothing mattered. He wasn't sure she'd accept that the accident was as simple as a deer in the road. But she hadn't said anything beyond a few inane comments about insurance and repairs.

They didn't talk on the short drive. Instead, she lit a cigarette, fumbling to flick her lighter as they sat at the stoplight—one of only two lights in Lawson.

"I thought you quit," he said.

She gave him a look and turned up the radio. They stopped in front of the athletic building. Football, as well as boys' and girls' soccer, also started today. The lot was crowded. Their car might as well have been on fire, the way it drew attention.

"You'll get a lift to work?" she asked.

"Yeah. Eric."

"Insurance company might call about the truck. Write down what they tell you, but don't make any decisions until we talk."

"Okay, mom."

"I love you. Run well. Go easy. Watch those stitches. Clean up after." She hugged him. Again, he noticed his dad's ring. It was always there. Like a—what was the word—a talisman. Mike used to think that's what it was. One time, when Andrew had asked why she wore it, Mike told him it gave her extra mom powers. Like super strength. Lately, Mike wasn't sure if she had super strength or none left at all. It was hard to tell the difference sometimes.

"Love you too. Work well."

His mom almost smiled. He stepped out, slung his duffel bag over his shoulder, and shut the door. He watched as she drove away.

When Mike turned around, there was Joe DeAngelo across the lawn, plodding toward the field house, carrying his helmet, pads, and gym bag. He spotted Mike and stopped mid stride, but his vacant expression didn't change. It was like a scene from an old western movie, two gunslingers sizing each other up in the middle of Main Street. He stopped walking, too, as he felt that dropping sensation again. There was that same pounding in his temples that had risen to a deafening roar just before the crash.

Joe seemed to hover in indecision, as though deciding whether to approach Mike. Mike glanced around tentatively. Everywhere he looked, eyes darted away. He continued, glancing ahead to see Joe ducking into the field house ahead of him. He was grateful that the football team had a separate locker room.

Eric caught up, blocking him before he could open the door.

"Dude, what the hell?"

"Sorry." Mike shrugged, stepping to the side and reaching for the door.

"Hey! You almost get killed in an accident and you won't even text me back?"

"I wasn't 'almost killed.' Don't be dramatic."

"My mom said that your mom said—"

Mike cut him off. "Jesus. Is anything my mom says rational these days?"

"Look, man. I don't know what…" Eric paused as some girls approached, all of them talking loudly. They were suddenly quiet. Lisa Belmont looked quickly from Eric to Mike. They'd both known her forever.

"Hey guys," she said, stopping. The others scuttled inside.

"Hey, Lisa," Eric muttered.

"So, um, some of us are getting together at my place later. My parents are around so it won't be anything too wild, but we'll have a few beers. Come on over if you want. Have a good practice."

"You too," said Mike.

She gave him a half-smile, before going inside.

Eric sighed. "Let's just get in there."

"Yeah." Mike reached for the door.

Eric grabbed his arm—the good one. "Hey."

Mike turned, looking at him. "What?"

"I don't care if we go to Lisa's. But can you at least promise me we'll hang out later? Like, just have a few beers or something?"

"Yeah."

Practice was tough. It was humid, with little breeze. Two-mile warm-up, then hills. Swanson was pushing them hard, trying to weed out the quitters. His arm throbbed, but the ibuprofen kept the pain at bay. The bigger problem was that Mike was out of shape, and midway through the hills, he wondered if it was from the smoking. He was sucking air, coughing. He laughed at himself.

Could be the weed. Or maybe the death wish?

Eric was back at the field house ahead of him, stretching, and tossed Mike his water bottle as he ambled in.

"You looked like shit on the hills."

"I felt like shit on the hills."

Steam spilled out from the locker room, a cacophony of running water, crude remarks, and laughter. The other guys were noisy, sharing summer war stories. Mike was in a hurry. He was eager to leave before the football team finished. He had no desire to see Joe DeAngelo again. And he didn't much feel like talking. Of course, they all wanted to check out the nasty cut on his arm. But at least it kept them from noticing any of the others.

He toweled off and started to wrap fresh gauze around his arm as the soccer team piled their way in from outside. Eric joined him at the row of lockers, snapping his towel at him. "Can't *wait* to do me some landscaping! You still need a ride?"

"Yeah."

They finished dressing and headed outside, trading small talk with some of the other guys and waving to a few girls coming out of their own practice.

Eric looked up at the pale sky. "Damn. Gonna be hot."

"It's August."

Eric rolled his eyes as they got into the car. "Okay, now that we're alone, you wanna stop talking about the weather? Maybe tell me what the hell happened?" He started the engine and rolled down the windows.

I should just tell him everything. Instead, he chuckled. "You know what happened. Deer the size of a grizzly decided to jaywalk in front of my truck. All things considered, I'm lucky as hell."

Eric sighed. He looked away out the driver's side window as they pulled out of the lot. "Yeah," he said, his voice quiet, "You're the last guy I'd ever call lucky, Mike, but maybe this time."

"Got any weed?" Mike asked.

"Yeah."

"Let's smoke."

"We just ran, man. And it's early."

Mike turned up the radio. "I could use it."

"Hold on, lemme get us out of sight." Eric pulled the car around the back of the maintenance building. Mike packed the bowl, wadding the stuff down. They each took a hit. He savored the warmth of it buzzing through him.

"Your arm looks bad."

Ah. Another serious look. "Do we really have to have another conversation about whether I'm okay?"

"Come on. Your brother just died. You just crashed your truck. You're all...I dunno, like..."

"All messed up?"

"Yeah, Mike, to be honest, you are."

He took another drag, and passed it to Eric. "I just wish I could have a normal conversation with *somebody*. Not psychotherapy. Like maybe my best friend could just talk about something normal? Know what? I'd be happy to talk about the goddamned weather."

Eric took a deep heave on the bowl, coughing. "Yeah. Okay." He emptied the bowl out the window, tapping it clean and tossing it into the glove compartment. "Looks cloudy, Mike. Might rain later." He jammed the transmission into drive. They went the rest of the way without talking.

Mike was relieved when they got split up at work, sent out on different jobs. Later, when he got home, he made three peanut butter and jelly sandwiches and poured a glass of milk. Sitting at the table, a sandwich in one hand and his phone in the other, he pored through some texts (one from Eric, reminding him about Lisa Belmont's house) and the usual stupid stuff in his feeds. By seven, he was ready to crash. *The hell with the party.* Everyone would be weird around him.

Like he was fragile. Damaged goods.

Well, you are damaged goods, buddy.

Mike trudged up the stairs, pulled the curtains closed, and stripped down to his boxers. He stood in front of the humming air conditioner, letting cold air wash over him. He reeked like grass and mulch, but he was too tired to get cleaned up. He flopped on the bed and stuck his ear buds in.

He went to his usual site, scrolling rapidly through the lurid thumbnails until he found tonight's inspiration. He watched, his pulse and everything else rising. But even this was hit or miss. He'd noticed lately it took him longer. And he didn't feel like it as often. It was the same for a few months after Dad died. But he was only in eighth grade then. It was worse now. He was seventeen. And twice over the past couple weeks, it hadn't even...well, *worked*, which scared the crap out of him. He didn't like to think about that.

Looking up for a second, he spotted the picture of Andy on his dresser out of the corner of his eye. *Shit.* His face prickled with heat and everything shut down. He stopped and threw the phone on the floor. He was shaking. He went to the bathroom and splashed some water on his face. He eyed the pocketknife on the windowsill.

No. Not that.

Back in his room, he picked up his phone and cleared the browser. His head was pounding. He needed some air. He threw on his clothes again, shuffled downstairs, and stepped outside into the humid night. He walked with his hands shoved in his pockets. It felt good to be outside.

He stopped abruptly. He'd wandered more than a mile, hardly paying attention to where he was headed. And now he was in front of the DeAngelos' house. He looked up at the massive home set atop a small rise, past the manicured front lawn. He'd worked on their landscaping earlier in the summer. Huge job.

He heard voices, then. It was an argument. From somewhere up the hill, maybe the backyard. Someone arguing. "Hell no!"

Joe. It was definitely Joe. The voices lowered again.

Mike looked over his shoulder. The street was empty. He scampered onto the lawn under cover of the densely-planted trees. There were arbor vitae—big ones, almost twenty feet tall—that formed a hedge row. He skulked along under them, then crouched behind a large boulder.

The DeAngelo twins were maybe twenty feet away, on a patio. The blue-green pool bathed their faces in pale light from below. They spoke in harsh, rasping whispers.

"…you little bitch? Think it'll change anything?" Joe was saying, arms raised.

"I'm just saying what if!" Alex hissed. "What if someone does?"

Joe shoved his brother roughly. "How the hell would they?"

"I dunno! Those texts! What if—"

"We deleted them."

"Come on. You know nothing's ever really deleted. Someone could—"

"Jesus, just let it go!" Joe opened the sliding door, and started to go inside.

Alex reached for Joe's sleeve. "But if we just…like…maybe Dad could…"

Joe slammed the heavy door shut, pivoted, and grabbed his brother by the shoulders. His voice was acid. "What! You want to go up to Dad, like, 'Oh hey Dad, you think it's bad that we were buzzed on vodka when that kid drowned? Jesus! What the hell do you—"

Mike ran.

Thoughts raced with him as he sprinted, faster than ever, down the dark streets.

"…we were buzzed on vodka when that kid drowned…"

They could have saved him.

They would have saved him.

The bastards were drunk when my brother died.

The spinning kicked back in and he tripped, tumbling, onto the grass on the side of the road. He wasn't even sure where he was. He grabbed fistfuls of grass, squeezing tight, the veins on his arms distended, eyes shut, jaw clenched. The stitches ached. He felt pinpricks of sweat break out all over his body. His heart began to pound, with such force he was sure it would burst.

Andrew's lifeless body in the hospital.

Andrew in the small, child-sized casket.

His mother's quivering hands clenching the lacquered pews of the church.

Sunlight glinting off the marble headstone at the burial.

The deep red, almost purple gleam of that first bead of blood chasing the blade on his arm in the bathroom.

The pine smell that afternoon in the woods, and the awful, rusted thing he'd used to tear the flesh of his arm.

The long expanse of yellow lines down the center of the county highway, stretching out in front of him, arcing gracefully into the sharp turn.

The buck, alive and startled, then lifeless and ruined.

Finally, most clearly, Joe DeAngelo: first at Andrew's funeral, rigid with downcast eyes. And then today. Just today, outside the field house, his eyes locked with Mike's across the expanse of the school's front lawn, without expression.

With a suddenness and clarity that surprised him, a singular thought coalesced. All the confusion and sadness and uncertainty and madness of the past three weeks disappeared, sucked out of his consciousness like water down a drain. His heartbeat slowed, and the tension in his muscles faded, replaced by a rush of warmth. The dizziness evaporated, and his mind felt sharp and ready. It was as if all the pieces of a jigsaw puzzle arranged themselves with unnatural speed, rotating and sliding around each other through some unseen force, quietly clicking into place for one clear picture.

Joe DeAngelo, on the ground, his lifeless eyes mirroring a clear blue sky.

*

"Mike, we're done." Liam tapped him on the shoulder. "We're done. Lunchtime."

"Yeah." Mike realized he'd been shoveling, working right along through the memories. He heaved the shovelful of dirt aside and stood up. They pulled their shirts on and gathered up their scattered sweatshirts, caps, and water bottles.

"We got everything?" Mike asked, grabbing the shovel.

"Think so." Liam hoisted the pick over his shoulder.

"Good." He started back down the path. "I'm starving. Let's go."

16

AIDAN'S VOICE WAS QUIET as the firelight danced on his face. He sat with his elbows clasped around his knees. "It was kind of a social media platform for homework. At first it was just my school. Like, sort of a homework exchange. You could post a worksheet for class and share answers. You got points for sharing something, and then you could use them to get stuff for yourself. Like a kind of currency…a homework trading post, I guess. It was called 'Closet Five.' See, we had this janitor's room in the basement of the school called 'Closet Four.' That was the sign on the door. Anyway, it's pretty much where kids always went to get away with stuff. Like, anything. It was out of the way, but for some reason it was never locked and there weren't any surveillance cameras there. So kids would go there to deal, trade homework, hook up, or do whatever.

"Well, Closet Four—the actual janitor's closet, I mean—had been a thing for the longest time. But then one day along comes this teacher, Mr. Sampson. What a stupid name, right? Anyway, Mr. Sampson went to our school, so he knew all about it. So he gets it in his head to shut it down. Saw it as his civic duty or whatever. He tells the Principal about it. A lock goes up on the door, and we get this lecture about behavior and honor and cheating and all this other crap. Whatever. Anyway, my friend Evan and I were in the cafeteria one day and these other kids are talking about how much it sucks, losing 'the closet.' Evan and I are into web design and coding, so we're thinking, like, why not make a virtual Closet Four? Except we decided to call it Closet Five, 'cause it was, like, a step up.

"So, like I said, it started up as pretty much a homework exchange. Just for nerds, I guess. Maybe twenty kids used it. The gamers. But then the cool kids caught on. Guys like Evan and me aren't exactly the center of attention most of the time. But once Closet Five got going, we became celebrities. The teachers didn't know shit. It's amazing sometimes, the stuff that goes on in a school that teachers have no idea about. Anyway, it gets bigger. Pretty soon kids at other schools were using it. And see, we set it up right. It wasn't a pay site at first. There was nothing to make parents suspicious. No credit card charges. It was all based on trades and points. I upload the big science worksheet, I get ten points. I need the quick problem set for math? That costs me five. It started out pretty harmless. I mean unless you have strong moral feelings about cheating on schoolwork." Now Aidan was moving along, and Mike noticed he was less hesitant.

"But then it started to change. By the end of sophomore year we had, like, a thousand accounts. Kids across the district trading essays, worksheets, all kinds of shit. We even got ahold of some final exams. Parents keep tabs on most social media, because they know about it. Not Closet Five. We figured it was only a matter of time before somebody got wise to it, but it stayed quiet for a long time. Anyway, kids started making deals in the chat room. It started out like...just...stupid stuff. Stupid jokes. Stuff like 'write my English essay. I don't have the points, but I'll wash your car.' Or 'I'll pose as your dad on the phone and call in to the office and say you're sick if you'll do my math all week.' Kids started using it to trade study drugs. Make threats. Bullying stuff. You guys have had all the anti-bullying crap in your schools, right? But it kept up. Soon kids were saying nasty stuff. Before long, the whole point system meant nothing anymore. Some kids started posting…you know, like, pics instead of homework. A couple girls started basically selling themselves in exchange for stuff. It went from 'write my paper and I'll walk your dog' to 'write my paper and I'll send you nudes.'"

He glanced up uncomfortably at Liz. "And then it went further. Like, 'write my paper and…and I'll…'" Aidan stopped, glancing around quickly, with a little nervous laugh. Mike traded a look with the others.

Seriously?

"At first we thought they were kidding. But it started getting real. Kids were trading pretty much *everything*. Stuff started getting posted faster than we could review it. We'd always had access to everything, and we'd kept up with it at first. We would delete stuff. But eventually it was impossible. Would have been a full-time job. I mean, we still had classes.

"Evan and I started freaking out. So we decided to put up a pay wall. We figured, if we make it cost something, then kids would back off. So we started charging a login fee. We kicked everyone off, and then everyone had to pay five bucks to get on for the first time, and then two bucks a month. Of course, we disguised it, so kids could use their parents' credit cards. We made it look like a charge for a gaming app. It showed up as 'GamerZoneFive' on transactions. But that didn't slow it down. Instead, we just got this huge influx of cash. Parents didn't really notice, because it wasn't enough money for them to care. So kids didn't back off. In fact, it *grew*. And since we were getting so much traffic, we started opening it up to ads, because why not? Before long, we were pulling in like five grand a month between the subscriptions and the ads.

"We were smart. Just in case it got found out, we didn't want the questionable stuff on the front of the site. So we kept the home page clean, and you had to know where to click—and use a password—to get to a hidden site *within* the site—like sort of a back room. We called that Closet Six. That's where anything went that could get people in serious trouble. Thing is, it cost another five bucks to get a login for that. Anyway, we kept it up for a while. One morning we looked at the site analytics, and the income, and we realized the site had pulled in almost four hundred dollars overnight. I know that's not a ton of money, but it was just *one night*. There were like twenty signups. But most of it came from ad clicks. The ads were sketchy. At first it was stuff like credit card offers, music streaming, travel sites, whatever. But soon we figured out we could host ads for, um, porn sites. And what can I say? Talk about optimized advertising. Man, they started getting a lot of clicks. Sunday nights were huge. I guess a lot of guys went on to get their calculus homework and got...you know, distracted." Aidan chuckled nervously again. Mike laughed along with the other guys.

"Evan was good at making fake I.D.'s. He'd been doing it for a while for kids to buy beer. He made one for each of us, and we used them to form an LLC in another state. That's a kind of company, if you guys don't know. It's good for separating business from your own name. Not hard to do online. Anyway, we had more than thirteen grand, and the ad money kept coming in. We got offers to host more ads. Soon it became a joke. Like, how many porn ads could we squeeze on to the Closet Six landing page? Before long it was mostly guys using the site. I guess the porn creeped out the girls. Anyway, you had people file sharing their English homework and clicking over to other stuff in the next browser tab. To be honest with you guys, I really got addicted myself. Kind of embarrassing. That's another story. Maybe you guys can relate to that."

He paused for a second, seeming to reflect on something. Then he shook his head and continued. "Closet Six got darker every day. Soon there was some serious shit on there. You wanted to mess with somebody, you started posting stuff on Closet Six. It started getting out of hand, but at the same time, money kept coming in, and we were like…celebrities at school. Soon we had twenty grand in the business account. We were worried about taxes and stuff. We started researching how to make it look like just a chat room, but that was getting harder with the amount of ad commerce going on.

"We couldn't help ourselves. The money was too exciting. We figured out that if we could drive more traffic, the ads would pay more. We had this idea for contests. You know, where you had to get votes, like ratings. It could have been something harmless like best painting or poetry. But kids wanted edgy stuff. So we opened it up in Closet Six. It was like, 'post your best stuff.' It could be funny, or cool, or whatever. Like your best skateboarding moves, or your best guitar song, or your funniest blooper video. We put some rules out there. We didn't want the FBI coming after us. Nothing violent or sexual. We said if anything like that came in we'd remove it. But anyone with a login could post stuff. We decided to give it a test drive, and only accept posts for one hour. Then, whatever got the most views over the next twenty-four hours would win. We didn't even say *what* you would win. It was almost like it didn't matter. Kids just wanted 'to win.'

"There was a lot of stupid stuff. One kid put up this photo of a turkey sandwich and wrote a romantic poem about it. Another kid on the swim team uploaded this video of him doing pushups in his Speedo to weird Eighties music. That one got a lot of votes. A cheerleader did her stretching routine in a bikini.

Aidan paused for a few seconds, and took a deep breath. "But one video got more hits than anything else. It got uploaded at the very end of the posting window. Like, just when fifty-nine minutes were almost up. It was weird. It started out harmless enough, and we were like, 'okay, what the hell is this?' It was just this series of sentences being typed on the screen. Low quality. Like someone filming a word processing document with their camera phone, right? You could tell someone was typing because the screen shook just a little bit, you know, and every once in a while, whoever was typing would make a mistake and fix it. So it started out with: 'These are all true statements.' And then it started in with some random funny stuff. Like, 'Tomorrow is Wednesday, and there will be tater tots for lunch, and they will be delicious.' Then it said 'If you smoke you will get lung cancer.' Then it dropped some huge gossip bombshell. I think it was, like, 'Ryan is banging Jessica.' Which was true, by the way. That got people's attention, I guess. Then it said…what was next…oh yeah. Then it said, 'At the lacrosse party last week,' well…" Aidan glanced up awkwardly at Liz. She showed no expression, and he continued. "It said that this girl got with these three guys on the lacrosse team, okay? And then it just kept going with stuff. Like dropping all this gossip. Ripping people apart. Started typing faster and faster. And every few sentences it would be something random and goofy and funny, like something just light enough to keep you from being totally disgusted…to keep you laughing. Like, 'It is a known fact that Mr. Davis—he's a chemistry teacher—was once a competitive tap-dancer.'" Aidan laughed at this. "Which is hilarious, see, because he weighs like three hundred pounds."

He brushed the hair out of his eyes and continued. "But then it said that this one kid had cancer. And then came the big whammy. It said, 'Emilio is gay. For real. Just ask Steve. Don't believe it? Check this.' Screen went blank, and this fuzzy, low-res photo came up. Like a screen capture from a night-vision camera. It was blurry, but it was clear enough to see these two guys on the football team, Emilio and Steve, lying in bed together, like, *together*. It wasn't like maybe they were just on a team trip for an away game, sharing a hotel room bed. No. It was pretty obvious what was going on. They were like the two best-known football jocks in the school. Emilio had this tattoo on his shoulder that everyone knew. You could see it plain as day in the video.

"So...so this goes up, and within ten minutes the site traffic is spiking so high, like, it's exceeding our server capacity. I mean, like, hundreds of hits coming all at once. It was like an avalanche. I hated it. I felt so bad for those guys 'cause..." He paused, brushing his hair away. Mike noticed that Aidan was shaking now.

"I have to tell you guys something, and I might as well just get it out there 'cause you'll figure it out. I'm gay, okay? Evan too. We were together." He was shaking hard now, staring at the fire, glancing intermittently up around the group. Mike saw tears in his eyes.

Aidan continued, speaking faster now. "Yeah. I figured it out when I was eleven, probably the same time you guys figured out you like girls. Assuming you like girls. Anyway, me and Evan, we weren't out of the closet, but people sort of knew anyway. And yeah, we'd been harassed about it...but this...this was just *wrong*. But Evan...Evan said not to take down the video. I don't know...it was like...thrilling or something. He said, like, 'let them take the heat for a while, too.' And I have to admit...it was. Like, it was sick, but it was sort of...it did feel good.

"But I got scared, really. More than Evan. I pulled the plug on it. I mean I shut the whole thing down. Crashed the site. It's funny how quick you can do that. A website seems so...so substantial. Like if you think of your entire social media profile, you think of it as this big thing. But it's really just...just some code. I just erased the whole thing. Bad URL address. Site does not exist.

"Evan was pissed. He stopped talking to me. It hurt. A lot. Everyone was weird at school. All these silent stares in the hallway. Steve and Emilio didn't come to school. Then it started. People had taken screen shots. I mean, nothing on the internet ever really goes away, I guess. It started showing up everywhere. Shit, I mean, like…we were dead. We knew it. Nobody knew who did it, but everybody knew who maintained the site.

"Emilio and Steve denied it. They came up with all these cover stories. It was a doctored photo, blah, blah, blah. Whatever. Sooner or later, obviously adults got ahold of this. It turned into this media shit storm. Guidance counselors. Cops. Even the freakin' FBI. Of course it led back to Evan and me. They wound up with our computers. It all came out. We both wound up arrested. I tried to defend Evan. He didn't do a damned thing to try to defend me. He blamed me for everything." Aidan paused, staring at the flames for a second. "He just ditched me."

He rubbed his temples before continuing. "It was complicated stuff. The site had hosted images of minors. But we were minors, too. The FBI figured out who posted the photo. It was this other kid on the football team, Ray Smith. Well, Ray Smith got his ass kicked. Kicked out of school. Some kids on the team put him in the hospital. Steve? It was weird with Steve. He just handled it, you know? Like he gave up denying it. He just…I don't get it, but it's like he didn't even care. I still don't believe it. That guy's like kind of a hero to me. To be able to just…carry on? Let it all slide off him? He even put out a statement about how yeah, he was gay. That it didn't matter. That he wasn't ashamed of it anymore. That he was even *glad* he was out now, you know? Holy shit…I mean a lot of people worshipped him for that. Like, serious respect.

"But not Emilio. The biggest thing was that Emilio…umm…" Aidan drew his knees up to his chest, clasping them tightly with his arms, rocking nervously in the chair. His voice quavered. "Emilio came after Evan and me. While the investigation was going on, there were all these threats. Our parents got threats. Evan's dad wound up getting fired after a fight at work about the whole thing.

But then this thing with Emilio. He went to Evan's house. He was drunk. Tried to break in. Evan wound up fighting him off with a baseball bat. Almost killed the kid. They both got arrested. God, it was a mess. Evan's still in juvie lockup over the whole thing. He didn't cooperate. I did. I spilled everything to the cops.

"Anyway...there's obviously more to the story. Lots of details and legal stuff. But I came clean. I told them what happened. What I did. Which, in the end, didn't come to that much. Oh...all the money? Seized, like drug money.

"Anyway...between that and the fact that I shut the site down...I guess it bought me some mercy. So I...I'm here with you guys. My family...my family doesn't know what to do. I think we're moving to Carolina to get away from the whole thing. There's all these lawsuits and stuff. I'm on all kinds of probation and I'm not allowed to use the web. Some of the stuff on Closet Six made a big legal mess because it involved minors. Like these tenth-grade girls sending nudes. It's...it's really bad. But I never really did anything. I just...I let it happen. I 'set the stage' for it. That's what they all kept saying. The prosecutors. The case officers. 'Set the stage.' Yeah. I set the stage, all right." He brushed his hair away.

Aidan hunched his knees up again, the same as before, and buried his head. He was crying again, no longer trying to hide it. "I wasn't gonna tell you guys," he said, his voice muffled. "I wasn't gonna tell you about myself. But I just decided, 'You know what? The hell with it.' This middle-of-nowhere shit is hard enough without putting on an act for six weeks. You wanna rip me apart for it, go for it. Fire away. I'm used to it."

Manny spoke up. "Ain't nobody here gonna hate on you, man." He looked around at them, as if to confirm it. Taylor nodded.

Liam shrugged and said, "No sweat." Aidan looked up at him, his eyes searching, a look of confusion there.

There was something about the whole thing that pulled at Mike. Something about Aidan…about how young he seemed. Like he just wanted to give the poor kid a hug. He didn't, but the instinct was there.

He's…innocent. Harmless.

Hurting.

Pathetic.

That's what it was. None of the other guys, himself included, were innocent or harmless. They were all hurting. But only Aidan was *pathetic*.

None of us is helpless. He is. What the hell is he doing here? It bothered him. That Aidan was here with them. Each of them, who did something violent. Who hurt somebody on purpose. But Aidan? There was something fragile about him.

Breakable.

Then he wondered: Why are you feeling like this?

Andrew.

It's because of Andrew.

But the pathetic, crying kid to his left was not his little brother, he told himself. *He's sixteen. A junior in high school. Just as responsible for himself and the stupid shit he did.*

But hard as he tried, it didn't fit. Aidan wasn't like him. Not like the rest of them.

No. He's not a selfish bastard like you. Or a dangerous one.

He's just a careless little kid who played with matches and got burned.

Just like a careless kid who went swimming and drowned.

Then, immediately, he was furious at himself.

Stop! Jackass. Don't compare them! Andrew didn't set up perverted websites. Andrew wasn't an attention craving, sick little…

Shit. Yeah, you were about to say 'homo.'

Not fair. Not cool.

You're pathetic, too.

156

17

IT TURNED OUT there were two more straight days of "trail maintenance," which took its toll. They were bruised and beaten. Mike couldn't remember being so tired, even after the toughest landscaping jobs. And so it was a great relief when Jim woke them up later than usual. Mike sat up, groggy, and looked toward the doorway. Jim stood there, silhouetted in the doorframe, and pointed over his shoulder.

"It's raining. Recovery day. I want you guys to clean the kitchen and straighten this place up. Get those clothes and the damp towels off the floor. Something's liable to nest in there and bite you where you don't wanna be bitten. Oh. And you've got one other individual assignment. This one's optional, but I recommend it."

"What's that?" asked Taylor, rubbing his eyes.

"Write a letter to someone back home. Someone you've hurt, or who has hurt you, or both."

"A letter?" asked Manny. "You're gonna deliver letters?"

"No. They're going to stay in your notebook."

"So, what's the point of that?" asked Aidan, coming down from the top bunk.

"It's a way of thinking things through. Reflecting."

"More head games," muttered Liam from the bathroom, through a mouthful of toothpaste.

"I think you'll find that you'll get out what you put in, Liam. And like I said, it's optional. Just a suggestion for a rainy day. But don't forget about the kitchen. That's not a suggestion." He turned to go, pushing the door open.

Liam came out of the bathroom and pulled on his t-shirt. "Hey, Jim?"

Jim turned, the door half open. "Yeah, Liam?"

"Gotta ask. Y'all come up with any of this stuff on your own, or does Liz call the shots?"

Jim's eyes narrowed. "It's a team effort, son." With that, he closed the door and Mike heard him head down the steps.

"Am I dreaming?" Manny muttered. "No work today? Just clean up and write some lame-ass letter?"

Taylor rolled over in his bunk. "Yeah."

"Gracias a dios. I'm going back to sleep, hermanos. Wake me up when it's breakfast time."

Mike dozed off, but woke up again shortly after. It was quiet in the cabin. Manny and Taylor were still sleeping. Liam and Aidan were gone. He could still hear rain on the roof. He lay there for a while, enjoying the peace. He went quickly through the cold shower routine, brushed his teeth, and, shivering, got dressed. He pulled on his waterproof jacket. Finally, he took his notebook and pen, laced up his boots, and stepped out into the cool mist. The rain was light but steady, really more a mist of fine droplets. Liz waved at him from the porch of the main cabin. She and Jim were reading.

"Hey, guys."

"Morning, Mike," said Liz. Jim looked up briefly, gave him a quick nod, then went back to his book.

"Seen Aidan or Liam?" Mike asked.

"Working in the kitchen." Liz gestured over her shoulder.

He stuck his head in the door. Aidan and Liam were seated close together. They had an array of snack bars, dried fruit, and bags full of trail mix laid out on the table. Apparently, they'd finished cleaning already.

"What're you doing?"

"Jim wants these put together," said Liam.

"Need help?"

Aidan shook his head. "Nah, we got it covered." He measured a cup of raisins.

Liam took finished bags and stuck them in a plastic bin. "We're good. Blondie and I got a system going." He elbowed Aidan, who smirked, not losing count.

"Um, alright."

Mike headed down to the dock, taking care on the slippery planks. It bobbed as he walked across it, sending small waves out over the gray surface. The plane pulled on its tethers. Mike sat crosslegged on a cooler under the overhang of the storage shed. It was a dry spot. He leaned against a pile of lifejackets, rearranging stuff until he was comfortable, then pulled out his notebook.

He paused, pen at the ready, and looked out over the lake. Low clouds obscured the craggy peaks. He could barely see the tops of the spruce trees on the far side. Despite the size of the valley, it gave it an enclosed feel, as though he were inside a snow globe.

He made a list, counting on his fingers as he went through the names. *Mom. Uncle Dave. Coach Swanson.* For a second, he had an idea: *Andrew.* He shook his head. *That's messed up.* But it wasn't. He knew he wanted to. *Not now. I will, buddy. But not now.* He picked some mud from his boot. *Start with someone easier.*

Eric.

He opened the notebook to a blank page.

Hey, man. So we're supposed to write a letter to somebody important. Like, somebody we've hurt. I guess that's you. I don't really know where to start. I could tell you the whole story, but I feel kind of stupid writing it all down in a letter that isn't actually gonna get sent. I'd rather tell you over a joint. Ha. Guess that's not gonna happen anytime soon. Or maybe I could send you this letter. I dunno know yet.

I think there's a 2-hour time difference, so right now you're probably just finishing up practice and on your way to work. Can't tell you how much I'd rather be doing that. I'm really in the middle of nowhere, man. It's not too bad here in some ways. I mean, I have to admit sometimes it feels good not to be in Lawson. Sorry. I guess that's not really fair, but it's the truth.

Since I'm probably not gonna send this anyway I guess it doesn't really matter what I write, but I should apologize to you. You've always been my friend, but I wasn't a real good one lately. There's some stuff that I don't know how to explain. Like the stuff I've been feeling. How bad it got for a while.

When this thing's over I don't think we'll be coming back to Lawson, so I don't know how much I'm gonna get to see you anymore. I guess I'm only realizing that now, man, and as I'm sitting here writing this I'm about to start crying like a little kid. But no matter where I go we'll stay in touch, and I promise I won't ever forget all the good talks and stuff we had over the years. I'm really sorry I've been a bad friend. You've been my brother for a lot of years.

Maybe someday we can go to college together or something.

He stopped writing. Suddenly his eyes were full and his throat was tight. He shut the notebook, looking around. Jim was walking onto the dock, smoking a cigarette. Mike wiped his face, sniffling. The dock creaked and shook as he walked.

"Am I interrupting you?" Jim asked.

"No."

"Want to be alone?"

"I dunno."

"Okay if I finish this?" Jim held out the cigarette. "Bad habit. We all have 'em."

"It's okay. Don't suppose I can have one?"

"Don't suppose you can. Sorry. What're you doing out here?"

Mike held up the notebook. "What you suggested."

Jim nodded. "Done?"

"I guess. I dunno. I could write more, but not right now."

"How was it?"

Mike stuck the notebook inside his jacket. "You want me to be honest?"

"That's the idea."

"Okay. I'll be honest. Writing that letter sucked."

"It can."

They both looked out across the lake.

"After Liz and I lost our son, I wrote letters to him."

Mike turned. "You had a son?"

Jim's eyes were narrowed. "Nathan. Nate. He was your age."

"What...what happened?"

"Drunk driver. Hit and run."

"Jesus."

"Took a year to find the guy."

"What did you..."

"I almost killed him myself, Mike."

"God, I'm sorry. I had no idea. Did I miss that? Do the others know?"

"No. We haven't said anything to the other guys."

"Oh."

Why me?

"Anyway, it was ten years ago. I get what you did to that kid, Mike. When I finally got that guy in my sights, well, if my partner hadn't been there..."

"How did you...how did you get over it?"

"You don't get over it. You just keep going."

"But, how?"

Jim took a deep drag on the cigarette and flicked some ash into the water. "You just...do. The world keeps turning."

"Yeah. It does."

"You remind me of Nate."

"Really?"

"Yes." Jim looked him in the eye. "Really."

"Um. Thanks."

"He loved hiking. He always felt best when he was out in the woods, or in the mountains. We used to take a lot of trips together."

Mike nodded. He ran a finger over the scar on his arm. "Is that why you and Liz started this thing? Because of him?"

"It is. Our priest told us we could either drown in anger or try to make the world better. We ended up with a lot of money from a lawsuit. More than we knew what to do with, actually. We wanted to do something that mattered with it. Something in his honor. So we started this a few years ago."

Jim pointed out at the lake. "If you were to go diving out there, in the middle of the lake, you might find a bunch of seashells on the bottom. Nate and I collected them during walks on the beach when he was a little boy. When we bought this place, I took the jar out in a canoe and poured them out. I wanted some part of him to be here."

Mike looked out at the water. "Why this, though? Why work with screw-ups like us?"

Jim took a drag and smiled. "You know Liz and I were both military, and then both cops. Those are two lines of work where you see a lot of kids go wrong. Mostly boys. Not every kid gets the chances or the family that Nate did."

"Does it help?"

"We've had some success stories, and I—"

Mike shook his head. "No. I mean, does it help *you*?"

"Yeah. It does. We call it Freedom Lodge for a reason." He turned to Mike. "It can get better, if you believe it can." He stood up and squeezed his shoulder. "I'll leave you to your writing."

The dock bobbed as Jim walked away.

"You don't get over it. You just keep going."

Mike had heard that before.

Uncle Dave had said almost the same thing at the holding center. After Mike told him what he'd overheard the DeAngelo twins say that night.

*

Uncle Dave tapped on the table with his pen. "Look, Mike. They're pressing charges. You're a minor—they can't sue you, but they're going to sue your mom. Now, we could bring this allegation of Joe and Alex drinking to the authorities. Make it a criminal matter. Subpoena these text message records. But it would be a long shot."

"Right…but couldn't we—"

"Listen. Civil matters are different. Burden of proof is lower. The twins are eighteen. If we threaten to make that charge…if we mention the texts, it will imply that we already have them. Because, from where they sit, how else would we know about them?" Uncle Dave was speaking rapidly now, twirling the pen in his fingers, talking more to himself than to Mike. "It might be enough pressure. One of the boys might just fold."

"So, we sue them?"

"No. I talk to the DeAngelos' lawyer. I keep it vague, but lay it out. He doesn't know what we have."

"But it's a complete gamble."

"Yes."

"Do you think…?"

"They know the judges up here, Mike. Believe me. It's in Mr. DeAngelo's interest to keep this quiet. It's not worth it to him to play hardball on this."

Mike's head hurt. *Just cover it up.* Some part of him was beginning to see the sense in it, and he fought it, swatting it away like a pesky gnat. "No. We have to go public. Fight. For Andrew."

"For Andrew, or for you?"

"Screw you!"

Uncle Dave looked back at him. "Your mom doesn't have it in her, Mike."

"But it's not just her fight. It's mine, too!"

"No, because you'll be in detention. So it *will* be her fight. And she'll lose. We go in guns blazing, we lose. We don't have enough."

Mike's mind was spinning. He turned to Uncle Dave. "So, we do it your way. Assume it works. They drop the charges? That's it?"

"There would also be a private settlement. A financial arrangement for your mom."

"Come on. Seriously? You're saying they'd *pay* us to stay quiet?"

"That's how these things work."

"How much?"

"We won't get greedy. Low enough to make it a no-brainer for them. But enough for you and your mom to make a fresh start. Somewhere else."

"And they go off to college like nothing ever happened."

Uncle Dave slammed the pen down on the desk. It made him jump. "Your mom is *broke.* Your dad's insurance money will not last long. If—no, *when*—the DeAngelos sue, that will be gone in a heartbeat! Forget the money. This is your future. And your mom's. You're all she has left, Mike! Don't you get that?"

Mike's felt the heat rising again. "So I'm just supposed to move on?"

Uncle Dave's voice was even lower than before. "You're never going to get over it. It's simple. Do you want revenge, or do you want a future for you and your mom? Gotta choose, Mike. And that's no choice."

*

He looked out at the lake. The rain had started up again.
A fresh start. That's really what this is.

18

LIAM SHIFTED FORWARD in his chair until he was perched on the edge, sitting up tall. He cracked his knuckles and stretched his arms. "Last but not least, eh?" His voice was low and measured, the Texan drawl coming on extra strong.

"So, like I told y'all before, my best friend died and then I put my soccer coach in the hospital." Liam paused, nodding. "It was during an off-season scrimmage last month. Coach pushed me over the edge, pulling me off the field for some bullshit. I got in his face; he got in mine. Started like some typical sideline ruckus. Y'all know what I mean. But then we took it into the locker room—he wanted to avoid a scene and all—and I just lost it. I mean I really lost it. Wound up slamming him against the concrete floor hard enough to put him in the hospital. Broke a few of his bones, too."

Liam looked around the group. "I doubt all y'all are big into the soccer world. I am. Well, I *was*. And I don't mean like something you do just to make friends or get the varsity letter. Nah. It was all about soccer for me. I didn't go to a regular school like you guys. Havershire Academy. Y'all prolly ain't heard of it. Boarding school in Virginia. Mixed right in there with other hotshot prep schools, except it's pretty much just a real expensive sports camp, with classes on the side. When you go to Havershire, you ain't really aiming for college right away. Some kids go, of course. But the main goal is to shoot for a farm team first, maybe college later. Anyway, soccer and lacrosse are the big ones at Havershire. Elliot—my friend who died— he and I had a future with it, big time. I didn't know him before, but he was from Texas, too. They recruited us at the same time, like a package deal. And this wasn't some pipe dream, boys. Nah. I'm talking about national team prospects. Olympics, okay? Any of you ever heard of *Realidad Futbol* magazine?" The Spanish came across fluently, like he spoke the language.

That caught Manny's attention. "Yeah. Of course!" Liam smiled at him.

Mike glanced at the others' faces. Apparently no one else had heard of it. But Mike was also looking for something else—any indication that the others were watching Liam like he was. He couldn't figure out what it was that was bothering him. It was something about the tone. About the easygoing, steady tone…like he was sharing a casual story with old friends. Maybe it was just the Texan accent. No, it was the way he was looking around at them as he spoke. *That must be it. The rest of us stared at the fire during our stories. But not this guy. Like he's at a weekend bonfire. Like, hand him a beer and pass the joint.* It was impossible to know what the others were thinking, of course, but Mike was sure he could detect something in Liz's expression again. Her analytical gears were turning. Sure, they must have been when the others were talking, too. But not like this. Just like last time he'd noticed her watching Liam. Her brow was furrowed; her head was cocked just slightly more than it had been listening to the rest of them.

Liam laughed, nodding as he continued. "Nah, you wouldn't have heard of *Realidad Futbol* unless you speak Spanish or were seriously into World Cup soccer. It's a Spanish magazine. Kind of like a European *Sports Illustrated* for the soccer world. Well, Elliot and I were on the cover last year after we spent a week at an international development clinic in Barcelona.

Manny just about jumped out of his chair. His eyes were wide. "Dios mio! I have that issue! That was you on the cover, cabrón? Damn, hermano, I knew you seemed familiar!"

Liam nodded. "Sí señor. They called us 'a dual phenom in the making.' And I guess we were. Believe me, we both took a lot of shit for the shirtless training photos. Guys would post them up around school to be funny. But that had its benefits, too. Havershire's a fine co-ed institution, and we became pretty famous if y'all follow my meaning." He paused, smirking. *Reminiscing,* Mike thought. "Anyway, all joking aside, it was a serious deal. We had every top tier college program looking at us. The national team coach traveled twice to see us play.

"Well, now, it's a damn long story as to why this coach and I weren't getting along, but y'all could say he pushed all the wrong buttons during that scrimmage. He was making all the wrong calls. Said some personal stuff to me. And you know, guys, when y'all are in the *middle* of it, heart rate up, like, in that zone? Y'all been there? Well, I was there, hermanos. And it just *sparked*.

"Of course, there's more to it. A backstory. There's always a backstory, right? Like I told you, Elliot died. It was last winter, just before Christmas." He paused, looking up at the stars. "We were real close. I told you we got recruited together. He was my roommate. I'll tell you more about him in a minute. But I gotta go even further back a bit. The boarding school thing is a long story. My dad's been in prison for the better part of my life. Sorry to lay another daddy-problem sob story on y'all. He got caught up in a very creative insurance fraud scheme. Made a lot of money real fast. Whole boatload of cash. Problem was, his primary client happened to be a shell company for a certain kind of shipping operation across the good ol' Rio

Grande. So that came crashing down when I was six, and he's been in federal lockup ever since. Texas judges don't take too kindly to people who help finance those vaqueros.

Manny's eyes narrowed.

Liam's tone lightened as he continued. "Anyway, my mother decided that would be a perfect time to get into her own little drug habit. You'd think she'd want to stay away from the industry, but no, she decided to keep up international relations. She's not in prison, but she's been in and out of expensive rehab resorts most of my life. She and my dad got divorced before I started second grade. Fortunately, my mother's parents are halfway normal and pretty loaded with cash, so I wound up with them instead of foster care. They were already in their sixties, though, so it was off to junior boarding school and summer camps for little Liam. They never spared a dime where I'm concerned. Best schools. Private tutors. Personal trainers. Top-tier soccer camps. I think part of it has always been to spite my mom and dad. But it's more than that. They hate my father. I didn't know how much until I got older. Anyway, it wasn't exactly a blessed union between my parents. Shotgun wedding in more than one sense. No sir, we were not a warm and fuzzy family unit. No siblings. Not a lot of family. So yeah, it's been boarding schools and summer camps my whole life.

"Anyway, last winter, just before Christmas break, we're at this house party with the rest of the soccer team and a bunch of girls. Elliot's girlfriend, Alicia, was there. Parents away, that sorta thing. Regular season was done—we'd gone undefeated. Elliot and I were slated to be the next captains. We all got messed up at this party. But Elliot and Alicia got real drunk. They went outside to hook up. There was this deck, and a really steep embankment over a creek. So they were like, you know, doing what people do up against this railing, and I guess they just fell. She got hurt pretty badly—she's still in a coma. But Elliot nailed his head on a sharp rock. Didn't make it." Liam stared at the fire for a few seconds, expressionless.

"It was tough on everyone. Y'all can imagine. We felt so responsible. I suppose we *were* responsible. Well, something like that happens at a place like Havershire, it's like taking a Louisville Slugger to a nest of hornets. Except all the hornets are lawyers. So yeah, there's our dead friend—my roommate, my teammate—and his girlfriend in a coma, frostbitten half to death. But hardly anybody spends any time crying, 'cause every one of those pricks is so busy covering his ass with daddy's legal force field. The parents who owned the house were screwed, of course. Elliot's parents sued them for about nine trillion bucks. Of course, nobody else could possibly be to blame. Not Elliot. Not Alicia. Not at Havershire, no sir-ee. Anyway, at the end of the whole mess, I'm the only one that comes out lookin' halfway decent, because I'm the one who found them and called the ambulance. Like it made a damn bit of difference.

"All right. I'm really dragging this out. Fast forward to that scrimmage. National team scout was there. My coach—really high-profile guy—he starts getting on me about the way I'm playing. Tells me I'm showing off for the scout. I'll spare y'all the soccer jargon. Anyway, he drops some shit on me, makes a crack about how at least Elliot was coachable. How Elliot wouldn't have pulled this 'showboat shit.' How maybe if I'd been halfway responsible and watched out for him, he'd still be playing. About how it's easy for me to show off now, without having to share the spotlight. That's when I lost it. Just…I mean, lost it. Took half the squad to drag me off him.

"Arrested right there in the locker room. And that was it. It was over. Prep school. Soccer. The future. Olympics. Everything. Anyway, I suppose I should be grateful, all things considered. It's a miracle I didn't kill him. Our family lawyer's a big shot from Austin. Knows every judge from coast to coast. Couldn't keep my dad out of the hot seat—don't know if Jesus Christ the Lord and Savior could've done that—but he worked this deal for me. Yeah, there's gonna be a lawsuit. No doubt. But good ol' granddad will cover that one. After this, who knows. Maybe they'll let me play in Spain, huh?" He crossed his arms and looked up at the stars. "That's my story."

19

ANOTHER WEEK PASSED. Things became routine. They were still exhausted every night, but they'd gotten used to it. The past few days had been busy, divided into two work crews. One scraped, sanded, and painted the main cabin. The other began digging a hole for a new outhouse. Progress was slow through the rocky ground. They rotated twice, but the work was non-stop. Between the big jobs, there was an endless list of small daily chores: refilling the water tanks, chopping firewood, laundry, food prep and cleanup, sweeping, mopping.

They rose in the silent, pre-dawn darkness each morning, shivering as they got ready. Liam was always the first awake, sticking with his solo fitness routine with impressive discipline. Mike had joined him a few times, but more often than not, Liam was finished by the time he woke up.

The evenings had gotten less intense; after all, Liam's was the last of the backstories. Now they knew each other's dirt. And while Mike still had a nagging, lingering sense that there was just something *off* about Liam's story—that it seemed too rehearsed, maybe—he'd stopped dwelling on it. Half the time there wasn't any "official" evening session. They would tell stories and jokes. Jim would talk about the Army. They would play cards. Sometimes Liz would lead them through a guided meditation, and occasionally she'd ask them to do some writing before bed.

As a whole, they'd become more relaxed. There was camaraderie. Taylor's dry wit and Manny's one-liners kept them laughing. Aidan was still quieter than the others, but occasionally he'd drop funny comments at random, which were all the more hilarious because they were unexpected. Liam could still be edgy, but he seemed less so, and Mike had started to figure he'd just been reading the kid wrong. He wasn't bad—not any more than the rest of them, anyway. He could just be…*blunt.*

To an outsider, it would look like a summer camp up there at Freedom Lodge. That's sort of how it was starting to feel. There were quiet times in the hot, late afternoons, all of them exhausted after work, when the only sounds were the breeze through the trees, the lap of water, the thud of the seaplane against the dock bumpers, and an occasional snore. Other times it was like a locker room, the space between the bunks a nonstop crossfire of crude humor. They'd torn a sheet of paper out of Manny's notebook, where they kept a log of "REALLY, REALLY AUTHENTIC DESIRES." It was a colorful list, and they kept it out of sight during Jim's cabin inspections. There wasn't much alone time, and whenever one of them disappeared for a few minutes—a little extra time out getting firewood, or going back to the bunkroom to get something he forgot, the wisecracks flew. Manny claimed he would hold out the whole time, but Liam called his bluff one day while they were painting. "Bullshit, amigo. You forget I'm a light sleeper. I heard you." Manny started to protest, something about itching mosquito bites, but then Aidan nodded, smiling. "I heard you too." The rest of them roared with laughter as Manny turned red. Finally, shaking his head and smirking, he muttered. "Okay, okay. Six weeks? That ain't self-control. That's just cruel and unusual, you pendejos!"

As for Jim, Mike had come to appreciate his steady temper and easygoing manner. As long as everyone did his job, he kept a level but firm hand on the tempo of each day. When someone slipped up, he let him know, and then moved on. Manny joked about Jim's "old man strength" after watching him wield the axe for ten minutes straight, barely breaking a sweat, or effortlessly maneuver the fully loaded wheelbarrow.

Liz had less of a daytime presence. When she joined them on the excursions, she hiked a few paces behind, listening. If she weren't there, it would have been easy to forget that they were both cops. Even the guns and cuffs had become so normal that he barely noticed it anymore on Jim—but not so on Liz. On Liz, it was always prominent—in part because the massive .500 was larger relative to her smaller frame. Her distance during the day was balanced, of course, by her deeper involvement in the evening sessions, when she always took the lead.

And so, by Liz's design, it seemed, the days had been dedicated to a pattern of activity, rest, work, and solitude. She'd encouraged them to use the notebooks to write freely as they reflected on their lives. Mike was surprised how much they were writing. A guy would sit up in a bunk or in one of the Adirondack chairs, scrawling thoughts in tiny script, pausing to stare off at a rock or a tree before resuming. For Mike, it wasn't always writing. He'd been sketching little pictures, and drawing rough maps of the area, trying to get his bearings. Liz stressed the importance of respecting boundaries and each other's privacy, and as far as Mike could tell, everyone had. The small black notebooks fit in their pockets, so they could carry them around.

The notebooks had revealed something else. Liam was a skilled artist. He'd shown them a few of his pencil sketches, which were incredibly good. Aidan appeared the most fascinated by this. Mike, Taylor, and Manny exchanged surprised glances when they found Aidan sitting close to Liam on the dock yesterday afternoon, watching him draw. It was a pencil drawing of the seaplane in the foreground and the landscape behind it, and it looked so real that at first glance, it could have been mistaken for a black and white photograph.

*

It was hard for Mike to tell how many days they'd been there. Was it a week and a half? Two weeks? Somewhere in that range, he thought, as he got dressed for the evening, lacing up his boots. His hair was still dripping. Water splashed in the other room as Manny and Taylor traded dirty insults in Spanish, both of them laughing. Aidan lay sprawled on his bunk, writing in his notebook. Mike was sore. His hands were raw from wielding the pick all afternoon—tons of trail work the past couple of days. The running joke was that Jim and Liz planned to convert the place to a luxury backcountry lodge, and this whole therapy program was just an excuse to get free manual labor.

The door opened. It was Liam. Now that Mike was clean, the reek of the other boy's sweat-soaked worked clothes was all the more pungent. He'd just finished taking off his grimy t-shirt—the door hadn't even swung shut yet—when Liz called after him. "Liam, Jim and I have to talk to you." Liam glanced at Mike and rolled his eyes. He smirked, balled up the t-shirt and chucked it across the room at Aidan. It landed on his face. "Hey! Shit! That's disgusting— Come on!" With that, the door swung shut and Mike heard Liam hop down the steps. He watched him out the window.

Liz stood leaning against the railing of the main cabin, gesturing as she spoke. Jim was next to her, arms folded. At one point, Liam must have asked a question. She pursed her lips—it was sort of a sympathetic smile—and shrugged her shoulders. Liam nodded slowly, then turned around and headed back toward the bunkhouse. Mike quickly ducked away from the window and busied himself rearranging stuff on his bed as Liam climbed the steps.

Mike turned around. "Hey, man."

"Hey."

"What was that all about?" Mike asked.

"Nothin'. Um. Just something about…just a family thing they wanted me to know about." He sat down heavily and worked at unlacing his boots.

Aidan hunched up on his shoulder and looked down. "Really? Everything okay? Normally they don't tell—"

"Yeah, blondie." He peeled off his socks. "Just…don't worry about it." With that, he finished undressing and brushed past Manny and Taylor on his way into the shower.

"What's his deal?" Taylor mouthed, pointing behind him.

Mike and Aidan both shrugged.

*

As they sat down for dinner, Liz declared it a free evening—no session. Instead, she said, it was time for a little reward. With that, she and Jim each hefted a box onto the table. Jim handed out ice-cold cans of soda. Liz reached into the other and pulled out some board games. Mike couldn't help smiling. Taylor looked around the group. "Is it weird that I'm seventeen and I'm as excited about board games and soda as I am right now?"

"Hell, no!" Manny reached for the box. "You're going down, pendejos!"

They played for hours. Liam lost out first. He'd seemed distracted, Mike thought. *Whatever's going on at home, I guess.* He figured he'd try talking to him again—he'd get up early and join Liam for his morning workout.

It wasn't long before Taylor and Mike were out. Manny and Aidan battled it out, and Manny finally folded with a fit of obscenities muttered in Spanish. Somewhere in the middle of it, right before he lost, Mike looked around and realized they were just a bunch of kids playing board games. It was almost…

Normal.

As he lay in his bunk that night, listening to the pop and hiss of the woodstove, he looked out at the bright stars and smiled in spite of himself. He'd confirmed it had been two weeks. Just two weeks had brought him—and seemingly, all of them—to a different place. A place apart from the confusion and anger of the past couple months. A place where he was starting to feel like maybe he could be at peace for a while, up here in these mountains, far away from his failures and his pain. Where he could rise shivering in the cold, pitch-dark dawn, lace up his boots, and push himself all day with the sun on his face, breathing clean air. Where he could wash himself with pure, cold water at the end of the day, and fall asleep in a simple cabin surrounded by others who needed to come out here, to the wilderness, to become boys again.

But then came the explosion.

Then came the fear.

20

THE DEAFENING NOISE jolted Mike awake with a violent spasm. It took a second to realize his ears were ringing, and he struggled to get his bearings. The awkward movement had left him lying at an odd angle on the bunk, legs hanging off the side, tangled in his sleeping bag. He had no idea what time it was. Shaking his head, he glanced around, confused by the bright orange glow coming from outside the cabin.

Outside.

Huh?

As he struggled to unzip his sleeping bag, he saw the others doing the same. Taylor. Manny. Aidan, clambering down from the bunk, missing a step, falling to the floor before groggily rising to his feet. The bunkroom was lit with a dizzying, pulsing glow. In the bathroom, the white tiled walls were ablaze in yellow and orange.

And the sound.

Thunder? It was like a constant stream. A rushing river.

Fire. It's fire.

Mike winced and ducked as another explosive thunderclap shook the cabin—this one not distant at all. Taylor was shouting, pointing out the window, which had been blown out—or, no, not out, but rather *in*. Only now did he realize he was standing on broken glass, a shard of it already digging into the side of his bare foot. Running a hand through his hair, he felt an odd, gravelly texture, followed quickly by sharp pain. His hand was bloody. Panicking, he brushed glass out of his hair, slicing his hand again, checking the rest of his body, relieved to see himself intact. The sleeping bag must have protected him from the biggest pieces.

Smoke began to billow into the room. Not wood smoke. Thick, acrid stuff. More like…

Chemicals. Gasoline. Burning plastic.

They heard shouting over the thunder.

Liz.

"Where's Liam?" He shouted it to Manny. He shook his head.

Out there.

He heard Taylor over the roaring sound of the fire and the ringing in his ears: "…explosion…the plane!" They lunged for the door, tripping over the clothes they'd left lying around.

"Shoes!" Aidan grabbed at them, pulling Mike back.

Of course. A fire. Debris. Need my shoes.

They fumbled around in the strange, pulsing light, grabbing whatever shoes they could reach. For Mike it was a pair of boots, definitely not his own. No time to tie them.

Outside, he shielded his eyes. The sky was still dark, with just the slightest paling of sky that signaled dawn—but the flames, even though they were a good distance away, were intense. He could feel the heat on his bare chest.

The plane. The dock.

Taylor sprinted toward the fire. The entire space was illuminated in the hellish red glow, flames snaking high above the melted, barely recognizable shape of the plane, which was tilted at a grotesque angle. The smell grew as they got closer, and Mike saw now that the flames were not just yellow, but an unnatural rainbow of burning plastic and melting fiberglass. The dock itself was engulfed, and chunks of smoldering debris were floating in the lake, some so distant that they appeared to be almost to the far shore. The lake *itself* was on fire, and Mike realized it was a slick of oil and gasoline.

Gasoline.

"Taylor! Wait!" He ran, tackling him, bringing the larger boy down. "We gotta stay back! The gas tanks!"

"It's already all burning! It's all gone!" Manny shouted down at them. The fuel shed was leveled, and the ground surrounding it was engulfed in flame, as though the pebbled shore itself was burning.

"Where the hell are Jim and Liz?" Mike shouted.

"I dunno!"

"Shit!" Aidan shouted, pointing toward the main cabin. A corner of the back deck was burning. It was a small fire, but it was growing. Mike looked quickly to the bunkhouse. No fire.

"Manny! Mike! Come on! Before it gets to the propane tanks!" And with that, Aidan ran to the main cabin, grabbing buckets. "Fill 'em from the cistern!" Manny clambered up the stepladder with a bucket in hand, throwing open the hatch, plunging it in. Scampering over the roof, he doused the flames, tossing the empty bucket to Aidan, who began filling another.

"Mike! Mike!" Taylor shouted. "Help me!" He turned midstride, leaving Aidan and Manny to deal with the fire. He sprinted to catch up with Taylor, who was lunging toward the dock. The heat grew more intense with each stride, but he was driven on by the sight in front of him: one figure carrying another, stumbling across the decimated pier, barely making headway. As they got closer, the chaos of flame revealed Liam and Liz. He had her body slumped over his shoulder in a fireman's carry. Liam screamed in pain as a burning board gave way, and he fell through the pier's decking up to his knees in the water. He stumbled, dropping the heap of Liz's unmoving body on the shoreline. "Help her!" he shouted. "Get her!"

Taylor scooped up Liz's body and Mike pulled at Liam's arms. He was slippery with sweat and lake water mixed with oily grime and blood. Mike couldn't find a solid foothold in the half-burned debris of the wrecked pier, and he felt the sharpness of the hissing, broken boards digging into his shins and calves as he squatted down, using all his strength to pull Liam to his feet. Free of the splintered mess, they clambered up the shore, not stopping until they were away from the searing heat. Gasping, they collapsed in front of the bunkhouse, grateful for the dew-covered grass. Mike could taste the smoke, the heat of it flaring his nostrils, making his eyes water. His stomach churned, and Liam, crumpled in a ball on his side next to him, vomited, heaving, clutching his arm, which Mike saw was bleeding heavily. Liam wore only his gym shorts and one shoe. He was gasping, spewing dark vomit between the heaving, gulping breaths. He was covered in ash, oil, and smeared blood.

"Mike. Liz." His voice was gravelly, and he coughed. "Help Liz. She—" He couldn't continue as a fit of coughing threw him back to the ground.

Taylor.

Mike leapt to his feet, sprinting further up toward the bunkhouse. Liz lay on the ground, and Taylor was doing mouth-to-mouth. Her face was pale, her eyes closed.

"Is she breathing? Is she breathing, Taylor?"

The other boy held up a finger, lowering his ear to her face. "Yeah. She is now. Liz!" He shook her shoulders. "She's unconscious." He shook her again, slapping her face. "Liz!"

Mike stood over them. "What can I do?" He tried to remember anything that could help. He took a first aid course in health class. He remembered something: *ABC. Airway. Breathing. Circulation. Elevate the legs for shock.*

That's it. Shock.

"Put her feet up. Get her feet up!"

Manny was there now, and Aidan, too. Manny was out of breath. "Fire's out over there. Wasn't bad. We just—Jesus! What happened?"

Mike pointed back at Liam. "Take care of him. His arm. And get him some water!" Manny looked, spotting Liam, still heaving on the grass. He scampered toward him. "Aidan! Get water!"

Taylor's voice was rushed. "Her pulse is weak. She's breathing shallow. But she's not waking up, man. She jus—"

He was cut off by another loud boom as something exploded. They ducked, covering their heads. When they looked up, the flames were brighter down at the dock, and a shower of sparks and flaming bits of something fell slowly, like snowflakes. Some tiny, glowing pieces landed near them and on them, burning pinpricks, and they smudged them out.

Taylor checked Liz again. "Get a blanket. Let's move her inside."

"What about the fire, man?" Manny asked.

Taylor looked over his shoulder, down at the dock. The plane was barely recognizable—a twisted mass of flame amidst the burning slick of oil. "Nothing we can do about that. It's on the lake. It'll burn itself out."

Mike ran inside, grabbing a sleeping bag. They draped it over her. Now Liam was stumbling toward them, Manny and Aidan on either side, holding him up. He was trying to speak between the hacking coughs.

"J— " He buckled over. "Jim," he managed, before crumpling to the ground, vomiting again.

Oh damn. Mike traded a panicked glance with Taylor.

"Where is he? Liam! Where is he?"

Liam couldn't speak, only shook his head, eyes downcast, pointing over his shoulder back toward the inferno.

Taylor was on his feet, pulling Mike with him. "Come on!"

But Liam grabbed them both, pulling them back to the ground. Mike was surprised by the strength of his grip. "You can't...he's...you can't," Liam's voice was barely audible above the noise and the ringing in his ears. And just then, another explosion sent them all to the ground. They covered their faces, Mike shielding Liz's unmoving body with his own. He buried his face in the cool grass, squeezing his eyes shut, his bleeding hands clenching, pulling, and digging into the clumps of cool earth.

21

LATER THE SAME MORNING, Mike was awakened by a sun-beam, and all he could hear was snoring from across the room. He lifted himself up on his haunches and looked around, taking a moment to re-orient. *Oh yeah.* He was in the dining room, sprawled on the floor, covered with an army blanket, a bag of rice serving as a pillow.

They'd carried Liz back to her room off the kitchen cabin, doing their best to situate her comfortably. She hadn't regained consciousness. Taylor had insisted they undress her to check for wounds. Mike felt uneasy as they'd taken off her filthy sweatpants and t-shirt, which were soaked in water and oil. He'd exchanged an uncomfortable glance with Taylor as they'd pulled off her pants, looking, sheepishly, relieved to find no obvious injuries. They'd wrapped her in blankets. Manny and Aidan had busied themselves caring for Liam, whom they'd carried in, too, and put in the adjoining infirmary bunk. Taylor had done his best to clean out the gouge in his left arm, disinfect it, and bandage it up.

Mike stood up—he felt a bit dizzy—and coughed, trying to stifle the noise. His eyes, nose, and throat were dry. There was sharp pain where glass had cut his foot, and he limped over to the sink, hoisting his leg up onto the counter to get a better look. *Not bad. Minor wound. You're used to those, anyway.*

He put his foot in the sink, running water over the cut. The morning sun was hot, and he could see now that his arms, hands, and face were covered in tiny cuts and abrasions. Looking in the reflection of one of the serving spoons, he saw that rivulets of dried blood covered his face and neck. Gingerly, he pulled another shard of glass from his scalp.

Across the room, Aidan and Manny slept. They were just as covered in soot and grease, but they slept soundly and didn't appear hurt. Apparently, their bunkbed had been far enough from the window to avoid the spray of glass. Lowering himself gently, Mike tested weight on his foot, wincing a bit. He padded across the floor into Jim and Liz's room. Taylor was asleep on the floor next to the bed in a tangle of sleeping bag. Liz hadn't moved, but he could see that she was breathing. He peered into the tiny infirmary. Liam was sound asleep. The bandages on his arm were bloodstained. *Your arm looks like mine now.* Mike grabbed a roll of gauze and some medical tape for his foot, wrapping it. Manny snored in the next room.

His foot done up well enough, he poured himself a cup of water in the kitchen. He drank it eagerly, surprised by his sudden thirst. He chugged a second. It made him nauseous, and he steadied himself against the counter. *Must be from the smoke.* Fine pricks of sweat sprouted from his scalp in a wave of itchy warmth. Recovered, he reached for the blanket and wrapped it around himself. He stepped outside into the chilly air, carrying the boots he'd kicked off by the door.

The odor was heavy on the air despite the breeze—like the morning-after smell of a campfire, but far stronger. The sun warmed his shoulders as he sat down on the steps. Every part of him was sore, like the day after a tough early season practice. He pulled on the boots, which chafed his feet. *Get some socks and your own goddamned boots.* First, he wanted to see what the hell had happened. He worked his way toward the shore. Debris was scattered everywhere.

The dock was nothing more than a few charred boards lying atop the stone foundation. Even more grotesque was the mangled, blackened skeleton of the plane. Body panels were missing altogether or melted into crazy shapes. It looked like someone had poured a vat of melted wax over a firebombed truck. The lake was a mess, chunks of foamy debris floating amidst swirling rainbows of a large oil slick. The breeze was blowing the mess westward, to his right, and he followed the shoreline, spotting wreckage for thirty or forty yards tangled amongst the rocks in the shallows. His boots crunched noisily on the crusted, oily gravel, as he came to where the fuel shed had been. The remains of the red metal canisters, several twenty-gallon drums, were split open, mangled and black, their sides wrenched apart by explosive force. There was a crater in the pebbled beach. It was just a foot or two deep but several yards in diameter. The force must have been tremendous.

And then it hit him: *Jim. Jim was...Jim is in here somewhere.*

He looked up, blocking the sun and scanning the debris. He didn't see anything. He walked closer to the shore, smelling something different now. A rotting odor, something really foul—and then he noticed that he'd stepped on the bloated carcass of a fish. The bile rose in his throat, barely held back, as his head rushed with nausea. Looking around, he saw that the fish were scattered all over the place, some of them on the beach, some *yards* from the water, some lolling lifelessly in the gentle waves that lapped at the shore. He closed his eyes, breathing through his mouth, trying consciously to hold back the vomit. After a moment, sure that he'd regained his composure, he opened them again, and continued his walk, picking his steps carefully.

He passed the pier again, about to give up, maybe go find the others. But then he spotted something, a bright glint in the sun, brighter than the pinpoints of light reflecting from the rippled water. It was floating. As he drew nearer, stepping over a log, he saw the glass face of a watch. It was attached to Jim's charred, mangled arm, which was floating a few yards away from the rest of him, amidst a cluster of dead, silver-white fish.

And then Mike was on his knees, buckled over, vomiting.

22

MIKE SAT WITH AIDAN, Manny, Taylor and Liam in the cool of a shaded grove. They were sprawled out, some lying on the ground, others leaning against tree trunks. The breeze was cool on his sweat-soaked t-shirt. Spots of sunlight pierced the trees to land on his arm. They were all breathing heavily from exertion. A heap of loose, upturned earth lay in the center of the grove. A simple cross, which Manny had pieced together with sticks and some twine, stood at the center of the mound. The air was pungent with odors of smoke, sweat, dirt, grass, and pine sap. Shovels and picks lay where they had dropped them. No one had said a word since they'd decided that Jim needed to be buried.

They'd hesitated only a moment after Mike found the body. Not one of them made it through the task of dragging the body ashore without vomiting. It was slow, difficult work, made nearly impossible by the wretched smells and grotesque sight. The corpse was badly burned. At one point, as Liam and Taylor tugged at a leg with the rake to free it from some debris, it simply broke off. Half-disintegrated tendons and ligaments gave way, leaving a ragged, gurgling mess of blood and torn flesh where the tissue came apart.

When it did, the trunk bobbed obscenely in the water, and Jim's ruined face—his melted eyes just two globs of reddish-gray pulp amidst webbed remains of clinging skin—seemed to nod at them, locked in a rictus of agony.

They used sticks and rakes to pull the body closer to shore, floating it onto a tarp. Taylor and Mike dragged it out of the water, quickly folded the tarp over, then again, holding their breath, and tied it shut with some cord. They dragged it up the shore until Taylor stopped suddenly.

"Hold on," he'd said, and started untying the tarp.

"The hell you doing?" Mike had asked, the smell hitting him.

"The gun," Taylor said, "and the sat phone."

They'd unfolded the tarp, and Taylor, using a stick, poked through the mess of guts until they saw the gun. It was useless, though: nothing more remained other than the metal frame and the barrel, and that was enveloped in a mass of melted-then-hardened-again nylon that used to be Jim's side holster. There was no sign of the phone. They were about to fold the tarp back over.

Mike held up his hand. For a second, a fleeting image of his dad's wedding ring on mom's chain necklace. "Wait. One more thing." Holding his breath, on the edge of losing it again, he reached for what was left of Jim's hand. His wedding ring was still there. Mike grimaced as he pulled on it, the bloated finger blue and spongy. It was stuck.

"Shit," he rasped, trying not to inhale. Tears were forming at his eyes, his chest burning as he continued to hold his breath. He tugged on it again, twisting it, and the flesh gave way. It slid free, wet with blood, water, and the slime of decomposing skin. He dropped to the ground, heaved, and vomited again. He wiped the ring on his filthy pant leg, and put it in his pocket. He would have also taken the West Point ring, but it was gone, along with the flesh of Jim's right hand.

"Jesus, Mike." Taylor's eyes were wide. They folded the tarp back over. Taylor secured it slowly, deliberately, deep in thought. The others grabbed hold to help, and together they dragged it past the cabins, through the perimeter fence, and up a gentle slope to this clearing.

Liam's arm injury had had little effect on him, slowing his digging only a bit. If anything, he was suffering more from the hacking cough that had come with the smoke he'd inhaled. Liz was still unconscious. Looking around, Mike saw a group of guys who might as well had just come off the battlefield. Uniform khaki utility pants, boots, and white tank tops, somber, streaked with blood, ash, dirt, and sweat, the mound of a shallow forest grave in the background— that's precisely what it would look like. The sky above them was vivid, electric blue, not a cloud in sight. Birds chirped.

Taylor swatted a mosquito on his neck. "We need to—"

Manny shook his head, cutting him off. "Not now, hombre!"

Taylor shot him a glare. "Yes, now. We need to find that other phone and get her help. We can't sit here. She's unconscious, and it looks like she took a hell of a hit to the head. That's one thing I remember from my EMT course. Head hits are bad news. Her brain could be swelling, and—"

"Cinco minutos, cabrón! Five goddamned minutes!" Manny threw the shovel he'd just picked up back down to the ground. It clanged on a rock. "Just give us a second to get our heads straight, man." He was panting now, his face red. He sat down heavily, wiping tears from his eyes. His voice was quieter, then. "Just a second to pray for him, hombre."

Mike looked around. They all had tears in their eyes. After a second, Liam stood up, wincing, holding his arm. His voice was softer than usual. "Manny, he's right. The radio on the plane is obviously gone. Jim's satellite phone is lost. But Liz had one. We gotta find it.

Call for help. They kept all kinds of stuff in the safe. The phones, our files, their guns and ammo. I'm sure it's in there."

Mike looked up at them. "How are we gonna open it?"

They all exchanged glances.

"Y'all reckon we can break it open?" Liam asked.

Taylor shook his head. "Won't be easy. It's a gun safe."

Manny reached for a pickaxe. "Maybe with this?"

"Worth a try," said Taylor. He picked up a shovel. He turned toward the grave, like he was going to say something, but then did an about-face and began trudging back to the camp. "Don't have a lot of choice, do we?"

*

They spent the afternoon taking turns going at the safe with the pickaxe. It wasn't bolted down, but it was heavy, and large enough to hold at least a couple of long guns. It took four of them to drag it from its space in Jim and Liz's room, down the steps, and onto the grass outside. It was solid steel, with thick hinges and a digital key-pad. Liam, clearly the strongest of them, had taken the first swing, holding the pickaxe tentatively, lining up his arc, then wincing as sparks flew and the spike glanced off the metal. He swore as he lost his grip on the axe, dropped it, and shook his hands out after the jolt. He looked around at them, eyebrows raised, and picked the axe back up. If the wound on his arm was bothering him, he barely showed it. The subsequent swings were more measured. Eventually, they decided to concentrate their efforts near the hinges, aiming to strike the small gap between the door and the frame, using the spike end. There was no way to know if they were making headway. Rotating shifts at it for the better part of an hour, all they'd managed to do is riddle the thing with dents and blunt the tip of the pickaxe. Aidan came close to piercing his own foot before Taylor snatched the tool from him and told him to leave it to the others.

Mike was in the kitchen with Aidan, cooking rice and rehydrating some meat for dinner. No one had had much of an appetite until now, but the exhaustion of the day was catching up with them. As he filled the pot, Mike's head whirled with questions.

They'd pieced together some of what happened. Liam claimed he'd simply gone out a little earlier for his workout—he'd been wired, probably from the extra sugar and caffeine from the soda the night before, he said—and was on his way back when the explosion happened. They'd all seen Jim out smoking at dawn before. The explosion happened just before dawn. And he did usually smoke on the pier—which was not right near the fuel shed, of course, but not that far, either. So that seemed to be the most logical explanation for the fire, especially given that Jim's body was out there. Liam saw Liz burst from the main cabin and sprint down toward the pier, shouting for Jim, carrying a fire extinguisher. He'd followed her, but by the time he caught up, she was flat on her back in the water, out cold. "Maybe she slipped. Hit her head. Breathed in too much smoke," he'd said. That's when he'd shouted for the others.

It added up. And Liam *had* saved Liz's life. There was no doubt about that.

Mike's thoughts were interrupted. "Hell yeah!" Liam shouted, after a particularly loud clang issued from outside. "Take that, bitch!"

Mike and Aidan traded quick glances and went outside. Taylor and Manny were holding the safe down, while Liam used the point of the pickaxe like a lever, wrenching the broken door from the steel frame. He'd managed to crack one of the hinges, swinging the door outward, and with a little coaxing with a crowbar, they were able to bend and snap it directly out of the other hinge. Soaked with sweat, Liam wiped his brow and sat down heavily in the grass. In the end, the door was too bent to open properly, but they managed to pry the top open a few inches, just enough. Aidan—the smallest—got down on his hands and knees, contorting at an odd angle to reach inside, feeling around blindly.

First, he pulled out a long, matte-black shotgun. Taylor took it from him. "There's the twelve gauge," he said, checking the chamber. "There's a few boxes of shot and slug rounds in there. Grizzly hunting, anyone?" Then Aidan lifted Liz's .500 out gingerly, holding it with two hands, looking at it wide-eyed. Taylor set down the shotgun and took it, opening the chamber, checking to see that it was unloaded. "Damn," he whispered, setting it on the ground. "That thing's almost as heavy as the shotgun." Aidan pulled out several boxes of ammunition. Next was a thick stack of manila folders, bound together with rubber bands. It took some coaxing to get them out, but finally they sprang loose. He tossed them on the ground. "I think we should burn those," he muttered. The rest of them chuckled nervously. He pulled out one smartphone, then another, and powered both on. Neither got a signal. "Well, we knew that, right? But where's the damn sat phone?" He went back to the safe. Finally, looking toward the sky in relief, he held up the satellite phone. "Sweet Jesus, thank you."

They crowded around him as he powered it on with a satisfying beep. The tiny display wasn't hard to read in the evening half-light, and something about its glow was comforting. Mike watched the startup sequence:

...INITIALIZING...

...SEARCHING FOR SATELLITES...

Aidan held it higher, walking a few paces closer to the lake, away from the trees.

...SEARCHING FOR SATELLITES...

...SEARCHING FOR SATELLITES...

...TRIANGULATING...

...TRIANGULATING...

…READY!...

Finally, the startup screen clicked off, replaced by what looked like a vintage flip phone display, a simple gray scale, pixelated readout of the time, date, and signal strength.

"We're in business!" Aidan said. "Wait…who do I call? 911?"

"Do it," said Manny.

But as soon as Aidan pushed the "9" key, the display changed:

…ENTER USER PASSCODE…

"What the hell?" he muttered, and tried again. "9" appeared, but the cursor simply blinked, anticipating another digit. He pushed "1," followed by another 1, then SEND.

…PASSCODE INCORRECT…

…ENTER USER PASSCODE…

"A goddamned passcode? Really?" He looked up at the others. "It should make emergency calls without a passcode." His face crumpled in confusion. He tried a few things, pushing various buttons. Aidan suddenly looked older and more serious than Mike thought possible. "These handsets are pretty old technology. They look like military surplus, not civilian models. No emergency call 911 bypass like any modern cell phone. And they've got it locked, guys. We can't make any calls without that code. We have to figure it out."

"What if we can't?" Taylor asked.

Aidan cocked his head, squinting at the phone's display. "Then I guess I gotta hack it."

23

LATER THAT EVENING, after they'd eaten, Mike sat with Taylor in Liz's room. He looked at Jim's ring, which now hung from her necklace.

"My mom wears my dad's ring like that," said Mike, his voice low. He pictured his mom smiling, the ring on her silver chain. "It…it matters a lot to her. I thought Liz should have it, too."

Jim had slept in a separate cot arranged head-to-head with Liz's. They decided to use it as a sort of storage space for all his stuff; certainly no one would be sleeping on it. Jim's sleeping bag was folded neatly, the pillow placed on top of it. Anything of his they'd found—clothes, equipment, anything—they placed on the bunk. They tried waking Liz up, but other than some subtle movements that seemed involuntary, she was still unresponsive. Outside, Liam was gathering wood for a fire in their usual spot, while Manny and Aidan finished raking up debris from the shore. They'd debated about whether or not it was worth building a fire, but in the end, they decided they might as well stay busy. After all, they had a lot to talk about.

Taylor's voice was low. "I swear, when Aidan pulled that gun out of the safe, part of me thought Liam was gonna grab it." He let out a low laugh, but Mike wasn't sure he was entirely joking.

Mike nodded. "Like, he'd grab it and say, I dunno…something *Texan,* y'know?"

They both glanced down at the gun, which was holstered around Taylor's waist. "Eh, what the hell. We were *all* eying it. Can't blame him for that. Still…"

"Still." Mike looked out the window again. It was getting darker by the minute.

Taylor pointed at Liz. "Somebody should stay in here with her, in case she wakes up or whatever."

"Should be you."

"It's not like I'm a doctor. Jesus. I only got halfway through EMT training."

"That's halfway more than any of us," Mike said.

Taylor looked down at the .500 on his belt. "Feels weird carrying the gun."

"I bet."

"But you know, it makes me realize that they always *were.* Carrying them, I mean. They always had them at the ready."

"For protection. Like, bears."

"Seen any bears, Mike?"

Mike looked at him, trying to read the expression. "No. But they're around."

"Right. They are. But so are we. And wearing this thing…the weight of it…it just…I'd almost forgotten that we're the criminals."

"Yeah." Mike nodded slowly. "I see what you're saying."

"Right. Well, I think you guys should take the shotgun to the cabin."

"Yeah. All we need is a goddamned grizzly bear to come charging in on top of all this." That did make him laugh, and Taylor too. The twisted humor felt good.

"Mike, seriously though, we gotta figure out what to do in the morning. If Aidan can't get that sat phone working, we've got no way to call for help. And we are *way* off the grid, man."

"What about hiking out?" Mike wasn't even sure they *could* do it if they wanted to. He thought back to the topo map Jim showed them—the incredibly rugged terrain they'd have to cross before they'd even get near the first marked trail. And some of those ridges...those were definitely technical climbs.

As though he were reading his mind, Taylor said, "We should find Jim's map."

"What about Aidan?" Mike asked. "You think he can hack the phone?"

"Maybe." Taylor didn't look hopeful. He looked out the window, and his expression changed. "Oh, come on. Seriously?" And then he was running out the door. Mike ran out after him. Liam had tossed the bundle of file folders into the campfire.

"What the hell are you doing?" Taylor shouted, running toward the circle of chairs. Mike sprinted after him.

The larger boy looked up, unmoved by the commotion. "What Aidan suggested." There would be no recovering the folders now; they were completely engulfed.

"Jesus! He was kidding!"

Liam stood up. "What the hell does it matter? That stuff is our past. We don't need it here." As if to make his point, he kicked what remained of a folder deep into the coals, where it sprouted a new, brighter flame.

Manny, hearing the commotion, came over with Aidan, holding a rake. "Hey, man! That might have been important. Like, notes on our progress to give the authorities! So we get some credit for going through this nightmare!"

Liam smiled, shaking his head. "Is that what this is Manuelito? A nightmare?" He chuckled, and spoke to all of them. "I know this has been a tough day. I get that. We're hurtin'. But no, amigo, this ain't no nightmare. In fact, I'd say we're doing alright." He looked around, waving his arm in a wide arc. "And in case you haven't noticed, there ain't no *authorities* here anymore. At least not any breathing, conscious ones."

They were all silent for a second. Mike looked around, and the steep valley walls seemed more imposing than ever against the darkening sky. The acrid smell of the fire had begun to fade, but it was still on the now-chilly air. They heard the cry of a hawk echo across the lake, and it only underscored Liam's point.

We're alone out here.

"We're 'doing alright?'" Taylor stepped closer to Liam. "You call this doin' alright? Jim is dead!" Taylor was shouting now. "The plane is gone! The radio is gone! The sat phone is locked! Do you have any idea where we are, man? Any idea how far we have to hike out of here? Liz could be dead before morning! And you think we're 'doin' alright!'" He was inches from Liam, who had barely moved a muscle. Mike's eyes darted to the revolver.

A few seconds passed. Mike's heart was pounding. Liam's voice came out low and mellow. He pointed down at the gun. "Might be going to your head a little bit. Ask Mikey-boy about that." He turned, throwing a glance in Mike's direction before looking back at Taylor. "Why don't we all just siddown?" He slouched into the nearest chair, slinging his leg over the armrest.

Crazy bastard. Mike's pulse was pounding—that old familiar rushing sound coming back to his ears. He felt the hot flood of...of something.

Calm down. Don't do anything. Don't do anything.

It was fully dark now, and the crackling of the fire seemed louder. No one else moved for a second, but then Aidan rustled in his chair. His voice was barely a whisper. "I think I can do it."

"How?" Taylor asked. "Speak up."

Aidan continued, louder now. "I...I think I can use one of the smartphones to bypass the code."

"You serious, hermano?" Manny asked, sitting down next to Aidan. Mike and Taylor sat down, too. Liam didn't move.

The firelight danced on Aidan's face. "I think so. It...it depends on the coding sequence, and...and how many layers of encryption we're talking...but the thing is just old and outdated enough that...well, if I can splice the sync cables, which I think I can do, then, see, there's this digital terminal interface that I can—" He stopped abruptly, looking around at their blank faces. "Sorry. Never mind. It's a bunch of geek stuff. Doesn't matter. But I think I can do it. We're just lucky they don't keep their smartphones locked, too. I was kind of surprised by that. Like, who doesn't lock their phone? But then I started looking through them, and there's like, nothing on them. Must not use their phones much. Old people, ya know?" He chuckled absently.

"Aidan!" Manny glared at him.

"Huh?" Aidan looked back at him.

"Well, go do it, chico!"

"Now?"

"No. How 'bout tomorrow? Of course, now, loco!"

"Don't get too excited. It's gonna take a while anyway."

"Why?" Liam asked, his head cocked to the side. "What's 'a while?'"

Aidan took a deep breath, and sat forward, his elbows on his knees. "It's...look. I can...I'm trying to keep this simple. It's like those gambling things with the number wheels that roll. Like in Vegas."

"Slot machines," Liam said, smirking.

"Yeah." Aidan grinned at him. "Right. Slot machines. So...it's sort of like a digital slot machine, okay? Here's the thing with passcodes. It's a simple form of security, just like the PIN number on an ATM card. But it's reliable and hard to work around. It's just designed to make it inconvenient and slow. See, I can just run a program to try every possibility. It's a four-digit passcode. That means ten thousand possibilities. Theoretically, if I could interface it, the smartphone could try ten thousand possibilities in just a microsecond."

"Lemme guess. It's not that easy," asked Liam.

"Right," Aidan said, nodding. "The problem is, this sat phone goes into lockout mode after five wrong tries. That's pretty standard. It's specifically meant to prevent what I'm trying to do. Without that safeguard, well...it wouldn't be too hard to do this with ATMs, right? Anyway, the lockout is five minutes...you can't try again for five minutes. So, do the math. We only get to try five combinations every five minutes. Which means we only get to try, um, sixty combinations an hour. That times twenty-four hours in a day...that's only...like fourteen hundred attempts every day."

"Why couldn't we just do that ourselves?" Manny asked.

Aidan rolled his eyes. "Because, Manny, that would mean someone sitting there punching in numbers all day and all night. And if he screwed up—even once, maybe skipped a combination by mistake—it could take forever. No. You need a computer to do it."

"You said ten thousand possibilities?" Liam asked.

"Yeah."

Liam thought for a moment. "So that's like...what? A *week* of this thing chugging along at that rate?"

"Well, it all depends on what the code actually turns out to be. It's gonna go through each combination, starting with 0000, then 0001, and so on. So if the passcode has a low number, say, like 2379 or something, it'll hit it a lot sooner than if it has a high number, like 9934. If it happened to have *zero* as the first number, it could be just a few hours, in theory. If we knew the first number, it would be much simpler. But we don't."

Manny looked confused. "So why not have it start with the higher numbers, then?"

Liam chuckled. "You're not the sharpest tool in the shed, are you, Manuelito? He's saying the first number is just as likely to be any number from zero to nine. Didn't y'all take probability?"

Manny's face grew flushed. "What's the probability you blow me, Tex?"

Liam smirked, shaking his head. "You'd like that, wouldn't you, maricón?"

Manny went to stand. Taylor reached up, grabbing his shoulder, calming him.

Aidan spoke up. "Um…in terms of probability, Manny, he's right. Unless we had some meaningful idea what the code could be, which we don't, then there's no more sense starting anywhere but zero." He stood up abruptly. "Okay. I should get started then, right?"

"Have at it," said Taylor. "The sat phone is next to Liz's bed. So are the smartphones. I've been charging all of them."

"Oh, shit," muttered Aidan. "That's the other thing."

"What?"

"Power. I'm not worried about having enough. These are small devices, and there's plenty of power from the solar panels in the main cabin. But obviously, we need to be able to keep both phones charged for this process to work. Problem is the charging port for the smartphone is also its data port. So I can't keep it plugged in while it's working. We'll probably have to stop to recharge it a couple times a day. So…yeah, that's another delay. I guess in theory, if the combination started with nine, we could be looking at more than a week.

"A week's too long," muttered Taylor.

"Too long? Doesn't seem too long. We can sit tight for a week," Manny said.

"Listen. If we can't call within a few days, she's dead," said Taylor.

"How do you figure that?" Liam asked.

Taylor shook his head. "Simple. Think about it, guys. If she *does* come out of the coma, great. She tells us the combination, and we call, and a chopper gets up here within a few hours." He kicked at a log, pushing it further into the fire. "But if she doesn't…Look. Something hit her on the head, hard. Problem is, there's not too much of a lump. That's bad. Knock to the head, you want to see a goose-egg. It means the swelling is going out, not in. I learned that in my training. No lump, good chance of pressure getting too high in the skull because of fluid build-up. Intra-something. Intracranial pressure. ICP. That's it. She could start having seizures. Maybe even a stroke."

"Yeah, but you don't know that," said Manny. His voice wavered.

"No, I don't. Either way, though, if she doesn't wake up, her body's gonna starve. We don't have any way of getting fluids into her. I don't see any IV tubes, and even if I did, I wouldn't know where to put them."

Aidan turned to go. "I better get on it, then."

Mike asked, "Anyone seen Jim's map?" He looked around. No one had. "We need to talk about hiking out."

"Hiking out? You loco, Miguel?" Manny asked. "You remember the view down from that ridge?"

"No. He's right," said Liam. "Aidan's phone thing might not work."

The possibility settled with a tangible weight. No one spoke for a little while. Mike thought out loud. "We do have good equipment. And plenty of food."

"I dunno," said Taylor. "We got good hiking equipment. But that's not hiking, Mike. It's Mount Everest kind of shit. Like, with ropes and stuff. Remember what Jim said? Gotta cross two passes until you even get to a trail, right?"

"It would be tough."

"More than tough," Taylor said. "Dangerous. We get hit with a storm out there, we're screwed. And somebody would have to stay here with Liz. We'd have to split up."

And that would obviously have to be you, Taylor, which means... Mike did a quick draft in his head. *Aidan's no hiker. He'd stay here and work the phone. Taylor stays with her. Liam's in the best shape, and I've got the most hiking experience. Yeah. It would be the two of us. Plus maybe Manny.* "Well, we definitely need that map before we can even think about it," Mike said. "I searched all over their cabin."

"Assume we find it. Two would stay, while three go?" Taylor asked.

"Maybe...But look. We can't do anything 'til morning," Mike said. The enormity of it was spreading in his mind, like a dark, billowing cloud of smoke. Now that he'd had some time to mull it over, the reality hit home.

Jim's dead.

Liz might be dying.

We're alone up here.

And no one down there even knows there's anything wrong.

He looked around him. Outside the circle of orange firelight, the darkness was thick. Thicker than most nights. He realized why. It had been clear most of their time up here, but tonight was overcast. No stars. And, he noticed, the wind had picked up. *Figures. It all goes to hell and the weather turns, too.*

The rest of them looked up, also surprised by the sudden change.

Taylor stood up. "Did the temperature just drop about ten degrees, or is it me?"

"Rain," said Mike.

"More than rain," Liam said. "Storm."

"Dios," muttered Manny.

Taylor zipped his fleece. "Hustle up and let's get inside. I'll stay with Aidan in the main cabin."

The storm center remained a few miles away, outside the valley, and the thunder wasn't as loud as Mike anticipated. He remembered a summer storm in the Adirondacks. He'd been hiking with Eric on a hot summer day. They were just coming down off one of the peaks, still above the tree line, when the weather rolled in so quickly they could barely get down fast enough. They hadn't seen it coming, distracted by the view in the other direction and a bag of trail mix. The temperature had dropped something like forty degrees in a few minutes. The wind rose from nothing to a gale, and the sky threw lightning and stinging hail at them. He remembered taking cover under some overhanging rocks like they'd been taught, sitting on their backpacks in case of a lightning strike, covering their ears to block the deafening noise. He'd been scared as hell when he looked at Eric and saw his hair standing up, charged with static electricity, and felt it in the hair on his arms and legs.

He figured a storm like that would be ten times worse up here. Thankfully, the bulk of it missed them. But still, the rain came in torrents, slashing at the bunkhouse walls, cascading down the windows in sheets. They'd nailed up a board earlier in the afternoon where the explosion had taken out the window, but it wasn't perfect, and it was drafty. The noise of rain on the roof drowned out any attempt at conversation. Mike and Liam built a fire in the stove while Manny shuttered the windows, and then the three of them huddled around it, silent, waiting out the storm. The shotgun stood in the corner, three boxes of slugs on the floor next to it.

When the worst of it passed, Mike put on his rain jacket and jogged across to the main building. He shut the door, removing the dripping coat. Aidan was messing with the phones. "Anything?"

"I think I got it started."

"You think?"

"Pretty sure. If it goes into lockout mode, it's working." He stared pensively at the smartphone before looking up. "Great weather."

Taylor came in from the bunkroom. "No change. She doesn't look good, though. Maybe it's just the different light, but I swear she looks paler. Her pulse is weaker."

"Any sign of the map?"

"No. I don't get it. I looked through Jim's stuff. Other books and papers. Flora and fauna guide, even a state road atlas. Some charts for flight routes. But not the detailed topo."

"What if he had it with him by the dock?"

"Maybe planning one of our hikes or something."

Taylor looked frustrated. "It's possible. Anyway, we can't hike out of here without a map. It's suicide."

"It's working," said Aidan. "Just cycled through and locked out. It's cooking."

"Good," said Mike. "Good job. At least something's working out."

"Hey. Don't count your luck yet. Remember. It could take a week."

Mike peered in at Liz. "Hope not."

"We should get some sleep," said Taylor. "Not much else to do tonight. Head on back. I'll stay here. Maybe we can figure something out in the morning."

"I'll stay here, too," said Aidan. "I want to keep an eye on this thing."

"You sure? You'll need to sleep on...on Jim's bunk."

"Won't bother him, right?" Aidan tried for a laugh, but it was forced.

Mike made his way back to the bunkhouse. It was warm inside, the stove fire roaring. Manny and Liam were already in their beds. Manny was reading the Bible. Liam was sketching something in his notebook. Mike undressed and brushed his teeth. Liam nodded at him and turned out the light.

Lying in his bunk, Mike stared at the ceiling, firelight dancing on it. *No. We aren't going to figure anything out in the morning.* Because, he knew, there was nothing more to figure out. The map was gone. Probably incinerated. And even if they could find it…

He looked over at Liam's bunk. Over the lip of the sleeping bag, he could just make out the edge of the soccer ball tattoo on his back and shoulder, moving slightly with his breathing.

Mike was tired. Too tired, he told himself, to be scared. *Not sure about that.* He tried to block it out. Instead, he thought about his mom. He could see her face, smiling.

Where am I, mom?

Where are you?

He reached for the cross around his neck again, toying with it. He wanted to pray. But prayer was not a thing for him anymore. Used to be. Church each Sunday. When he was little, nighttime prayers with Dad and Andy—kneeling at bedtime, hands folded, eyes shut tight with belief. Apparently, it hadn't counted for much. The universe—and whoever ran it—didn't seem interested in a positive relationship. He wasn't sure how Mom could look at it differently, but somehow she did. She still held to her faith, like it was some divine quadratic formula that could solve the unsolvable, inexplicable equation—*no, make that non-equation*—that had become their family story.

*

He was five when she took him to pick out his first bike. They'd been talking about it for weeks. The plan was to go out for pancakes on the way. Dad was supposed to come too, but he got a last-minute overtime shift at the mill.

So he gave his dad a big hug, then he and Mom left. Mike scarfed down a full stack of blueberry pancakes, squirmy with excitement. He'd had a series of tricycles and scooters, but this was the real deal. He wanted a red big-boy bike with training wheels. Luckily, they found one.

When they got home, Mike unbuckled even as she was putting the car in park. He bounced, waiting for her to open the back and help him wrestle the bike onto the driveway.

"Hey! Hold on, buster! Put your helmet on!"

But Mike was already straddling the seat, testing his grip on the handlebars, the bike leaning on the training wheels. "In a second, Mommy!" He found the pedals. He wobbled toward the sidewalk. "I'm doin' it! I'm doin' it!"

She jogged to catch up and pulled him to a stop. "Put this on." She did the strap. Mike rode and Mom jogged, catching him every once in a while when he threatened to tip. They went around the block. Sitting on the front step, Mom helped him take the helmet off and ran a hand through his mop of sweaty hair.

"You did great, baby boy."

*

The rain had stopped, and there was no wind, so Mike could hear the crackle of the fire again. Occasionally, there was still thunder, but it was distant now. Miles away. And as he lay there, staring up at the flickering shadows, he realized something.

I have to get back to her.

He needed to get through this. He needed to *survive.*

Exactly the opposite of…what he'd come so close to doing. His heart pounded.

24

THE FOLLOWING MORNING was overcast, and unusually cool. The light had a different quality—the sun was nothing more than a pale eye behind featureless clouds. Mist covered the lake, and Mike watched it move in tendrils as he stood on a fallen log, peeing into the woods. He finished, padding back to the bunkhouse. Liam was doing his workout routine, the wound in his arm apparently not affecting his pushups.

Mike went inside. The cabin had begun to smell. They hadn't done any laundry since the fire, and the musk of body odor, smoke, and dirty clothes was thick in the still air. Manny was still snoring. Mike pulled on his last clean pair of underwear and his scuffed-up utility pants. Doing up his belt, he realized his body had changed.

He went into the bathroom and looked in the mirror. He was trimmer for sure—but he felt leaner and stronger. *Harder.* His hands were calloused. His feet, too. The blisters of the first day's hike had faded. His nails needed trimming. He was very dark. Not the surface burn you'd get from a weekend at the beach. No. He was tan like those older landscaping guys at the end of the summer, like the ones that did it full time, all day, every day, their skin like leather. The scar on his face had faded to a ridged line, hardly visible now with his darker complexion. Same for the other tiny cuts and scars. He smelled bad, he knew, but he didn't want to douse himself in cold water until the day warmed up a bit.

"Morning," huffed Liam, shouldering past him as he pulled off his sweat-soaked shirt. "Checking yourself out? Lookin' hot."

"Screw off." Mike went back into the main room. He threw a balled-up t-shirt at Manny, waking him up. Manny's eyes fluttered open and he stretched. "Buenos dias, cabrón." He stretched. "What time is it?"

"No idea. Get up. I'm going to get the others."

He heard the splash of water from the other room. Liam whistled. "Oh, baby, that's *fresh!*"

Manny threw Mike a look, rolling his eyes.

Over in the other building, Aidan was already up, adding water to some powdered milk for cereal. "Hey," he said.

"Anything with the phone?"

"Not yet. But it's still cranking. Something happened with Liz, though." Aidan gestured toward the other room.

He heard water splattering in the bathroom, and Taylor called out. "Is that Mike?"

"Yeah," he answered back, stepping into Liz's bunkroom. She was unchanged, if maybe a little paler. "What happened? Is she waking up?"

"Maybe," said Taylor, stepping back into the room now, toweling off. "Aidan heard her make a noise last night." He got dressed as he talked. "I came in and turned on the light, and she mumbled something. Have to assume that means she's getting better, not worse." He tucked in his t-shirt, water dripping from his hair. "If nothing else, I think it means just a kickass concussion instead of something *really* bad. But I don't know. She could wake up and not know her name."

"So you think she's really waking up?"

"Dunno. A sign of consciousness is something, though."

Taylor stepped closer to Mike. Glancing up toward the door, he grabbed his arm, pulling him out of Aidan's angle of view. His voice was a whisper. "Listen. You know as well as I do, this is gonna start falling apart. It's only a matter of time before something...I don't know what. Just, *something* happens, y'know?"

Mike nodded.

Aidan poked his head around, and Mike reflexively took a step back.

"Everything okay?"

"Yeah," muttered Taylor and Mike at the same time.

*

There was still no sign of the map. They'd scoured both cabins. They'd gone through everything. Mike looked around as they ate lunch. The kitchen was a mess; they'd definitely not kept up with Jim's standards for cleanliness. Nobody seemed to care. *As long as it won't draw the bears.*

"If we can't find it, we'd be crazy to try," Liam said, chewing on a mouthful of peanut-butter and jelly. "No trails? Terrain like this? You can't get anywhere without a topo map."

"What if the password thing doesn't work? Then what?" asked Manny.

Aidan swallowed a bite. "It'll work. It just—"

"But what if it doesn't, hombre?"

"Listen," said Taylor, putting down the rest of his sandwich. "I've thought about something." He pointed at the phone-on-phone contraption, silently working away on the counter. "Aidan says it could take up to a week to work. From what I remember on the map, Jim said it would take at least three days to hike to the trail. At least. Probably more, especially with bad weather. Well the way I see it, hiking out is really dangerous. I think we all agree on that, right?"

Everyone nodded.

"Okay. So, hear me out on this. I figure, let's wait at least three days. I mean, let's let Aidan's contraption work for three days before we send anyone out."

"Why three days?" asked Manny.

"Manny," Taylor said, "think about it. If we send anyone out, it's gonna be *at least* three days before they even have a chance of contacting anyone. And that's *if* they get a cell signal past those further ranges. Or *if* they happen to reach someone on the hiking trails at the edge of the wilderness zone. So doesn't it make sense to at least give the sat phone that long to work? It's hedging a bet, but..."

"He's right," said Mike. "Play it out, Manny. If we hike, it's gonna be you and me and Liam, right?"

Manny nodded. "That's what I figured."

Mike continued. "Okay. So let's say you, me, and Liam tromp out there. We got plenty of food and water, warm clothes, it's all good. We get a day out, doing okay. But then we get to a point where we gotta get down this ninety-foot cliff—no way around it, okay? Except we don't have climbing gear, do we? And even if we did, none of us knows how to use it. So yeah, we tie some half-assed knot and try using ropes to get down a vertical that we can't hike down. And we fall. So then we're lying there with broken legs, screaming and bleeding. Maybe a storm's coming in, too. And that's when back up here, the sat phone lights up. They come get Liz, Taylor, and Aidan. But then they'd have to search for us, too." Mike started speaking faster.

"Except they *can't* because of the storm. And by the time they can, they can't find us, 'cause we're in a deep gorge, covered in snow, and we've got no way to signal. Needles in a freakin' haystack.

And even if they do manage to find us…" His heart was pounding now, but his voice remained level. "By the time they can get a rescue crew down to us, two of us have bled to death and there's bear eating the other one. So yeah, I think we give the phone at least three days." He looked around. The others were staring at him, bewildered— except Liam, of course. Liam looked…what was it?

Amused.

"I see you've thought this through, Mike," he said, an odd smile on his face. "Kind of a worst-case scenario, don't you think?"

"We're *in* kind of a worst-case scenario, don't you think, Liam?"

Liam shook his head. "I think it could be a lot worse. But you're right. Three days. If we can't get a call through three days from now, we go. Agreed?"

Mike looked up at him, meeting his eyes, trying to read into them. *Nothing.* "Yeah. Agreed. Manny?"

Manny shrugged. "Like we got any choice?" He turned to Aidan as he gestured at the tethered phones cranking away on the counter. "Work your magic, little man."

25

T HEY SPENT THE ENTIRE AFTERNOON clearing debris. They fished the larger pieces of loose wreckage from the water using long tree branches, and dismantled the charred remains of the pier. After some trial and error, they managed to devise a makeshift skimmer using foam, sticks, and towels, and it worked pretty well at gathering up the oil slick still floating on the surface. They used buckets to scoop up the concentrated muck, then shoveled as much of the greasy beach gravel as they could into the wheelbarrow, dumping it into a hole they dug a few yards into the forest. Birds and small scavengers had already picked away most of the bloated, rotting fish. They disposed of what remained, putting it into the hole with the filthy gravel before covering the whole mess with soil. The wind and the storm had already diffused much of the ash and debris, so by the time the sun dropped below the western ridge, the shoreline looked much better. Better. Not fixed. No, there was no erasing what had happened. The burned-out fuselage of the plane remained sprawled on the rocks like the skeleton of a dead bird, its wings bent and broken.

Every fifteen minutes or so, Taylor had been jogging back up to the main cabin to check on Liz. There'd been no change, except for an occasional incoherent murmur, same as before. At one point, after coming back to the beach, Taylor motioned to Mike to come back up to the cabin with him. When Taylor opened the door to the bedroom, Mike flinched at the stench.

"Holy...did she?"

"Yeah. Can you help me?"

Ah, damn.

"Yeah."

Carefully, they lifted Liz from the cot, placing her gently in the infirmary, trying not to bump her elbows as they passed through the narrow doorframe. Taylor cleaned her up, and Mike felt his cheeks burning at the indecency of it, torn between his desire to look away and the need not to be a wuss about it, especially since Taylor was doing the dirty work, apparently unperturbed. He felt childish about the whole thing. *For God's sake, grow up.* Back in the bunkroom, Taylor pulled the soiled towel from the cot, wrapping it up in an oversized garbage bag. Mike realized, then, that Taylor must have put the garbage bag on the cot underneath the sheet in advance.

"I wouldn't have thought of that."

"I didn't either, the first time yesterday. Took some cleaning in the middle of the night."

"Wait. The first time? You mean you've been doing this right along?"

"Only twice before. She doesn't have any bladder control, obviously. But I guess she's got to be pretty well...cleared out by now. You saw the color of the urine. She's really, really dehydrated. It's been three days—well, two and a half—since the explosion. Since she had any water."

And as Taylor carefully laid out another garbage bag, then another clean sheet, Mike felt something other than the sheepishness of a moment ago. It was a rush of admiration. For kindness. For humility. After they moved Liz back into place, situating her on the cot, covering her naked body, Taylor tucked the sheet around her shoulders and brushed a stray lock of her hair back into place.

"You're doing a lot," Mike said, sitting down heavily on Jim's bunk.

Taylor shook his head, arms crossed. His voice was low. "We need to get her out of here." They both watched her breathing for a moment. Taylor looked toward the door. "Let's get back outside."

They helped the others finish the cleanup job, wearily tossing the shovels, wheelbarrow, and buckets into a pile. It hadn't been a sunny day, or a particularly warm one, but they were grimy, greasy, and hot anyway. Nobody complained about the cold water. They were all too wiped out, too exhausted to care. The bunkhouse had become like some backwoods frat house—any measure of modesty was gone. As Mike stood in front of the mirror shaving, Manny and Liam showered behind him. He could see the physical change in all of them. Everyone was ruddy and lean. Calloused, scraped, and scuffed from all the time outside. All edges and angles. Both Taylor and Liam had given up shaving, and the past couple days had resulted in an all-on beard for Liam. He looked older than ever, Mike thought. Then again, they all did.

Dinner was bland, brief, and quiet. They threw together the easiest assortment of food they could, taking what they wanted individually and piling it on their metal plates. There was more than enough food, so there was no thought of rationing. It was a far cry from the sit-down meals with Jim and Liz. *Just a couple days and things are so different.*

Midway through the meal, which had been mostly silent except for the guttural orchestra of chewing noises, Liam took a deep swig of water and set his cup down loudly on the table. "Know what? I'd *kill* any one of y'all for a cold beer right now." He leaned back, tipping his chair as he stretched his arms over his head, smiling.

It startled all of them, and a few seconds of silence passed before anyone moved again. Manny almost choked on a mouthful of food. Aidan chuckled nervously. Mike exchanged glances with Taylor and Manny before looking over at Liam, who was shaking his head, smirking.

"Good thing there's no beer, then," Mike said.

*

It was a cold night, and Liam had the fire stoked inside the circle of Adirondack chairs. The flames were bright. The shotgun was propped against one of the chairs, a small satchel of slug rounds hooked around the stock. There was something comforting about having the guns nearby, even though there was something unnerving about it, too. Mike hadn't held a gun since that day at school. He wondered where that revolver was now. Inside some evidence locker somewhere.

Evidence. Of the crime. Your crime.

Nobody talked; all of them just sat there, staring into the fire.

"I've never fired a gun," said Aidan, his voice breaking the stillness.

Liam let out a low laugh. "Little dark tonight, blondie. Ain't safe. Maybe in the morning?"

"Whatever," the smaller boy said. "That's fine."

Liam shrugged. "Aw, what the hell. Y'all wanna feel the rush? Let's do this." He stood and picked up the shotgun. "Come here."

Mike looked at Taylor, then turned to Liam. "What are you doing? Why waste the ammo?"

Liam rolled his eyes. "Calm down, Mikey. We've got plenty of slugs. You expecting a firefight? Bear invasion?"

Mike threw up his hands. *Maybe, jackass.*

Liam stood close to Aidan, showing him how to load the slug into the chamber, rambling on about the safety and the semiautomatic action, and where to point it. "Whoa there," he said as Aidan took hold of it, "keep the barrel pointed down, Jesse James."

"Like this?"

"Yeah. C'mon over here." Liam took a few strides away from the fire. Aidan followed, and Liam, huddling close, in a sort of trainer's stance, maneuvered him into the proper position. "Put your legs like...yep. Now relax your shoulders..."

Liam inched closer to Aidan, in all but an embrace as he guided his arms into position, the barrel aimed out into the lake. Aidan's face was flushed in the firelight.

"There. Now...steady it...it's gonna kick back pretty hard on y'all, okay? Get a good, solid grip. Like this." Liam put a hand over each of Aidan's, squeezing. "Okay. Three. Two. One!" The muzzle flashed with the deafening shot, and the kickback jolted Aidan back against Liam. He relaxed his grip, letting the gun drop to his side. The sound echoed across the lake. Mike's ears rang.

"Holy shit!" Aidan said breathlessly. "That was awesome. That was..." and he turned abruptly now, pulling away from Liam. His eyes darted to the others, then back at Liam, then down at the ground. Then, more quietly, "That was great."

Liam shrugged, hooking his thumbs casually into his pockets. "Like y'all could take on the world, right? Here." He took the gun from Aidan, pulling open the chamber, and double-checked to see that it was unloaded. He ambled back to the chair, set the gun down, and sat, a smug look on his face.

Aidan sat down too, excited, hunched forward on the chair. He was fidgety. He picked up a stick, poking at the edge of the fire.

Manny, seated next to Liam, threw him a sidelong glance. "You enjoy that?"

Liam nodded, eyebrows raised. "I think Aidan did. Right, bud?" He reached over, giving Aidan a light punch to the shoulder.

Abruptly, Aidan stood up. "I…I should go check the phone. And I'll check on Liz." He headed up the footpath toward the main cabin.

When Aidan was out of earshot, Mike spoke up. "What the hell, Liam?"

"What, Mike?"

"You know damn well what he's talking about," said Taylor. "The bullshit with Aidan."

"Or maybe it isn't bullshit," said Manny. "Maybe Tex here really wants the little guy."

Liam shook his head. "I just showed him how to fire a gun. I think y'all are seeing something I'm not."

Mike felt the anger rise. *If you don't wipe that grin off your face I'm gonna…* "Listen, man—" But then Aidan was coming back, and Mike stopped midsentence.

Aidan sat down heavily. "Nothin' to report. She's still out, and nothing on the phone. Still locked, still cycling."

It was quiet for a few moments, the fire crackling, an occasional loud pop and a spiral of sparks.

"Why'd you burn those files, Liam?" Taylor leaned back in the chair, legs outstretched, his hands folded behind his head. He didn't look at Liam; just kept looking up at the sky.

"No need for 'em," Liam said.

"How do you figure?"

Liam nodded. "I already said it. Those files were our *old* lives. All the stuff we're here to move past. We're here to burn that shit, aren't we?"

Mike wanted to argue with him, but Liam had a point. He had no idea what was in his file. How much more than he'd told them? How much did Liz and Jim know? What was in his psych report?

He looked around the group. *They're all glad he burned them, too. Shit. We're all grateful.*

And as if reading his mind, Liam said, "Okay. Y'all want to talk about what's in those folders? Y'all want to go there?" He leaned over, reaching for another log from the stack of firewood behind his chair, and tossed it on, sending up sparks and a new burst of bright flame. "Let's do it then. Let's keep up the therapy. We don't need Jim or Liz, do we? We can get real by ourselves, minus the two cops listenin' in." He cocked his head, and looked at Mike.

"Whaddya say, Mikey? Maybe y'all can tell us all about that little school shooting plan of yours." He glared at Mike for a second before turning to Manny. "Whaddya, say, Manuelito? Quieres decirnos toda la verdad? Eres realmente inocente? Solo perdido en los pecados de tu hermano?" Manny's eyes narrowed. And then to Taylor: "And how 'bout you, Idaho? Want to tell us the real story about your little slaughter-fest? Want to tell us how bad it really got with daddy before y'all—"

Taylor was on his feet in a second, his chest heaving. "Shut your face, Liam!" His hand was on the .500. They all staggered to their feet.

Except Liam. He hadn't even twitched. "Whoa there, tiger! Gotcha all riled up on that one, eh?"

"Liam, I swear to God…I swear to God, man." Taylor sat back down heavily, shaking. Manny, Mike, and Aidan sat down, too.

"Y'all need to cool your jets. Especially you, Taylor, but *all* y'all," Liam said, his voice level. "What y'all saw right there? Idaho goin' for that cannon he's got slung just below his righteous, volunteer firefighter's heart? That's exactly why I burned those folders." He kicked a log deeper into the fire. "Y'all *wanted* 'em burned. 'Cause with those folders burned down to ash, we can keep on pretending to be a decent bunch of guys, can't we? We can keep pretending we aren't wild animals."

When he stopped talking, the fire was the only sound. A log hissed. Mike's heart had been pounding all through Liam's tirade, and it was only starting to slow now as he looked out at the lake. It was still.

Liam spoke louder now, leaning forward in his chair. "Know what? Screw it. Y'all really so interested in those folders? Okay. Tonight's therapy session is called 'Shit About Me the Rest of Y'all Fuckers Didn't Know.' Three rules: First, it's gotta be something true. No bullshit. Second, be quick. No more twenty-minute sob stories. Cut to the damn point, Manny. Rule three: no follow-up questions. Whatever everybody has to say is what he has to say. So how 'bout it? Y'all in?"

No one said anything for about ten seconds, and Liam chuckled. "Okay. I'll start then. Here goes: I was doing my best friend's drunk girlfriend right before they fell. Right before he died. Boom. Done. Who's next? Mikey-boy? Idaho? Manuelito? Blondie?"

Mike racked his brain. *Alright, jackass, I'll play this stupid bullshit game if it'll shut you the hell—*

Manny spoke up. His voice—for the first time—sounded shaky. "I...I called the cops on him. On my brother. I was pissed and I tipped them off." He kicked a log into the fire, glaring at Liam.

Then words came tumbling out of Mike's mouth before he even finished thinking. "My truck. It wasn't an accident." They all turned to look at him. His heart was pounding, but like before, spilling this stuff felt—in some odd way—good. *Honest. Clean.*

"My old man was a drug dealer on the side. I helped him," said Taylor, breaking the silence. "Paramedics can get stuff. He started using. We both did. That's what the fight was really about."

The fire burned lower. Their faces were reddish in the glow.

"You're up, blondie," said Liam.

"I don't really have anything else." He was rocking back and forth, fidgety as all hell, Mike thought.

"Not good enough, Aidan." Liam's voice was flat and cold. "Not good enough."

"What do you want to know? You want to know whether I got one on when you were showing me the gun? Yeah. I did. Practically shot it in my pants when I pulled the trigger, okay? Good enough?"

Liam smiled at Aidan, whose eyes were brimming with tears.

"All right, screw this," said Taylor. "Liam, nobody wants to hear it. Nobody gives a shit anymore. We're lost. There's a dead guy buried over there, a woman's maybe two days from dead, and we're sittin' around this fire listening to your bullshit!" He got up abruptly, zipped his fleece, and stomped off. He shouted over his shoulder. "Keep going if you want! I'm gonna go see if Liz is still alive."

Liam shrugged, shaking his head. Aidan was crying. Manny just stared at the fire.

Mike got up and followed Taylor. He could hear Liam chuckling.

It's falling apart.

*

Nothing had changed. Liz looked the same. From time to time she would move a little, and make a quiet sound, but nothing more. The phone kept on cycling. Together they straightened things up a bit, cleaning up some of the food that was left out.

"Maybe she'll wake up tomorrow," Mike said.

"Maybe." Taylor turned to go to the bedroom, but stopped and looked back at him, leaning against the doorframe. "Mike?"

"Yeah?"

"That thing about your truck…"

"Yeah?"

"Just…" Taylor looked down at the floor, then back up at him. "I've been…I've been in that place, too."

Mike nodded, staring at a place on the floor. "Wake me up if anything changes with her."

"I will. Except...Mike?"

"What?"

"You still feel that way? Like you did?"

And a flurry of thoughts hit Mike then: *No. No, not even a little bit. What I really feel like is surviving. Getting the hell off this mountain and seeing Liz wake up and getting back to Mom and getting out of Lawson and making a fresh start somewhere really far away.*

"No. Not at all," he said, his voice quiet.

"Me neither. Maybe all this shit happening is like...changing it."

"Maybe it is."

Taylor glanced over at the smartphone, the numbers scrolling. "Seeing that phone makes me realize something."

"Huh?"

"Remember how Jim was talking about our being away from our phones and everything? I don't miss mine. Not anymore."

Mike realized he hadn't thought about his phone in a while now. He imagined all the notifications. The avalanche of meaningless, ignorant shit that had probably piled up online about him. *I don't want to see any of it.* Mike nodded. "I don't miss all that."

"I don't think I want one. I mean after. When this is over."

"Yeah. Maybe not. Goodnight." He stepped out the door.

Mike passed Aidan on the way back to the bunkhouse. The smaller boy walked quickly, his shoulders hunched. "Night, Aidan."

Aidan didn't stop or slow. He headed for the outhouse. "G'night." His voice was tight.

Manny was getting into his sleeping bag back at the bunkhouse. He must have brought a burning log in from outside, because there was good fire going in the stove. "Where's Liam?"

"He said he wanted to stay out for a while."

"Where's the shotgun?"

Manny gave him a quizzical look. "It's right there. I brought it in." He pointed to the far corner.

"Okay."

Mike brushed his teeth. On the way to his bunk, he peered out the window. He could see Liam and Aidan standing on the shore of the lake, silhouetted against the moonlit water. "Manny."

"Huh?"

"See those two out there?"

Manny shuffled over and looked over Mike's shoulder. "Yeah."

"What the hell is Liam up to?"

"I'm not sure I wanna know, amigo."

"He's playing with Aidan's head," Mike whispered.

Manny clapped him on the shoulder. "Just his head he's playing with?"

"You think?" Mike turned, looking at Manny, who was climbing into his sleeping bag.

"Dunno what to think about that cabrón, man. That was some loco shit tonight."

When Mike looked back out the window, they were gone.

26

A HALF HOUR LATER, Mike lay awake. Manny was snoring. Liam's bunk was still empty—he hadn't come back yet. The fire had burned down to a red glow in the stove. Pale, blue-gray moonlight streamed through gaps in the curtains, but the room was dark.

He spotted something sticking out from under Liam's pillow.

His notebook.

That nervous dropping feeling hit Mike's gut. He looked at Manny—still snoring—and padded over to the window. No sign of anyone.

Hurry.

He reached for the notebook but paused, making a mental note of exactly how it was positioned. Without disturbing the pillow, he pulled it gingerly, looking once more over his shoulder at Manny. Mike opened the notebook in a shaft of moonlight. The first couple pages were unremarkable—a series of scrawled reminders about the rules, a rough sketch of the camp. But then he found the entry about "authentic desires" from a couple weeks back. At first, he thought he might have been looking at a joke. But there was something about the writing—the deliberate, neat handwriting—that didn't *feel* funny at all. And Liam's list made no sense:

Cravings	*Authentic*
Monkeys and bananas	*Sharks like seals*
Cats	*Dogs*
Horseshoe Crab	*King Crab*
Stallions	*Mustangs*
Chocolate Sprinkles	*Rainbow Sprinkles*
Creamy Peanut Butter	*Crunchy Peanut Butter*
Rear-Wheel-Drive	*Four-Wheel-Drive*
Cirrus Clouds	*Cumulus Clouds*

Other parts were just as weird. At one point—when they'd been asked to write about a list of intentions for daily life—Liam filled a page with incoherent ramblings:

When the dragon reaches the cave, he grumbles for some scrambled eggs. "I never knew she felt that way about hot sauce," her husband remarked. Once upon a time in a faraway land lived an ostentatious Labrador with a very lustrous coat; sadly, he was accursed with obsessive compulsions—usually involving ladies' underwear. Yet, only the trees know how hard the wind blows. The electrician found the problem quite shocking!

It went on like that. Mike turned the pages quickly, his heart racing. It all alternated between complete nonsense and photorealistic pencil drawings. On one page, a remarkable sketch of the seaplane—on the next, a series of eloquent sentences about root vegetables.

He turned another page to reveal an explicit sex scene. Like the other drawings, incredibly detailed. A guy leaning back with a woman on her knees in front of him. For a second, Mike felt a rush of excitement.

Jesus. He blushed and flipped past it.

Toward the back was the remnant of a drawing. It was a bare foot. The rest of the page had been torn out.

Manny stirred, and Mike quickly tucked the notebook back under the pillow, carefully aligning it just as it was. He wiped the sheen of sweat from his face.

Gotta tell the others. Manny. Taylor. About Liam being out in the middle of the night. About the rambling, incoherent stuff in his notebook. About…what? He didn't know what it all meant. But it meant *something*.

He was about to wake Manny up, but he caught movement out the window.

Shit.

He crept back to his bunk, sliding back into his sleeping bag. He shut his eyes as he heard muted footsteps outside. Then the subtle creaking of the cabin door. Mike closed his eyes almost all the way, feigning sleep.

Slow down. Breathe deep.

Don't.

Move.

Liam glanced at Manny, then Mike.

Just stay still. He'll be in bed soon. Just don't move. Ride it out 'til morning.

But Liam wasn't getting ready for bed. Instead, he was being as quiet as possible, slowly, carefully putting things into a small canvas bag. *Damn.* At one point, Liam peered over his shoulder, glancing at him and Manny. Then he continued rummaging through his footlocker, quietly gathering stuff. After another minute or so, he stood up and padded to the door, stepping cautiously to avoid the squeaking floorboard near the west wall. He was barely in Mike's angle of vision now, but Mike could tell he was opening the door, turning the handle carefully. Seconds later, he was out. The door latched with just the slightest click. Outside, Mike heard a single twig snap.

What the hell are you up to?

Mike waited twenty full seconds—it felt like an eternity—then slid quietly from his sleeping bag, shivering in the chill. He quickly pulled on his sweatpants, fleece jacket, winter cap, and a thick pair of hiking socks. He hesitated, thinking about shoes, but decided to keep things quiet, and stuck to just socks. *Ground is dry enough by now.* He stepped outside. He could smell the lingering odor of the fire, and the air was thick with the sweet smell of pine and night breeze off the lake. He crouched low, sticking to the shadow of the building out of the relatively bright moonlight.

There. It was just the slightest hint of motion. Half a second later and he would have missed it. But it was definitely Liam, heading into the forest. Past the outhouse.

He's headed outside the perimeter fence.

Mike's heart was beginning to beat heavily.

Go get Taylor.

Get the gun.

No. No time.

You'll lose him.

So he followed, avoiding the gravel footpaths, his sock-clad feet silent on the mossy ground. As he passed the outhouse, he formulated a cover story just in case he ran into Liam. *I was just out taking a leak and thought I heard a noise. Christ, man. What the hell are you still doing out here?*

Then he was at the edge of the forest. He peered into darkness. Forty, maybe fifty feet away, Liam was opening the wire fence. Just the slightest squeak of hinges. Squinting, he could see now that Liam had a backpack. One of the full-size internal frame packs. They'd each been issued one, although they hadn't used it yet. Jim had said they'd be doing some multi-day hikes soon.

He took a deep breath, heart still pounding, and made his way further into the woods, stopping every few seconds to look up, watching for any sign that he'd been detected. So far there was none, and now Liam was scampering across the clearing where they buried Jim. He followed for another thirty seconds or so, moving silently from tree to tree, always keeping distance. Abruptly, Liam stopped and went rigid. Mike crouched, holding his breath, watching as Liam turned, listening. After five seconds that seemed like five minutes, he was on the move again. This time Mike hung back further. After another minute or so Liam stopped again, checked his surroundings, and turned off the path, disappearing behind a huge boulder.

Damn. Gonna lose him now.

But Mike could hear him. He must have been just a few feet off the path. There was the swish of nylon, then another sound…something he'd heard before. *A plastic tarp. Someone folding a tarp.* Liam emerged again, back on the path, looking around for just a moment before heading back toward the cabin. *Without the backpack.*

Mike knew he'd managed to stay out of sight. The problem was, he wouldn't be in his bunk when Liam got back.

Maybe he won't even notice.

Idiot. Of course he'll notice.

He was spinning his mental gears as he watched Liam walk past him, not more than twenty feet away now, oblivious. He wanted to check out what was behind the boulder, but he had to get back within a couple minutes of Liam. If he didn't, his cover story wouldn't work. So he gave him a lead, then followed, remaining as silent as possible, keeping his distance.

Shit. He's gonna latch the fence.

It's not that Mike couldn't open it—anyone could. It was meant to deter animals, not people. But those hinges squeaked. There was no choice, though. He couldn't hop it. It was eight feet tall with razor wire across the top. The only way around it was to get into the lake and wade out at least fifteen feet.

An image of Jim's bloated, rotting body bobbing in the lake.

No. That ain't happening.

Besides. How would you explain that?

"Oh, hi, Liam! I just felt like freezing my balls off, so I went out for a midnight swim!"

Crouched down again, he heard the gate swing shut, and the latch clicked. He could see Liam walk past the outhouse, headed for the cabin.

Damn.

And then it came to him.

I got up to take a leak.

But I also decided to check on Liz. So I was in the other cabin.

He watched Liam climb the steps to the bunkhouse, open the door, and go inside. Mike flipped the latch on the perimeter fence and pulled the gate open, just seven or eight inches, wincing at the noise.

Crouching low again, aware he had only seconds before Liam would realize he wasn't in his bunk, he half-sprinted, half-crawled to the far side of the kitchen, which put him out of sight. Regaining his composure, he stood up and walked around the corner of the building, headed for the bunkhouse.

The door opened. Liam was standing there, leaning on the door-frame.

Mike pretended to be startled. Which wasn't hard, because his voice was shaking for real, his heart pounding harder than ever. "Oh, shit! There you are! Scared the crap out of me, man." He climbed the steps.

Liam's voice was a whisper. "Sorry to scare ya, Mike."

"Well…yeah, I got up to take a leak. Decided to check on Liz." He did his best to look perplexed. "Wait. You're dressed. You been out by the fire pit all night?"

Liam didn't miss a beat. He pulled something from his pocket. It was a pack of Jim's cigarettes. "I nabbed these from Jim and Liz's room. I should've offered to share. I was talking with blondie for a little while until he went to bed. Then I was sittin' out there by that fire after y'all went inside, and I just decided to stay and look at the stars, smoke a couple of these." He shook the pack, nudging a cigarette out with his thumb. "Want one?"

Mike was glad for the darkness. "Nah. But I'd kill for a joint right now." He forced a quick laugh.

"Suit yourself," Liam said, shoving the pack back in his jacket.

Mike paused. "Yeah. Right. Okay. Cold out here." He reached for the door, opening it slowly.

"Forgot your shoes?" Liam asked, his voice a little different.

Mike hesitated as he swung open the door, just for half a second, before continuing inside. "Yeah," he whispered. "I really had to go."

"No headlamp?"

"Couldn't find it. Jesus. What is this, twenty questions? Let's get in there before we freeze." He ducked inside.

Liam followed him in, closing the door with a subtle click. Manny stirred, rolling over, the swish of his sleeping bag drowned out by a single loud snore before he settled back to sleep. Mike undressed in the darkness, his back to Liam. He noticed his headlamp resting right on his footlocker, in plain sight. *Shit.* "Night," he whispered, climbing into his bunk.

"Night, Mike." He heard Liam zip into his sleeping bag.

I need to talk to the others.

Now.

But he couldn't. Had to wait until morning. He couldn't act any weirder than he already had. Questions raced through his head, colliding, merging, and dividing again, until they were nothing more than a confusing jumble.

That journal.

The backpack.

Stashing supplies.

He's planning to sneak away. Why?

What's he running from?

Why has he waited this long?

Why didn't he leave tonight?

Then he thought of something else. Something big.

The map. I bet he has it.

And then, a thought so dark and cold that it made him gasp.

If this was his plan all along…does that mean?

No. That was an accident.

But Liam had been the only one out there. And now he had Jim's cigarettes, and a lighter. A *lighter*. An odd dropping sensation hit him, like he was careening downhill on a rollercoaster.

He set the fire.

He killed Jim.

Because now that made sense, too. If Liam had been planning to make a run for it all along, then it made even more sense that it wasn't an accident.

And Liz.

They'd assumed Liz had been injured trying to rescue Jim.

We got there before he could finish her?

Mike lay awake, facing the wall, his heart pounding, his dry mouth now flooding with spit. It was the same panicked fear he used to feel as a little kid after watching scary movies. When he used to be sure that the monster was lurking near his bed. His fists clenched the sleeping bag tightly around him, and he squeezed his eyes shut.

Oh God.

For a second, he thought about springing from the cot, going for the shotgun, and shouting for the others.

But Mike didn't do that.

Because he couldn't move.

Because he wasn't sure enough.

Because he might just be going crazy up here.

He lay there, trembling.

27

HE WOKE UP after what could have been two minutes or two hours of restless, fitful half-sleep. It was pitch dark in the cabin, the moonlight gone. Still before dawn. He looked at his watch. 4:06.

Shit. He hadn't meant to fall asleep.

Manny's snoring was louder than usual—alternating guttural rumbles and airy whistles. Liam was asleep, the soccer ball tattoo barely visible. Mike couldn't just lie there anymore. He was ready. He had to move. He had to see what Liam had stashed. To get proof.

Now.

He slid out of his sleeping bag for the second time that night.

Liam didn't move.

Thank you, God.

He pulled on his cap and grabbed his sweatpants and fleece jacket. He took the headlamp this time. Again, he thought of taking the shotgun. But it was too much. Too heavy. He'd make noise. He stole a final glance at Liam—still unmoving—before he pulled the door shut, easing the spring mechanism of the doorknob instead of letting it click. He stayed to the edge of the stairs—where they squeaked less—taking care to avoid the railings. He breathed only once he was down on the ground, after taking a few crouched, silent strides away from the cabin. Then he was down and moving swiftly through the darkness. There was a moment of indecision: Should he get Taylor first?

No. No time. Check that stash. See what's there.

The earth was cold enough to numb his bare feet. He hardly noticed the sting of pine needles, twigs, and pebbles on the uneven ground. Approaching the gate, he checked over his shoulder, his eyes accustomed to the darkness now. There was no sign of anyone. He shuddered in the breeze. There was fog over the lake, and tendrils of damp mist snaked through the forest around his feet. He could hear the waves lapping on the shore, and the hush of wind through the treetops.

Hurry.

Crap. The squeaky gate.

But he had to pee. So he did it on the hinges. Under any other circumstances this would be hilarious, he thought, as he strained to build pressure, aiming and soaking the lower hinge. Just in time, he realized there was no way he could hit the top hinge, which was at eye level, so he cupped his hand, gathering enough of the warm urine—*this is ridiculous*—to slosh over the top hinge.

It worked.

Great. You're a genius. Now move it.

He hurried, fully enveloped in the forest's gloom, still unwilling to flip on the headlamp. He nearly missed the hulking boulder. For a second, a fleeting doubt: *did I dream the whole thing?* But then it was there, and he circled around, nearly tripping on the plastic tarp at his feet.

He flipped on the headlamp, sure that the boulder and trees had him hidden. The tarp was wrapped around a bulky collection of stuff, folded over twice to prevent rain or groundwater from reaching the contents. He stopped himself long enough to make a mental note of its appearance—the angle, how it was arranged. Unwrapping it, he spotted the backpack. There was also the small canvas bag Liam had been packing last night. He unzipped the various compartments and side panels, rummaging through them. There was Liam's waterproof jacket, a lightweight tent, a sleeping bag, and a camping stove. Ten or twelve foil packets of dehydrated food. No sign of the journal.

A box of shotgun slugs.

And...

Bingo.

The map, rolled up in its clear waterproof case.

I don't think so, Liam. Adrenaline pulsed as he shoved the rolled-up map case into his waistband. He rearranged the backpack and reassembled the tarp, leaving everything exactly as he'd found it, minus the map. He was sweating, trembling, energy coursing through him. It was the same thing he'd felt the morning he put that gun in his gym bag, back on the day when all this started. A lifetime ago.

Satisfied he'd left no trace, he flipped off the headlamp and scrambled over the low brush, back out on the path.

And stopped.

Because a massive wolf stood no more than ten feet from him, its head cocked and snout testing the air. The thing was easily twice the size of the coyotes back home. Its gray-black fur seemed to absorb the moonlight. It issued a low, canine growl—a pitch lower than any dog he'd ever heard; so low, in fact, that he *felt* as much as heard it.

Oh Jesus.

Mike went lightheaded for a second, but then there was a fresh, warm rush of adrenaline.

He tried to remember what Jim said.

Avoid eye contact. Don't turn your back. Back away slowly.

Wait. No. That was for a bear. Or was it? Shit.

His breath came in shaky spurts as he stumbled over plants and rocks, barely keeping his footing as he backed up. He was looking at a spot of ground near the wolf's huge paw, fighting the instinct to glance up, aware now that he could smell the thing's musk and the stink of its breath. At the edge of his vision he could see its eyes, two sinister points of white, returning the pale glow of starlight. It breathed with a husky, irritated, impatient sound. Mike's tongue felt wrapped in cotton. The wolf growled again, then huffed, shifting weight on its haunches, its forelegs tense.

Oh God. He braced, sure it was about to lunge at him. His eyes darted around, looking for a branch, a rock, anything he could use to fight.

But then, with a quick intake of breath and a low, guttural snort, the wolf scampered off. Despite its size, it barely made a sound in the underbrush. Mike slumped to the ground, breathing hard, his hand on his chest. He realized now he'd been gripping the map with white knuckles, brandishing it like a weapon. He was tingling everywhere, and that nauseating, electric hum was back—the same thing he'd felt after stumbling out of his wrecked truck. His stomach heaved for a moment, but he held back the bile, burning his throat. All these involuntary responses were related, he knew, to the magnitude of the danger—to another brush with death—as was the sudden, spontaneous shudder of nervous laughter that started somewhere deep inside him, rushing upward along his spine.

The Buck of Fate.

The Wolf of Fear.

And then he remembered why he was supposed to be quiet, shaking the fog from his mind, focusing.

Liam.

It made him laugh again through his crazy tears, though, because, because...

242

Because maybe he really is a goddamned werewolf.

Above him, the sky showed pale beginnings of dawn. Mist swirled around his bare feet.

Get back.

*

He went straight to the main cabin. Aidan was asleep on a mat in the kitchen, the smartphone contraption plugged in, cranking away next to him. Mike stepped over him into the other room and crouched by Taylor's cot. He shook his shoulder, whispering. "Taylor, get up."

"Wha—what is it?" Taylor's eyes fluttered open, a confused expression wrinkling his face in the dark room. Mike's headlamp was aimed upward, illuminating the place with an odd, shaky light. "What the….?" He raised himself up on his elbows. "You smell like…did you piss yourself?"

"Shh. We need to talk. Now."

"What time is it? What the hell is going on?"

"It's late. I mean it's early. Christ. I dunno. Shut up and listen," Mike shook his head, wondering where to start. "Just listen to me." And then he showed Taylor the map, swinging the headlamp down, pointing at it. "Liam had this."

"Whaddya mean he had it?" Taylor sat up now, still half in the sleeping bag, swinging his legs off the cot.

Mike jabbed at the map with his finger, his voice a shaking whisper. "Not just this. He has a whole bag packed, stashed outside the fence. Food. Clothes. Everything. He's planning to run, Taylor." Mike looked at Liz, still motionless on the bed except for her shallow breathing. "And…and I think he did that to her."

"Hold on." Taylor shimmied out of the bag, pulling on his pants.

Aidan walked in, rubbing his eyes. "What's going on?"

243

Mike ignored him. His words spilled out in a rush. "I think he did it, man. I think he set the fire. I think he killed Jim. And I think he's planning to escape."

"Mike, this is…this is nuts. Why do you—"

Aidan's eyes were wide. "What the hell happened?"

Mike grabbed Taylor by the shoulders. "It's not nuts!" He nearly shouted it. He said it again, trying hard to speak calmly. "I'm not nuts."

"But there's no way—"

"Listen!" His words tumbled out again. He explained everything. The journal. The map. Taylor looked stunned. Aidan had an odd expression on his face.

Whatever. Aidan's weird.

Mike almost mentioned the wolf, but stopped himself.

No. They'll think you're completely whacked. And besides…a strange thought popped into his mind. Something that didn't really make sense, something irrational: There was something about the wolf…something that was just…*his* about it. He remembered the thing's eyes, its smell, the low, rumbling growl. He didn't want to share that with anyone.

"Okay, okay. Calm down," Taylor said, snapping Mike back to reality. He was up now, pulling his t-shirt on and buckling his belt. "So he's making a break for it. But that still doesn't mean he…he *killed* anyone, Mike. It doesn't make sense."

Aidan was looking out the window. His voice wavered. "But…um…hold on. Why would he wait this long? Why not leave right after the explosion?"

"It would be too suspicious if he took off right away."

Taylor nodded. "You're saying he hung around. Even helped us, so we wouldn't suspect anything? That he acted normal just to play us?"

Mike shook his head. "Nothing normal about that guy, Taylor. He put on the whole rescue act, carrying Liz out of the fire, then acted like he was stranded up here just like the rest of us."

Aidan stood up, his arms crossed. "But he got hurt doing that. His arm!"

Mike rolled his eyes. "All part of the act."

"But…where would he go?"

"Canada. He could disappear up there."

"But that's so far!" Aidan gestured out the window.

"It isn't—"

"It is if you're hiking!" Aidan looked frustrated.

Mike jabbed his thumb at the map. "It isn't that far. And it's so remote—"

Taylor shook his head. "You're right. He could do it. He could do it without passing any roads."

Mike pointed at the broad, remote *nothing* between the camp and the border. "No police checkpoints. Nothing."

"He could hunt with the gun," Taylor said.

Mike nodded. "He's in good enough shape. He could do it. He planned it. You guys remember how he was studying the map?"

The door opened in the other room. They all tensed, frozen for a second. Taylor reached for the .500, hands trembling as he loaded it as quickly as he could. Mike braced, moving toward the walls.

But it was just Manny, rubbing sleep from his eyes. "Buenos dias! Hey! Whoa!" He raised his hands, taking an involuntary step backward. "What the hell, Taylor?"

Taylor lowered the gun. "Sorry."

"Jesucristo, locos! What the hell is goin' on this morning? I wake up and nobody's in the cabin and—"

"He's gone?"

"What? Who?"

Mike grabbed Manny by the shoulder, shaking him. "Liam! Was Liam in the cabin?"

Manny shook his head. "No. No, loco, that's what I was just saying. Now what the hell is—"

But Mike was out the door, running for the cabin, the others trailing after him. He charged up the steps and threw open the door. Manny followed him in. He looked immediately to the corner where they'd left the shotgun leaning against the wall. It was gone, along with the boxes of slug rounds. Liam's bunk looked just as it might any morning, his sleeping bag strewn across it. But most of his clothes were gone.

"Manny, how long ago did you get up?"

"Few minutes, man. I was wondering why nobody was—"

"Did you see him at all?"

"No! Like I said, nobody was here!"

Mike paced around the cabin frantically for a few seconds, before he rushed back outside. "Come on."

The perimeter fence was closed. *Thanks for the courtesy*, he thought, remembering the wolf. They passed through it, jogging down the path now, to the spot. He could see the corner of the tarp before he reached the boulder. The ground was more trampled than the surrounding woods; anyone could see that now. And the tarp was empty, lying in a heap, left behind in a hurry.

"He's gone." He slumped to the ground, heavily. "Now what?" He looked up at the others. Manny and Taylor looked baffled.

But Aidan looked different.

"Aidan, what is it?" asked Mike.

The smaller boy stared at the empty tarp, shaking his head. He had tears in his eyes. "I…I can't…he…"

"Aidan, spit it out!" Taylor shouted. Aidan looked up, startled, bracing himself against the boulder.

"He said he'd..." Aidan's voice trailed off. More tears welled in his eyes.

"What? What did he say?" Mike asked.

Aidan shook his head, his expression changing to anger. "I was supposed to go with him."

Mike glanced quickly from Aidan to Taylor, then to Manny, then back at Aidan. He was about to say something, but Taylor's fist swung so fast he didn't have time. It slammed into Aidan's jaw with a deafening crack, and the smaller boy was flung back against the rock. Blood poured from his open mouth as he coughed and sputtered. Taylor was about to spring on him, about to kick him in the gut, but Manny and Mike tackled him. "Get off me! Get off!" Taylor shouted, spit flying from his mouth onto the dirt.

"You done, loco?" Manny and Mike backed off. Taylor stood, brushing dirt off. He was breathless, glaring at Aidan. "What the hell do you mean you were supposed to go with him?"

Aidan huddled against the rock, wiping blood from his chin. "I mean he was gonna take me. He...he told me I...I had nothing to go back to. That I could escape. Start over. With him."

"Oh, Jesus Christ." Mike rubbed his hands through his scalp. "Oh, Jesus. Aidan, what did you do?"

"I helped him get supplies. And... I knew he had the map..."

This time it was Manny. "Cabrón!" he shouted. "You knew he had the map, you little fag?" Aidan shielded his face. Then it was Mike and Taylor pulling Manny away, struggling, his limbs flailing, spit flying from his snarling teeth. "Lemme go. He's gonna kill us up here! Gonna kill Liz!" Manny screamed, an indecipherable roar.

"Stop it! I'm sorry!" Aidan was weeping now. "I'm sorry. I'm sorry."

Mike felt oddly calm. Somehow. Even with this madness. This chaos. Punching and kicking and bleeding and shouting all around him. He was level. He was...

In control. I'm the only one in control.

"Taylor, gimme that gun."

"What? I..."

"You lost your temper. Gimme the gun."

Taylor nodded. "Right. Maybe it's better if you take it."

Aidan watched, his eyes darting from one to the other, as Taylor unstrapped the side holster, passing it to Mike.

He slung it over his shoulder. "Everyone back to the cabin."

They walked quietly. No one talked.

Mike led.

28

THEY SAT AT THE TABLE after checking on Liz. Mike sipped from a cup of water. "We need to stay calm. If we lose our shit, things are gonna get worse. Agreed?" They all nodded. "Aidan, tell us what you know."

Aidan looked up, his eyes full of tears again. "Mike…you guys…you gotta understand, I didn't think…"

"We don't care, Aidan!" Taylor snapped. "Nobody gives a shit about your little love affair with the psychopath. Just tell us where he was going."

Aidan wiped his eyes. "Like you said. Canada. He was going to run for the border." He shook his head. "The hell with him. He's a liar," he muttered.

Taylor slammed his fist down, startling him. "What else did he take?"

"Enough," Mike said. "Both of you get out of here. Let me talk to him alone."

Taylor shook his head. "I'm not going anywhere without that gun, Mike."

Manny's eyes widened. "No way, Mike. You wanna have a little alone time with this maricón, you give us the gun."

Mike nodded. "Fine. Then take it. Just step outside and let me talk to him." He handed the weapon back to Taylor. "Try to cool off. And Taylor?"

"What?"

"Keep an eye out for Liam."

Taylor got up. "Yeah. Okay." Manny followed him outside.

Mike looked at Aidan. "Just tell me what happened. I need to know how to fix this."

Aidan covered his face with his hands. His voice was muffled. "I'm so sorry, Mike. He..." He broke down again. "I never...I'm always..."

"Breathe, bud."

Aidan wiped the tears. He took a deep breath. "Okay. Okay. Just gimme a second." He looked out the window, shaking his head. "We got along. Like, when we were on the work shift together. He'd listen to me, y'know? Like, after my story. He talked to me. It was like he understood. He was...he made me feel alright."

"I know. I get it. It was the same with me."

Aidan chuckled, a dark expression taking over. "No, Mike. I don't think it was quite the same with you."

"What?"

"He would mess with me. I know the type. It's happened before. When you're like me...sometimes other guys will just...like, tease you. Like, hint at it, then back off. One day, when he and I were paired up doing trail work, we really...I dunno, like, really bonded, you know?"

He reached for his journal, which was in his pocket. He unfolded a piece of paper stuck inside. "He made this drawing of me." It was photorealistic, incredibly skilled. Aidan in an Adirondack chair, his face lit by the firelight. "He made me feel so good when he did that.

Like someone *cared*." Aidan reached deep into his pocket. "And then…then he made this one." He unfolded another drawing.

A self-portrait. Shirtless. There was no doubt it was Liam. It was like a photo. *Including the goddamned soccer ball tattoo.* And it was missing his right foot, where it had been torn out of the notebook.

"Seriously?"

"Stupid. I know. Anyway, I caught him packing stuff up. Night before last. After we finished burying Jim. That night of the storm. You guys were all asleep. I caught him sneaking out with gear, and a box of food. He told me I could go with him if I kept my mouth shut. That I *should* go with him. That maybe it was *meant to be* that I caught him. We went for a walk, and we talked, and he…we…"

"Jesus Christ. Aidan, are you for real? Couldn't you tell he was just using you? Why didn't you tell us?"

"I swear to God I almost did, but," he looked down. "But I…I wanted to go with him. And I didn't think it would do too much harm, really. I mean, us leaving you."

"You're nuts." Mike glared at him. "I mean, don't you realize what he…that…I mean…what, you were just gonna disappear off the grid with him and live happily ever after in the Canadian wilderness?

"I can't go back home."

"What?"

"It's not like your situation, Mike. You and your mom can move to a new town. You can make a new start. My…everything is….my dad lost his job. Evan? Boyfriend back home? Over. Nobody wants me, Mike! I'm, like, toxic. So, disappearing? Yeah, that worked for me. But I didn't…I swear to God I never thought for a second he did any of this. I just…I just figured he was taking advantage of it."

"But now he left you behind."

"He played me. He cooked up all this bullshit about my coming with him so I wouldn't say anything."

"To buy him some time."

Aidan looked defeated. He stared at the table and furrowed his brow. "Yeah." And then, abruptly, he looked up. "Hold on."

Mike was startled. "What?"

"Did you see the other sat phone in that backpack?"

It was a stupid question. "No. It was lost in the fire, remember?"

"What are you talking about?" Taylor asked, walking inside. Manny stepped in, too.

Aidan glanced sheepishly at the other two, then turned back to Mike. "I realized it just now. It's been on...on the edge of my mind...like a word you can't remember but it's right there and then you—"

"Aidan, get to the goddamned point."

"Okay listen." He pointed to the sat phone. "*This* sat phone? The one we've been trying to hack? It was Liz's, right? Well, Jim carried the other one. And now I think Liam has had it all along."

Manny looked up at the ceiling. "Dios mio."

Mike and Taylor traded confused looks. "What makes you think that?"

"Think about it," said Aidan, his words tumbling out. "Jim and Liz are cops...well, like, retired cops. Whatever. It doesn't matter. My point is, this is a court-supervised thing, right? So they're up in here in the middle of freakin' nowhere with five juvenile delinquents. Five minors. Don't you think they must check in from time to time? A case officer? A judge? The local Sheriff's office? A call? Or at the very least a text message? Like, 'hey, everything's normal up here, all okay' or something like that?" He looked down at the smartphone, its display pulsing, illuminating his face with pale, bluish light. "And today makes the third full day since the explosion. Three days, guys."

Mike was nodding now. "Holy shit. Taylor, Manny. He's right. We've been thinking about this backwards. They probably would have sent someone by now if they *hadn't* heard from Jim or Liz."

"Right," Aidan continued. "Which is why I think Liam has had the other sat phone all along. I think he's been posing as Jim, sending 'okay' messages for the past few days. I mean, I don't know that for sure, but it adds up."

"If you're right, that would mean no one down there has any reason to think there's anything wrong," Taylor said.

"No," said Aidan, "and nobody's going to, as long as he has that phone."

"Hold on," said Mike. "That means he must have the password."

Taylor nodded. "Must've gotten it somehow. Maybe he watched Jim type it in. He was probably spying on him. Watching the check-in routine. I bet Jim checked in early in the morning, at the same time Liam did his workouts."

"Oh, shit," said Aidan, bringing his hand to his forehead.

"What is it?"

"Of course. *Oh shit*. That means he can also probably *change* the password for the whole account. For all phones on the account. Oh shit!"

"Hold on. What?" Mike was trying to keep up.

Aidan pointed at Liz. "So even if she wakes up and remembers the password she and Jim had, it won't work anymore."

"But won't your thing there still figure it out?"

Aidan laughed, shaking his head, glancing out the window toward the other cabin. "God, he is one smart bastard." He stood up now, pacing. "No. See, it *won't* figure it out. Because he probably keeps changing it. Of course! I bet he's already changed it again. To a low number, something the program has already tried. So it will just keep cranking, get all the way through 9999, while we sit around waiting. And then it'll just start over again at 0000, and it'll look like it never worked at all." Aidan banged his head against the wall. "I'm so damned stupid!" He made a fist, slamming it against the window frame. Spinning around, he leaned against the wall, looking up at the ceiling, exasperated.

"Yes, you are, rubio." Manny shook his head.

"We *all* are." Taylor. said, gesturing toward the mountain pass. "Meanwhile, he's gone, with no way for us to communicate, as long as he keeps changing the account password. Maybe he throws us a bone, sets it and leaves it, so we can call for help eventually."

"Well, sooner or later his battery will run out, and he won't be able to," Aidan said.

Mike nodded. "But that would still give him enough time to escape. Give him, what, a few days' lead?"

"Yeah, maybe," said Aidan. "But meanwhile, Liz..."

Manny threw up his hands. "I still don't get it."

"What?"

"Why? I mean why *do* all this?"

Mike thought back. Then it hit him. "Remember when Jim and Liz pulled him aside? They told him something, remember? He said it was something about his family."

"Yeah, right," said Manny. "He was acting weird after that."

There was frustration in Taylor's voice. "It had to be something big. To set him off like that?"

"Like what?"

"Who knows? Something really—"

They looked around at each other. Mike stood up. "It doesn't matter. We need that phone."

"But he's got the gun—"

Mike went outside. The rest followed. He spun around, shielding his eyes from the sun, looking up at the distant passes. "No. We don't need to follow him."

"Why?" asked Taylor. "We need that phone, Mike."

Mike pulled the map from his waistband. "But he needs *this*. He'll come back for it as soon as he realizes he doesn't have it."

"What if he doesn't?"

"He will. He has to." And then, after a few deep, rushed breaths, he shouted, as loudly as his voice would go. "You need the damned map!" The commotion sent birds scattering, but then a deep silence settled quickly back over the forest. "He has to come back," he repeated, more quietly now, looking out at the dense woods surrounding them. "Let's be ready for him."

Around them, the forest loomed.

29

MANNY, TAYLOR, AND MIKE were bringing in firewood when they heard Aidan shout through the screened window of the main cabin. "She's awake!"

All three sprinted back. Aidan was holding Liz's hand. Her eyes were open, moving lazily around the room. Taylor snapped into action. "Water. Mike, get her water." He knelt down next to her, putting his face close to hers. "Liz. It's Taylor. Can you hear me?"

Her eyes darted directly to him, and then, hesitantly, she turned her head slowly, wincing. They heard a sound like someone cracking knuckles, and she blinked hard, her body seeming to shudder a few times, her knees and feet moving under the blanket. Her eyelids fluttered, then her mouth opened just a bit, her tongue sliding out over chapped, cracked lips. Mike knelt on the other side with the water, and her eyes went wide when she saw the bottle approaching. She lifted her chin eagerly, her arms straining to reach for it. Mike held the straw to her lips, and she drank eagerly, most of it spilling.

"Slow. Slow, Liz." Taylor said, nodding and smiling, tears at the corners of his eyes. "Mike, she needs salt. We gotta get her blood sugar back up. Look for some packets of rehydrating solution.

They're orange." Mike came back with a few. Taylor tore one open, poured it into the bottle, then shook it vigorously. She drank more, most of the liquid again spilling down her chin.

Working together, they were able to help her sit up, propped with more pillows. She couldn't speak for the first ten minutes, and showed no interest in anything but sipping slowly. Finally, she spoke. It was barely audible.

"J…Jim."

The four boys glanced around the room at each other.

"He's not…" began Taylor.

"Fire," she managed. "The plane."

Taylor was nodding, his brow crumpled in frustration. He looked to Mike, desperate.

No sense bullshitting here. "Liz. Jim…Jim didn't survive the fire," Mike said, his voice as gentle as he could make it. "It's been a few days now, and…" An odd expression came over her face, and it occurred to Mike that she was crying, but without any tears.

She's too dehydrated to make tears.

She reached for Mike's hand now, squeezing it with surprising strength, and turned her head. "Liam…"

They traded glances again. "He's alive, Liz, but…" Her eyes darted around nervously now, her entire body beginning to tremble.

"Where?" she managed, clearly agitated.

"He's run off. He…" Mike looked up at Taylor, who was shaking his head. "Don't worry about that now, Liz. You're safe here. Just drink right now."

She inhaled deeply, clearly in pain, and tried to shuffle more upright. They helped her. She drank more, eager but with surprising restraint, Mike thought. She seemed to grow stronger by the minute. After closing her eyes for a few seconds, she opened them again, looking at the gun in its holster, strapped around Taylor. "My

258

gun..." And then she looked less at ease, glancing around at them, clearly registering more by the second. "The phone."

"Shhh," said Taylor, feeding her more of the water, her eyes darting around the room now. "We'll explain everything to you. We're in a little trouble, Liz, but..." She spit out the straw, coughing, sputtering. "Hold on! Hold on!" Taylor said. "Slow down."

"Jim?" she asked again, her voice fading, eyes closing.

"Jim's not here right now, Liz. Keep drinking." He lifted the straw.

"Drinking..." she said, her voice barely audible, before working the straw between her lips again.

Aidan stood at the foot of the bed. "Liz!" he said, his voice loud and abrupt enough to open her eyes. "Liz, what's the code? The code for the sat phone? We need to call for help!"

She looked up at him drowsily, her brow furrowed again, squinting. "Call. The sat phone."

"Yeah. The sat phone. We need the code for it, Liz. We need to try the—"

"6804," she whispered.

Aidan ducked away immediately, reaching for the sat phone on Jim's bunk.

"But why would it work if he's been changing—" Mike began asking.

"Because maybe he didn't figure that out." Aidan began messing around with the setup, then disconnected the cords. He punched the code into the sat phone, a fine sheen of sweat glistening on his excited face, still bloody from Taylor's punch. But it quickly faded to disappointment, and he looked up, shaking his head, before reconnecting the cords and starting the sequence back up. "We need the other sat phone or we're screwed," he muttered. "Liam will just keep using it to change the account password until he runs out of batteries. That could be a long time."

"But where's Jim?" Liz asked again, looking around, eventually looking right at Mike. "Mike, where is he?"

"He's dead, Liz. Jim is dead." He got hard stares from the others, but he shook them off. "He died in the fire. His ring…it's on your necklace." She watched his hand as he reached for the cross on his own. Then, hesitating, she looked down, and held the ring. Her eyes pooled with tears.

"We think Liam did it," Aidan said, his voice shaky, the words rushing out. "He took off with the gun. And we think he's been using Jim's phone to send okay messages. If so, he took off with that, too. And we're trying this thing here that I rigged up with your phone to try to cycle through the codes, but now we know that if he has that other phone, that's not gonna work and—"

"Aidan!" Mike snapped, his voice loud enough to jolt him to a stop. Liz, looking more confused than ever, turned to look at him. "She's barely conscious."

Liz shook her head. "No, I'm…we…" Her eyes rolled back.

"Just drink," said Taylor, holding the straw to her lips again. She sipped, then passed out again.

30

LIZ NEEDED TO SEE THE GRAVE. She asked to go as soon as she woke up again, and despite her condition, no one could argue with her. They wanted to ask her questions about what happened. About what she'd told Liam. But Mike told them to wait. *This first.* She couldn't walk, so Manny and Mike took turns carrying her. She'd lost so much weight, it was almost effortless. *Like carrying a little kid.* Taylor walked ahead with the .500 in hand, pointed low but ready, with the safety off. He and the others scanned the perimeter, half-expecting Liam to emerge with the shotgun. The map, rolled up tightly in its waterproof case, was tucked into the waistband of Mike's pants, hidden under his shirt.

They plodded along slowly, no one saying a word. The cloudy sky cast a flat, gray light over the forest that muted the colors and made everything look tired. Even the usual chorus of birds and insects seemed to shy away. As they passed through the perimeter fence and up the gentle slope to the grassy clearing, the first drops of cool, misty rain began to fall. Liz was unfazed by it, staring at the makeshift cross that leaned haphazardly in the freshly turned earth. The smallest of weeds had begun sprouting in the fecund dirt, their tiny green stems and leaves trembling slightly under the weight of raindrops. As they approached, Mike felt Liz's body stiffen, her previously weak grip on his shoulder tightening until it hurt.

"Put me down," she whispered.

Mike set her down gently. They all stood back, watching her, unsure of what to do, unsure even of how close to stand. She sat unmoving at first, then willed herself forward, crawling on hands and knees toward the cross. Manny took off his jacket and placed it over her, but she pushed it away, and when she turned, they could see that her face was soaked from tears as much as from the rain, her hair hanging down in ragged, twisted clumps, becoming plastered to her neck and back. The loose dirt was turning to mud, and the oval-shaped mound became a bleeding scab on the grassy forest floor, little rivulets of brown water trickling down the sides. She buried her hands in it, her fists clenching, white-knuckled. And then she collapsed on it, the side of her face in the mud, weeping openly now. She tore the ring from her neck, the fine chain drawing blood before it snapped. She gripped it in a white-knuckle fist, and began to pound the pile of dirt, her chest heaving, her emaciated form skeletal under soaked clothes. It was a horrific sight, a woman writhing in the mud.

That's her dead husband.

Her dead son's dead father.

It hit Mike with the blunt force of a locomotive, his face twisting in agony as he fell to his knees. This is what his mother has suffered.

Dead son.

Dead husband.

And you almost took away everything else.

You almost robbed her of her only other baby.

You monster.

Mike wept, pushing the others away as they tried to lift him, unable to speak, unable to explain, unable, in fact, to move. He rolled over, lying flat on his back, shuddering and cold, the wet mud seeping into his pants and collar as he looked up at the forest canopy, eyes squinting, the rain blurring his vision until everything was a twisting gray and green kaleidoscope.

It was Liz that reached for his hand, and he looked up to see her mud-soaked face, all tears and rain and wet hair, sharing in his pain. And it was Liz who pulled *him* to *her*, Liz who held his head in her lap, Liz who brushed the hair from his eyes. The others stood by, still watching for the silent wolf in the woods, and let the two of them weep together as the rain fell harder.

When it was time to go, Mike picked Liz up, brushing off Manny's offer of help, and carried her all the way. He had no thoughts of Liam during the slow, messy walk, his boots sloshing through the black-brown mud.

*

No one spoke for an hour. Liz was able to bathe—they took the time to heat some water—and dress herself. She managed to drink some broth and more rehydration solution, and even eat some solid food, before passing out in her cot again. Mike sat out on the front porch in the rain, holding his head, his mind spinning: his brother, his mother, Liz, Liam, Aidan, the wolf, the map, Jim, the explosion. He sat out there for almost a half hour before heading to the bunk-room to take a shower. When he got back to the main cabin, Manny handed him a steaming cup of coffee.

"Fuerza, hermano. Strength."

"Thanks."

"You're a good man, Miguel. You got patience like my abuela."

They spent the rest of the morning fortifying their position. They moved all their stuff from the bunkhouse to the main building, forming a protective perimeter around Liz and the map. Taylor kept the gun loaded. Mike hid the map under Liz's mattress. They discussed it all in hushed voices, glancing nervously at the windows, aware that Liam could be anywhere. They all agreed on one thing: The map was the only hand they had to play. It was the only reason Liam would come back, and therefore their only chance to get the other phone.

Mike carried a final duffel bag across the wet ground, headed for the kitchen. Manny caught up to him, loaded down with his own stuff. They both wore their waterproof jackets, and the rain made a loud pattering sound on the hoods.

"Mike," Manny said, looking around, scanning the perimeter.

"Huh?"

His voice was hushed. "I seriously think that dude might try to take us all out."

Mike stopped, as much out of surprise as anything.

Manny continued: "I mean, think about it. You pull all the loco shit he's done, and then you realize all the rest of us have figured it out, and what do you do? I mean, really, man, that pendejo is trying to *disappear*, right? Run for the border and all?"

"I guess, yeah," Mike replied, both of them quickening the pace as the rain fell harder.

"Then really, man, it makes sense." Manny looked genuinely frightened. "I'm serioso, man. Not kidding. Take us all out, nobody calls nobody, no reports, and he's got what, like, a week, maybe even two weeks of lead time before anybody knows anything's happened!"

Mike heaved open the door, holding it for Manny as they maneuvered the hefty duffel bags in. "Shit, man. I dunno."

He stopped abruptly, noticing Liz. She was upright in the bed now, and Aidan was spoon-feeding her some broth. "Hey, Liz."

"Hey," she said with a weak smile. But the smile faded quickly. "Taylor explained everything to me." She looked around at all of them as she took another sip of broth, and Mike was floored by the remarkable change in her strength. Her color had returned, and while she was still emaciated, there was a vigor and energy he hadn't expected. It was like her collapse at the grave had flushed out the weakness.

"Liz, the night before the fire. What did you and Jim tell him?"

She nodded. "You remember his story, right? When his friend Elliot fell down that embankment, along with that girl?"

Mike looked quickly around at the others. He remembered what Liam said around the fire the other night. *"I was doing my best friend's drunk girlfriend right before they fell. Right before he died."*

Liz continued. "We got a call from the detective covering that case. The girl—Alicia—she came out of the coma. She hadn't spoken yet, but it was a big sign of progress. The detective asked us to tell Liam and gauge his reaction. They were still piecing it together, but based on some forensics, it seemed to them there was more to the story." They all processed this for a moment. "Well, I think it's clear now that's the case. Obviously, we can't underestimate Liam at this point. Maybe you guys could tell. I've had my eye on him from—" Abruptly, she began coughing, her face contorted in a grimace of pain. It took her several seconds to regain her composure. She wiped some spittle from her chin. "His case concerned me from the beginning. But Jim pushed. Wanted to work with him. After all, he cleared the psych evaluation, just like you guys, so I decided to give it some time. But my gut was right."

Mike sat down on the bed. "Do you remember what happened that morning? The explosion?"

She shook her head. "Like I told Taylor, things are still fuzzy. I do remember Jim went out for his usual early morning cigarette." She paused, eating a spoonful of broth. "We were up extra early, about to review Liam's case file. We'd been arguing about it the night before. Based on the way he reacted when we told him the news, I wanted to have him extracted. Jim said I was reading too much into it. Assuming too much. We agreed to get some sleep and look at it with clear heads in the morning. Anyway, I was just getting dressed when it happened. When I ran out, Liam was there. He was shouting something about Jim, pointing at the burning plane. We ran down to the pier together, but by then it was all on fire. Everything. The last thing I remember is—is Liam by my side as we tried to get closer to the plane." She rubbed her head, wincing as her hand traced the lump and the scar. "I think it's safe to assume he did this to me."

Mike nodded. "Liz, what I don't get is…how did he get placed in this program?"

Liz shook her head. "He's hyper intelligent, Mike. One thing you didn't know about him is that he had a perfect score on the SAT. *Perfect*. And his early school records? Off the charts IQ. Anyway, I think we all see how sharp he is now. Those screening evals are good…they're usually failsafe. Not always, though. A true psychopath—which is what I now believe Liam is, and I say that clinically—would be motivated to outsmart and fool the screening mechanisms. And Liam is smart enough that he would have researched those techniques. Psychopaths make excellent liars. Anyway, when it comes to this program, we have to rely on the data we're given. Usually it's good. So, either Liam played the system really well, or somebody screwed up somewhere, or both. In some ways, obviously, Jim and I got it wrong. There were a few things in his case file that have me thinking now. He obviously has a reason to run."

"You think he tried specifically to get placed in this program? Close to the Canadian border?" asked Aidan.

Liz looked out the window, absently. "Maybe. He's smart enough. Or maybe he just saw the opportunity once he got here."

"What if he doesn't come back?" Manny asked.

"He will." Mike said, looking at Liz. "He has to, right? You can't cross this terrain without a map. He said so himself. We're close to the border, but we're not that close. And he needs to know how to avoid trails and roads."

Liz nodded. "I agree. He needs the map. And besides, he knows he's got leverage—he knows we need the phone."

Manny's tone was insistent. "But guys, what if he doesn't? What if he just decides to take off and chance it without a map? I mean it's possible, right?"

"It's possible, but—"

And then three rapid shotgun blasts sent them all ducking for cover. Mike found himself on the floor next to Taylor and Aidan. Manny pulled Liz from the cot, and they tumbled to the floor on the other side. Taylor clicked off the safety.

"No. It's all right. Put the safety back on. Those were far away," Liz said between coughs.

"But not that far—"

"Maybe just outside the fence—"

"In the forest—"

"What's he—"

"It was a signal," Liz said, heaving herself back up on the cot with Manny's help. "He wants to negotiate."

*

Taylor stayed back with Liz, the gun, and the map, while Mike, Manny, and Aidan fanned out, looking for Liam—or for something. There was no sign of him, but that wasn't a surprise, since Liz was sure the shotgun blasts had been at least a half mile away—definitely outside the perimeter fence. Just past the outhouse, Mike spotted it: A torn out sheet of Liam's notebook was rolled up, sitting on a rock that had been placed conspicuously in the middle of the path, with a miniature pyramid of pebbles acting as a paperweight. There was no way anyone could miss it.

"What the hell?" said Manny, as Mike picked up the paper and unrolled it, reading aloud:

"Even trade. Sat phone for map. Just Mike. <u>No one else</u>. Mountain pass we went to on the first hike. Seven P.M. sharp. Don't be early or late. I mean it. No one else. No gun."

He let the paper drop to his side and looked up at the others. "Just me."

"Why?" asked Aidan.

"Doesn't want to be outnumbered," said Mike, whispering. "And he knows I took the map."

"We can't send you up there alone!" Manny said, pointing up at the pass.

"I think we have to."

"You trust that cabrón, Mike?"

Like I trust a freakin' wolf.

"Of course not. But I think he'll do like he says. As long as he feels like he's in control. Come on. Let's show this to Liz and Taylor. It's almost four o'clock now. Time is tight." They started walking, and Mike looked up at the distant western pass, high above them.

31

MIKE CLIMBED THE ROUGH-HEWN PATH, his muscled legs working like pistons, his steps sure and even as he clambered over the rocky, uneven ground.

It was as if the whole ordeal—from the moment they arrested him at school—had been preparing him for this. If there were ever going to be a reason for it all happening, this was it. It didn't make any sense, but it did.

Because it has to be me.

It had to be him, and he had to do it.

For Liz. For Jim. For Taylor, and Manny. For Aidan.

But it was more than that.

It was for Dad. Dad always did what was right.

It was for Andy.

It was for Mom.

It was even for Eric.

But more than anything else, Mike knew it was for himself.

This is why.

He didn't feel hunted. No. *I'm the hunter now, you bastard.*

Beyond where they'd gotten to with the trail work, the way wasn't clearly marked. But he recalled enough from memory—after all, they'd done this a few times as a group. Besides, there was only one approach to the pass that made any sense. And if there were any doubt, it was erased by Liam's boot prints, fresh and clearly visible in the mud. He couldn't have been too far ahead of Mike, which made sense if he'd begun his climb around the time of the shotgun blasts. *Smart,* he thought. *Gave himself plenty of distance before signaling us.*

Mike carried little: just a light day pack loaded with his rain jacket and wool cap, some water, a compass, his knife, his headlamp, and some emergency rations. And, of course, the map, tucked securely into the main compartment. They'd argued about whether he should go at all. They'd argued about the gun. Taylor definitely wanted him to take it; Manny agreed. But both Liz and Aidan said no. Liz had been the most adamant. She believed that if Liam were to see him with the gun, things could get violent quickly. *A gamble.* That's what she'd said. *Some gamble,* Mike thought now. *Like playing chicken with a freight train. With your shoelaces tied together. Oh, yeah—and there's a psychopathic cowboy driving the train.*

But the longer they'd gone back and forth, the more it became clear that there was no real alternative. Taylor and Manny suggested they just wait a few days until he gave up and ran out of batteries on the phone. When he did, he wouldn't be able to send "all okay" messages, which would mean the authorities would begin trying to contact them. Or, even if they didn't, Liam wouldn't be able to change the password anymore, so it would only be a matter of waiting for Aidan's contraption. Now that Liz had come out of the coma, they could wait it out.

"True," she'd said. "But we need to give him the map."

They'd immediately protested—all of them. "Why should we?" Mike asked.

She'd explained it all in her quiet, firm voice.

"We get him the map, he leaves. That's what he wants, right?"

"Yeah, but—"

"No. Listen. If we don't, things could get out of hand. It would escalate the situation."

"So lemme get this straight," said Taylor. "You're saying we *want* to give him the map, even if he won't turn over the phone?"

"That's exactly what I'm saying."

"It's dangerous for Mike."

"It's more dangerous if we don't. Trust me on this, guys. This kind of person...he won't back down."

"So we just let him get away?" Manny asked, shaking his head.

Liz nodded. "Once we can call, it'll be one eighteen-year-old kid against the Montana State Police, the Border Patrol, the Royal Canadian Mounted Police, the National Park Service, local law enforcement, maybe even the FBI. It's not like crossing into Canada is going to solve his problems. Not to mention, once they see the size of the reward, every backwoods nut-job from here to Alaska will be tracking him like a bloodhound."

"What reward?" Manny had asked.

"The one I'm going to post." Her voice had been cold.

In the end, they'd decided she was right. For now, only two things mattered. First, taking Liam out of the equation. And second—if possible—getting the phone. Mike said it clearly enough himself: It was worth it either way. Even if Liam wouldn't give up the phone, he'd leave them alone and they'd be rescued soon enough. Of course, they all knew the part he didn't say out loud.

It's worth it either way...unless things go really wrong.

Now, as he hiked, Mike felt powerful, his legs and core and heart and lungs working in concert, like a machine, propelling him upward. He was drenched in sweat, despite the overcast sky and chilly air. He glanced at his watch: 6:10. He paused, chugging some water, and looked downhill behind him. Far below, the camp was nestled in its narrow hollow, but there was no movement. *They're all inside. Manny's freaking out, probably talking nonstop. Taylor is pacing, wondering if I'm gonna come back alive. Alive and with the phone. Aidan's staring at the damned screen. And Liz…she's just…she's trying to think past this. About her life without Jim.*

And then there's me. Huffing it up to the wolf's den.

Above him, off to the west, the sky was darker, and he knew it could mean another thunderstorm. *Mountain pass in a lightning storm. Great plan, Liam.* There was no thunder, though, and he hoped the weather would hold off. He shoved the water bottle back into his pack and turned upward, moving quickly. At the steeper parts, he scrambled on all fours, his calloused hands gripping rocks and branches, pulling, pushing upward. His chest was heaving, the aerobic machine humming. The evening light was a gray haze, making everything dim and dreary. A breeze cooled his hair, carrying the scent of damp pine. It reminded him of the Adirondacks back home. A couple years ago, he and Mom had taken Andrew on a climb.

*

"You can do it, buddy!" Mike was twenty feet ahead of Andrew. They were on one of the toughest stretches of the path up Mt. Haystack. Mike was excited to be climbing this one with him—it had one of the best views once you broke the tree line, and Andrew had never seen it. He was seven. It was a push to convince Mom to let them go on ahead alone, but she finally relented. She was probably a half hour back, plodding along at her slow pace, stopping to look at flowers and tree bark. It always drove Mike nuts. He missed hiking with Dad. Dad went fast.

He missed everything with Dad. He'd been dead a year and a half.

Andrew stopped, calling up in a high, cranky voice. "I'm tired, Mikey! I need a break!" His brown hair was plastered over his forehead, his white undershirt a mess of mud and gravel from where he fell a half hour ago. He scraped his knee, and a smudge of blood had mixed with the dirt and smeared down his leg.

"Come on. We just had a break." Mike stopped on a boulder, one leg bracing his weight as he looked downhill.

"You sound like Dad!" Andrew said, winded.

The path they were climbing dropped down steeply behind them, at least thirty degrees. There hadn't been a switchback for a while now. That's what Dad had always said about these mountains. "Adirondack trails aren't like out west," he'd said on a trip a few years back. "No way. These are old logging trails that follow streambeds, and they're pretty merciless. Mountains may not be as high here, but the hiking's probably tougher. I'll take you to Rocky Mountain National Park and you'll see what I'm say-ing! Compared to these, those trails are like four lane highways."

"There's a rock in my boot," Andrew said, interrupting the memory.

"Come on!"

"Seriously, Mike!" Andrew sat down heavily, dropping the pack on the rock next to him. He unlaced and wrenched the boot off his foot. Steam rose from it. He turned it over, and a pebble dropped out. "There you are, you little piece of shit."

Mike laughed. He loved when Andrew swore. He only did it around Mike, and the words always sounded funny in his little brother's high-pitched voice. "Feel better? Here." Mike tossed him a water bottle.

"Are we almost there?" Andrew asked, squinting up at the path ahead.

"Almost. This is the hardest part. I'd say ten minutes 'til we hit the tree line. Then it really opens up. You'll feel like a new man."

"I'm trying to go fast," Andrew said, re-tying his boot. "As fast as you."

Mike smiled. "You're an animal. You're a mountain goat! Okay, ready? You go ahead and set the pace. I'll follow."

*

He savored the memory, taking a breather before he kept going on a particularly steep section. *Not too many switchbacks on this trail either, Dad.* But then again, this wasn't really a trail, was it? He was breaking past the tree line now; he could tell from the stunted growth of the pines and spruce around him. Low shrubs and mossy lichen coated the sloped ground. Another glance at the watch told him it was just past six-thirty.

Damn. This is gonna be tight. He adjusted the lumbar strap on his backpack and took another swig of water. His temples were throbbing. He reached in the side pocket and grabbed a handful of trail mix, stuffing his mouth and downing it as soon as he could chew it. Almost instantly, he felt the surge of energy from the chocolate. Zipping the pocket closed, he brushed his hands on his shorts and got moving again.

You're a mountain goat!

The low-growth trees eventually gave way to scraggly shrubs, and soon he was hiking on bare rock. The clouds were low and close, and he got the sense that he was climbing into them. The breeze had picked up now without the cover of trees. He figured he had about another ten minutes to the pass. If Liam was up there now, Mike couldn't see him. But that worked both ways: Liam wouldn't be able to see him, either. The angle and steepness of it would keep him out of sight. In fact, looking back down toward the camp, Mike realized that was true for the entire hike up. Maybe he could have brought backup, after all; Liam probably wouldn't have been able to tell. As he got closer to the top, the way meandered between and around a number of large boulders. Part of him expected to turn a corner around one of them and walk smack into Liam.

And the shotgun.

He stopped, breathing hard, to take a sip of water. When he did, he became acutely aware of the drop in temperature. The breeze wasn't a breeze anymore—it was wind. He looked around and listened. The sky was dark gray now, but there was still no thunder. Squatting down, he unzipped his backpack and pulled out the waterproof shell and his wool cap. He shouldered the pack and began climbing again. He could see the edge of the pass looming above him. The final section was steep—he remembered having to scramble on all fours, making switchbacks in several places. But it wasn't far. Maybe a tenth of a mile, tops. The watch told him six fifty-two.

Just a few more minutes. Go. Move!

He worked hard, blocking out thoughts of everything that could happen, trying to focus on just the climbing. Just the pure movement of it. Pushing with his legs, exchanging carbon dioxide for oxygen. His calves and quads burned.

Breathe. Push.

And then he was there. It took a second to acclimate to the level ground. There was a flat space of perhaps forty feet before it dropped off steeply on the other side. His ears were plugged, and he moved his jaw to clear them. The wind was buffeting him now, coming across strong from the west. The view opened up, the massive ridges and snow-capped peaks still visible for miles despite the growing darkness. Far off, the faintest hint of a sunset painted the clouds with pale washes of orange and red. *God, that's beautiful.* Granite cliffs rose steeply on either side of him, the higher stretches of this ridgeline looming hundreds of feet above. He looked all around. No Liam.

Where are you, you bastard?

And then, from somewhere near him: "Y'all got here right on time."

32

MIKE SPUN, CROUCHING, arms outstretched, bracing himself for whatever might come at him. Liam stepped out from behind a boulder. Surprisingly, the gun was strapped to his backpack, which Liam was unbuckling and lowering to the ground. "Bitch of a climb, eh? Need some water?" He held out his water bottle.

"I'm here for the phone. I have the map."

"I was hoping we could chat first." Liam unscrewed the cap and took a sip. "About our options."

"Don't wanna chat, Liam." He thought about Liz's advice: *'He's going to try to manipulate you. To bond. He'll be persuasive and reasonable, at least at first. Don't let him get to you.'* A strong gust of wind buffeted both of them, and they shielded their eyes until it passed. "Just give me the phone and I'll give you the map, like you said."

Liam's voice was louder now, raised over the increasing wind. "Y'all are the smartest of all of 'em, Mike. That's why I just wanted you to come up here. Not Taylor with the gun, or Manny and his drama. Or even the little blond fag." He chuckled. "Although he's kind of cute in his own way, eh?"

"Liam. The phone."

"Get to that in a second. First—"

"Give me the phone."

"Calm down! Just take a breather, Mike. Listen to me. I want you to consider something."

'Don't let him get to you.' Mike felt his pulse rising. "What?"

"I want you to come with me."

Mike looked over at Liam's oversized pack. The shotgun. "You really think you'll get away with it, don't you?"

"I'm gonna disappear, Mike. Come with me. Start over. Isn't that what Liz said? That we came up here to make a fresh start? What do you have to go back to, anyway?"

"Is this the line you used with Aidan?"

"Come on. It was bullshit with Aidan. But I mean it with you."

"I'm going back, Liam. To my mom. To finish school. To have a life."

Liam smirked, shaking his head. "Y'all know you're always just gonna be the kid that brought a gun to school."

"No, I'm not."

Liam smiled more broadly. "Yes, you are. That's gonna follow you forever. Don't you get it, Mike? What college will take you? What company will hire you? This is a chance, hermano. To get off the grid. To run. Canada's less than a week's hike from here. Maybe less with the two of us moving fast, together. I'm gonna get up there and then I'm gonna disappear. People do it all the time. You know the backcountry. I could use you. I have enough gear."

'I could use you.' It struck him. *He's scared.*

"I'm going home when this is over."

But you're not, really, are you? Home is over. Home is dead. And for a moment, despite himself, he envisioned running. Disappearing. Leaving it all behind. Everything. Everyone. *Even mom.* The thought wrenched his gut.

278

Jesus, no.

"We're really so alike, Mike. We both lost our dads. We're both survivors. We're the strongest ones. But we go back to the world, and we're nobodies. We're has-beens. You know it. We're the same."

"We're nothing alike! *Nothing!* You killed Jim."

Liam rubbed the stock of the shotgun. "It was a fire, Mike."

"A fire you started."

"Prove it."

"I don't have to *prove* it! Just tell me the truth!"

Liam nodded, running his finger along the barrel of the gun. "Okay. Yeah, I set the fire. It was to set the stage, Mike."

"Set the stage? For what?"

"To get away. Look. I didn't *try* to kill him, but he got in the way."

Mike's voice was low. "He caught you."

Liam nodded. "Red handed, so to speak. Had to light it up a little ahead of schedule."

"And Liz…"

"Liz was an accident. Collateral damage."

Another crack of thunder. The lightning was close now. Tears were on Mike's cheeks, and his voice wavered. He felt a sudden urge to piss. "They told you that girl was coming out of a coma."

"Yeah. Kind of a problem there."

"That's what this is about, isn't it? Your friend didn't fall off that cliff, did he?"

"Man, you wanna know it all! No, Mike. He didn't fall."

"You pushed him."

"He caught me with his girlfriend."

Mike felt dizzy. "Oh my God. You said she was drunk. Almost passed out."

Liam shook his head, a grotesque smirk forming. "I told you guys I'd been getting with her! Well, we were about to, right out there in the snow. That's when Elliot came outside and found us. It was real bad timing on his part."

"She was drunk! You were gonna…"

"Y'all done preaching at me?"

"And your friend caught you. So you killed him."

"I did. But this was not entirely intentional."

"And she saw you do it. So then you pushed her too."

"Man, I don't know what she saw. She was so out of it. But I couldn't risk it. Look, amigo. There was a good chance she'd never come out of that coma. But now she did, and if she remembers, it's over. So I'll be long gone by then."

"You're…evil."

Liam chuckled. "Evil. Getting mighty dramatic, compadre. Look, Mike, I still like you. We're brothers, in a way. See, you're a killer, too. Oh, you might not have actually killed that kid, but if there were no one there to stop you, you would've. Y'all would've kicked his brains in with those steel-toed boots. Y'all are no different."

"Give me the phone!" Mike's teeth were clenched, his hands balling into fists.

Liam's eyes narrowed. "Where's the map, Mikey?"

Mike reached back, patting his backpack. "Here."

"It's a trade, then."

"I want the phone unlocked."

Liam cocked his head, and put his finger to his temple, pretending to think. "That's not happening. I'm gonna get some distance before y'all call out the Texas Rangers on me. Don't worry. You know blondie's little looping cell-phone hacking deal will crack it once I stop changing the code."

"That could be another week, Liam! Liz could still be in danger! Who knows what the hell you did to her head!"

"Bullshit. I've been watching y'all. She's fine. If she was well enough to visit Jim's grave, she'll make it."

"I saw the crap you wrote in your notebook. Oh yeah. I read it. Monkeys and sharks and all that shit! I knew you were weird. Had no idea you were insane. Now give me the phone!"

"Cool your jets, Michael." Liam walked slowly toward the backpack. Mike was trembling now, watching every move. There was an instantaneous, dizzying rush of adrenaline coursing through him as he saw Liam reach for the shotgun. For half a second, he considered turning to run, but there wasn't time. Liam had the heavy weapon shouldered and pointed at him in an instant. "Now, gimme the map."

"Liam, just—"

"The map. Now. No more games." He paused, his head cocked to the side, peering at him over the gun's barrel. Staring him down. *Like the wolf.* "That wasn't nice, peeking into my notebook. Y'all know I could kill you. Or maybe I'll just blow your balls off." He lowered the barrel, smiling. "Still a virgin, Mikey?"

Mike swallowed hard, his hands trembling now. Slowly, he unclipped the waist strap and sternum clip, pulling the backpack around to his front. "I'm getting it. Point the gun somewhere else, Liam."

"Wait." Liam edged closer, gesturing with the gun. "Now, y'all don't have that big 'ol grizzy-killin' pistol in there, do ya?"

"I don't." And to prove it, Mike opened the pack wide, showing Liam. "See? Only what I need to survive up here on this godforsaken mountain. That, and the map."

"Throw it over here." There was a sudden white brightness, brief and intense like a camera's flash. Seconds later, a roll of low, reverberant thunder seemed to travel up *through* the mountain.

"We gotta get off the ridge. That storm will be here in minutes." Mike gestured with the rolled up-map.

"Throw the map over here."

"Gimme the phone."

"I don't think so, pal. Look. Tell you what. I need a couple days. Then I'll stop changing the passcode. I swear."

"Hand it over!"

"Hey!" Aidan's voice was loud, raised over the rising wind. Mike's eyes darted sideways. The small boy stepped out from behind a boulder, the .500 outstretched, aimed at Liam, his arms trembling and his long, blond hair whipping around his face. "Drop it!"

Liam laughed. "Well hey, there, blondie!"

"Drop it! Now!"

"Aw, come on, Aidan."

"I'll do it, you fucking liar!"

"Y'all really that pissed?"

"You used me!" Aidan's face was contorted with anguish.

"Get over yourself. You enjoyed it." Liam turned to Mike. "Hey, as long as we're all being honest here, I gotta tell you. I've never really played for both teams before, but Aidan here has really expanded my horizons. I swear this kid can—"

Aidan shouted. "Shut up! You used me! Just like Evan. Just like everyone else." His eyes were soaked with tears.

"Don't take it so personally. I needed you distracted, you little shit. Y'all helped me figure out everything about the phone. And when you saw me packing up, I knew you'd tell—"

"I'll kill you." Aidan's arm trembled.

"Y'all don't have the guts," Liam said, his voice different somehow. It was a subtle shift. Softer, quieter. And then slowly, deliberately, he began lowering the shotgun to the ground. For a second, Mike thought maybe it was over. Maybe this was going to go okay. That maybe, in the end, it would be Aidan who took Liam down.

But there was something else.

It was Liam's eyes. Something cold and terrible. Something hungry. Something...*canine*. And with a surreal slowness, Mike watched Liam pivot the gun as he lowered it to the granite rock surface. Mike was unable to say anything—the shout didn't have a chance to rise fully in his throat—before the eruption of fire and a deafening crack. The shotgun flew backward without Liam's shoulder to brace it. And it was only out of the corner of his eye that Mike saw Aidan topple, almost as if a giant, invisible arm had punched his legs out from under him. The .500 was pitched out of Aidan's hands and went flying over the cliff face. By the time Mike could see what had happened, Aidan was down on the ground. His right foot—what *used to be* his right foot—was a mangled, bloody mass of bone and tissue. For a few seconds, all three of them just stared. Aidan's brow furrowed in bewildered fascination.

And then a flurry of movement, like a slow-motion action cut in a movie rapidly shifting back to real time. Mike lunged at Liam, fully airborne, landing on him and wrestling for the shotgun. They struggled, rolling, and Mike could hear Aidan's low, guttural grunts rising to high, panicked, continuous shrieking. As Mike rolled and ducked and punched and clawed at the unbelievably strong monster on top of him, he saw Aidan sitting upright against the boulder, his hands squeezing the blood-red stump of his leg, his face contorted in agony as he screamed. Somewhere in the midst of this, rain had begun pelting them—hard, gray, sideways rain. The wind was unrelenting, the sky a furious, twisting mass of dark clouds.

And then his wet hands lost their grip on the shotgun for a fraction of a second, just long enough for Liam to overpower him. Dazzling sparks accompanied a crushing blow to his temple as the larger boy kicked him in the head. When he could see again, blinking against the rain and the wind, it was Liam who filled his field of vision, standing over him, chest heaving, the barrel of the shotgun less than a foot from Mike's face. There was another blinding flash of lightning, and an eruption of thunder. Mike felt the ozone crackling in the air.

Liam didn't flinch. He yelled toward Aidan, never taking his eyes off Mike. "That was real stupid, Aidan! Real stupid!" And then to Mike: "I told you to come alone! Alone, Mike!" He shoved the gun closer, just inches from Mike's mouth.

I'm going to die.

And it was so clear then: *I don't want to die.*

Andy, I don't want to. Not anymore.

Mike found the cross on the chain around his neck, squeezing it between his fingers. He couldn't talk. He couldn't really see now, either, because the rain was filling up his eyes. Rain, and maybe blood. But then Liam stepped away, and Mike rolled to his side, crumpling, trying to wipe his eyes. Slowly, he got to his knees, then stood, his balance off, the wind and rain pelting him.

Liam's voice was still coldly level and calm despite everything. Raised a bit over the wind, and a bit breathless from their struggle, but not angry or panicked. "Take off your belt, Mike."

"What?" Mike looked up to see Liam shouldering the oversized backpack, first one strap, then the other, switching the shotgun from one hand to the other, keeping it trained on Mike. Liam had grabbed the map; it was now shoved into his waistband.

"Shut up and listen! Take off your belt. Make a tourniquet for his leg. Make it tight. Real tight, or he'll die."

"The phone!"

"Screw the phone! You don't have time to talk to me about the phone. And you don't have time to come after me. He's gonna bleed out."

Mike's voice turned pleading. "You bastard! Give us a fucking chance!"

"Do his leg!" Liam looked quickly over at Aidan, writhing on the ground. He paused for a second, then looked right back at Mike, right in his eyes. "No phone. Now do his leg! And I'm warning you. Don't come for me, Mike. Don't come for me or I'll kill y'all. All y'all. I mean, it, Mike. I'll start with this little fairy, and I'll do you last. Or maybe Liz." Liam backed away, keeping the shotgun pointed at Mike, his face oddly expressionless, until he reached the western edge of the pass. And then quickly, like an animal, Liam crouched low, his back to them, and ducked over the ledge out of sight.

Just then, in the bouncing beam of his headlamp, Mike spotted a metallic glimmer. It was the .500, maybe ten feet away. He scrambled down, retrieved it, then hustled over to the far ridge, scanning, the meager beam of the headlamp barely reaching fifty feet down into the gloom of the precipitous slope. He stood, pointing the massive pistol downward, his finger trembling on the trigger. There was no sign of Liam.

Go after him. Get the phone.

But Aidan's screaming had faded to low moans now. "Mike. Help."

No. Let him go.

He turned around. There, at his feet, was Liam's notebook. He grabbed it, and ran back to Aidan. Flipping the safety back on, he tucked the gun and notebook into his backpack. Mike unclasped his belt, the wet nylon slipping easily out of the loops like a slick snake. He dropped to his knees, hoisting Aidan's decimated leg up, and tied the tourniquet. He made a loop, found a short stick, and twisted it as tight as he could. Aidan's face was ashen in the half-light, his soaked hair plastered to his head. As if in league with Liam, the storm had also moved beyond the pass. The rain tapered off, and the wind was dying. But it was dark now. Mike put his headlamp on.

"Mike." Aidan's voice was weak.

"Quiet."

"Mike, I'm sorry—"

"Shut up. I'm carrying you down."

"The phone...he..."

"It doesn't matter." He hoisted the small boy over his shoulder, holding him tightly as he began his descent. "I'm getting us down." And he did, using strength from somewhere deep and true and wholly unknown to him until then.

33

THE HELICOPTER, buffeted by wind, bounced and rocked as they rose out of the valley and crossed the western ridge. The noise of the rotors drowned out everything, even dulled by the headset covering his ears. Mike looked out the window—first at the spot where he'd confronted Liam—and then at the vast expanse of ridges and peaks beyond it. The sky was clear this morning, and he could see for what might be hundreds of miles. He looked off to the north.

Could he make it? All the way to Canada? Somewhere down there, Liam was hiding. Or dead. All it would take is a wrong step in the darkness. *Or a run-in with a wolf.*

It didn't matter. He was going to see his mother. In just a matter of hours. Tonight.

There was a young Montana State Trooper strapped in across from him, next to Manny. Taylor sat beside him, staring out the window on the other side of the chopper. It was too loud to say anything, and that was good, because he sure as hell didn't feel like talking.

Liam's phone must have run out of batteries—or maybe something else happened to him—because it had taken only another day for Aidan's rigged up device to crack the passcode. It was a shame he wasn't awake to see it work. But the kid had lost so much blood he was barely hanging on. Mike had wondered if he would make it out at all. They all knew he was going to lose his foot. The tourniquet that saved his life also guaranteed that. When the phone did finally work—with a hilariously anticlimactic beep—it was Liz who made the call. Mike, Taylor, and Manny had run outside with her, watching eagerly as she dialed and held the phone to her ear, nearly in disbelief that it could work. Somehow, she'd managed to remain composed as she spoke to the dispatcher, calmly explaining their situation. Hearing it retold, Mike could barely believe it himself.

It was less than an hour before the heavy reverberations of approaching helicopters echoed across the valley walls, and two aircraft touched down. The noise—the first machine he'd heard in a long time—was jolting, and it seemed to make the entire valley tremble. The first was a big National Guard medevac chopper, and that took Liz and Aidan. Mike, Manny, and Taylor had watched as the flight nurse and medic, assisted by the pilots, carried the injured boy across the clearing to the helicopter, the downdraft and noise of the whirring blades buffeting them. Liz waved them away as they tried to put her on a gurney, walking alongside Aidan instead, holding his hand. The second helicopter was marked MONTANA STATE POLICE. And now, as he rode along, guarded by the bewildered-looking cop strapped in across from him, he couldn't help smiling at the irony.

Oh yeah. I'm still a junior convict. And so are they. Scuffed up and bloody and scratched and dirty, lean and scruffy and gaunt. And they smelled. Yeah, he could smell himself and the others now, confined in the cramped helicopter.

Mike's pants were stained with Aidan's blood—despite the tourniquet he'd been bleeding so much that Mike was sure he'd lose him. He'd talked to him, but Aidan was delirious and only half conscious. It had been unbelievably hard, but something had carried him on despite the unbearable, searing pain in his legs. He'd stopped only once, after nearly dropping Aidan when he slipped on a wet rock. After ten minutes, he'd had tunnel vision, everything throbbing and numb at the same time. He prayed that the others would come running. And then they had. He'd made it nearly halfway down on his own, barely conscious himself, utterly exhausted and delirious with pain, when Taylor and Manny found him. Together, the three of them hobbled down to the valley floor, sharing the burden of Aidan, going as fast as they could. They'd peppered him with panicked questions about what happened, about where Liam had gone, but Mike's answers were only half coherent, and eventually they'd given up, putting all of their energy into carrying Aidan and half-carrying Mike. He'd collapsed on the floor of the cabin when they got there, and he only vaguely remembered the commotion of the other three caring for Aidan. Just bits and pieces of it, really: talk of blood loss and shock and elevating his legs.

It's a wonder the kid's alive.

He glanced over at the cop, who was staring at him. Taylor was asleep, exhausted, despite the noise and the rough ride. He had stayed up all night with Aidan. Manny had a blank expression, leaning against the fuselage, gazing out the window. Mike turned back to his own window and looked out.

The mountains went on forever.

No way you make it out there, you bastard.

34

HE'D BEEN THROUGH THE WRINGER since landing at the hospital's helipad. There was a quick medical evaluation, all under guard. They'd taken his vitals, asked lots of questions, and given him water. He'd kept asking to call his mom. And, insanely, it seemed, they wouldn't let him at first. They assured him that she'd been notified, that she was already on her way.

Since then, he'd been interrogated by three separate detectives. He'd told the same story to all of them. Liam's confession. He'd hesitated—afraid, for a moment. Of Liam. But he realized that was something he could never hold on to. Maybe even more than that, Mike found he just didn't care anymore. He was too tired of running scared. And he wasn't going to hide a thing for that monster.

He'd turned over the journal to the cops, but not before tearing out one of Liam's drawings. It was the sketch of the plane and the lake. *So real. Like a photo.* It was smudged with dirt, the paper brittle after having gotten wet. He'd ripped it out while they waited for the helicopters, and he'd stuck it inside his own notebook.

Each of them listened without saying much, scribbling notes. They brought him food and water right away, but it was only after the second detective finished that they gave him a break to get cleaned up. The hot shower felt strange, and he watched as the dirty water sluiced off his body, swirling into the drain. He'd scrubbed hard, and his skin felt raw and clean in a way he'd forgotten. When he stood in front of the mirror, he barely recognized himself. He reached for the cross around his neck, spinning it, feeling the cool metal. He'd shaved, too, and discovered that the scar on his face had smoothed over even more. He had new bruises from the fight with Liam, including a nasty shiner from the kick he took to the head, but the old cuts were almost gone.

He'd asked about Manny, Taylor, Aidan, and Liz. They'd told him very little, only that the others were undergoing similar questioning, and that Aidan and Liz were both going to be okay. He'd asked about Liam—if they were searching for him—but the detectives said nothing.

And now he sat in the hospital room, wearing the blue nurse's scrubs they'd given him. He looked out the rain-spattered window, waiting for the next interrogation, hoping he'd be allowed to see the others. Hoping that his mother would be there soon.

There was a knock at the door. He stood up quickly, thinking it might be her, but it was the detective again. The second one. Or maybe the first, he couldn't remember. An older guy with glasses. "Come with me, son. Mrs. Crane wants to see you." They walked down the corridors, took an elevator, and crossed into a different wing. The electric lights and man-made, right-angles of the hospital building felt foreign to him after all that time outside.

Liz was in a hospital bed, an IV line in her arm. She looked better. The detective left them. She smiled weakly. "You clean up well, Whittaker."

He sat down in the chair, his knees brushing against her bed. "How are you feeling?"

"Better. The headaches are duller now. They've got me on some meds. It was one hell of a concussion. Nice crack to the skull. I got lucky. Guess we both did."

"Did they find him yet?"

Her smile faded. "No. But they will."

"You really think so?"

"They will, Mike." She touched Jim's wedding ring. "He can't hide out there forever, and there's no way he's made it to Canada by now."

"What if he does?"

"Make it to Canada?"

"Yeah."

"Truth is, it doesn't mean much. Canadian authorities would take over. They'd find him, and then it wouldn't take long to get him extradited. Not under the circumstances."

"Are you sure?"

"But what if he makes it out of Canada?"

"He won't."

"But he—"

"Mike." She put her hand on his. "When does your mother arrive?"

"Don't know. Soon, I hope. I tried calling but she was on the plane still."

"Shouldn't be long, then."

He walked over to the window, watching the raindrops cascade down. "Liz?"

"Hm?"

"What happens to us now? Me and Manny and Aidan and Taylor?"

"I don't know yet."

"I mean, does this change anything? Like, what we've been through?"

"I think it changes everything, yes."

"But…"

"Legally? I don't know."

He traced a finger down the length of the window, keeping pace with a raindrop. "Are we going to have to do prison time now?"

She chuckled. "No. No, I'm sure it won't come to that. At least not if I have anything to say about it."

He turned from the window and sat down heavily in the chair, rubbing his eyes. "I'm sorry."

"What for?"

"I'm standing here asking about myself and you're…you're in that bed, and Jim's gone.

She pursed her lips, looking down, holding the ring again. "Yes, he is."

They were quiet for a minute.

"I guess I didn't really get to say thank you yet."

She wiped her eyes. Her voice was strained. "Well, you…" She stopped and looked at him, nodding. "You're a good boy, Mike. A good young man."

He felt heat rising in his neck and face now, and the burn of tears coming. He blinked them away. "Okay. But I really want to thank you. I don't just mean for helping us get rescued. I mean for before. For helping us—helping *me*—figure things out. I mean before everything went wrong, when we were having those conversations by the fire. That was the first time things started to make sense for me."

"I know."

"And it was the same for the rest of us, too. I mean except for…well."

"Yes."

"And we all just…well, even though everything happened the way it did…" He was struggling now with how to word it. "It worked anyway, Liz."

She reached for him then, and he bent down, embracing her. It was a tight hug, awkward with her lying in the bed, but he held her tightly. "It worked anyway."

He pulled back, and she held his hands in hers. "I want to keep working with you, Mike."

"What do you mean?"

"I don't know what's going to happen to you, no. But no matter what, you're going to have probationary supervision. With a court-approved official, that is. I'd like to take that on."

"But how can you do that? I mean, you've gotta sort everything out now, and without Jim, and you've gotta—"

"Mike." She looked him right in the eye, squeezing his hands tighter now.

"What?"

"Jim's gone. My life doesn't stop. And I want to help you."

"I don't even know where we're going to live."

"Doesn't much matter."

"But you live in Phoenix. What if we aren't anywhere near you?"

"We'll work it out, Mike. Don't sweat the details right now."

"Sweat the details?" He chuckled, sitting back down, pulling away from her. "It's not just details, Liz. It's like…my whole life is completely up in the air right now. I don't even know if I'm going to some juvenile prison or home with my mom or…or even where home is. For all I know she's already up and moved to California! I don't even know—"

"Mike!" She was smiling, laughing. "Stop."

He looked at her, bewildered.

"I know Jim already said this, but you remind me of our son, Nate. You're strong, but gentle. He was like that." She straightened a crease on the hospital blanket. "You know, he was a runner too. Used to get up before sunrise and do these long runs. Sometimes I'd go with him. God, he was strong."

Mike scratched at his thumbnail, his eyes downcast. "Jim told me about the seashells. From their walks on the beach. The ones on the bottom of the lake."

"Did he?"

"Yeah. And…and I…well, we couldn't find Jim's West Point ring. It's in there too. With those shells, I guess."

At this, he looked up and saw tears welling in her eyes.

"I'm sorry. Maybe I shouldn't have…"

"No. Thank you for telling me." She smiled again. "I'll work with you, Mike. Even if it has to be remotely. And I want to meet your mother."

He stood up and went back to the window. "You will." He stared out at the rain-soaked parking lot. It was getting dark. Beyond, in the distance, he could just barely make out some of the mountains. He was thinking about Liam now. Everything that happened on the pass. "I don't understand him."

"Who?"

"Liam." He traced another raindrop with his finger. "I don't understand how someone can be like that."

"He's a classic case in a lot of ways, Mike. His behavior, and the stuff in his notebook made it clear…some pretty textbook psychopathic tendencies, and—"

"Jesus. Stop!" He whirled around, glaring at her. "Stop talking about him like he's your patient! He murdered your husband! He tried to kill Aidan up there! And back home…he…he killed that other kid, and he put that girl in a coma!"

She stared back at him, her eyes hard. "I *know* what happened up there, Mike."

"So, can't we just say what it is?"

"What do you mean?"

296

"That he's just…that he's evil! Does he have to be crazy? Does he have to have an excuse? Like some psychiatric condition that makes it…I dunno…like, excusable?"

"Of course it's not excusable."

"Then don't use that word."

"What word?"

"Psychopath. It's like it…like it explains it."

She raised her eyebrows. "Well, Mike, it does explain it."

Mike shook his head. "I don't get it. How you can sit there and say that? How can you be so cool and calm about it?"

"Look. For one thing, I'm a scientist, so I can't help but see the clinical side of things. That probably helps. But more importantly, I've had to learn the hard way not to allow terrible things to define my life. Don't you think we wanted to kill the drunk driver who took our son from us? Do you think Jim and I could have carried on with our life if we held on to that sort of hate? That's exactly why we started the program. Because that hate would have destroyed us. And it could destroy me now. But I won't let it."

"I don't understand how you can control it."

"Because I don't try to control it."

"What the hell does that mean?"

"It means when you've been through enough shit, you eventually figure out that you can't control most things in life, Mike. And that you just have to live. Haven't you figured that out yet? Dad gone? Brother gone? You can't control it, can you?"

"No!" he shouted, startled by the force of his own voice. "No, I can't! I can't control a goddamned thing!"

"Wrong. You can control how you live. And you did that up there. You saved us, Mike. You saved Aidan. You led."

"That was different! That was up there in the middle of nowhere and—"

"It doesn't matter where it was. It showed who you really *are*. You chose to save Aidan instead of chasing Liam. You chose to save a life instead of getting revenge."

He was breathing hard, his heart pounding. "It's not that easy, and—"

Her voice was low, almost a whisper. "Don't talk to me about easy, Mike."

"Sorry. I just…"

"Don't be sorry. Listen. You need to focus on your life *now*. Not Liam. Not me or Jim. Not that lifeguard, or your brother, or your dad. Right now, it's your mom and you. That's everything."

He looked up at her. "You'll help me?"

"I'll help you. I promise."

"What about those other kids? His roommate…Elliot. And that girl he hurt. Their parents need to know what he told me."

"Let us take care of that."

"But I feel like I should…I dunno. Like I should…meet them? Tell them?"

"Maybe someday." Liz looked at him, her head tilted, with the slightest curve of a smile. "You've changed, Mike."

"What?"

"You were lost in your own head a few weeks ago. Now you're thinking about everyone else. People you don't even know."

"Well, maybe."

"No, not 'maybe.' You are. Because that's who you are, Mike."

There was a knock at the door, and the detective opened it. "Michael, your mother will be here in a few minutes. We'd like you to meet her downstairs."

He turned and looked at Liz. "I've gotta go."

"Yes, you do."

"I'll bring her up to meet you."

"Yes. Go. Oh—Mike?"

"Huh?"

"Thank you for this." She pointed to Jim's wedding ring.

He smiled, nodded, and stepped out.

35

THE RED ROCK MESAS OF SEDONA were bathed in morning sun. He felt the heat on his arm as he rode with his mom in the new SUV, windows down. "It's beautiful here pretty much all the time," is what Mom had said on their first night in the hotel a couple weeks ago. "This is the place." And he'd agreed.

They'd worked it out with the courts. He'd be able to continue "rehabilitative therapy" with Liz once a week down in Phoenix, just a couple hours away. Other than periodic check-ins with a local cop, things had settled into a normal routine. He'd transferred into the school without too much turbulence—just a conference call with Liz, the principal, and the guidance counselor. Mom had been looking at houses—the real estate was upscale out here, but the money from the arrangement had come through as promised. She planned to pay cash for a modest place, as soon as they found the right one. She'd been interviewing for jobs. She was happy. It was a side of her he hadn't seen since before they lost Dad.

Stopping for coffee had become part of their morning ritual. They sat outside at their usual spot, a little café with a cactus garden on the patio.

Mom reached across the small, wrought iron table, her hand on his. "Are you keeping up on your end?"

"I am. Are you?"

"I am, Mike."

They'd made some promises. Part of the new start. She would stop drinking. And he would stop smoking. And the other stuff. No cuts. Mike had showed her. Did his best to explain. The truck, too. Everything. It was in Liz's office, during a family session weeks ago. They'd wept together, for so many things, and made their promises.

No more secrets.

That was the big stuff. But there were other, smaller things, too. Little things that they'd decided about the new life they were building together. Dinner together, every night. No social media. They both got simple flip-phones. They joined a church, and started going to Mass again. And they'd always have a project. That would be a given once they bought a house—it would have to be a fixer-upper in this town. In the meantime, it was art classes. Their tiny extended-stay hotel suite was littered with canvasses and watercolors. A series of not-very-good desert landscapes adorned the walls.

"Are you happy here?" she asked, squeezing his hand.

He smiled. "I'd be happier if they'd give me back my driver's license."

She laughed, the lines on her face deepening. "Maybe soon. Baby boy, I'm so happy here." She looked at him, and the smile faded.

"What is it, Mom?"

"It must be hard. Starting over at your age. Do you miss home?"

He ran his finger across her ring. "I miss Andy and Dad. I miss Eric. But no, I don't miss home."

*

The juvenile court judge in Montana allowed one trip home—four days only, with a daily probation check-in with Liz. So he and his mom flew home for one night, then took three days to drive a rental truck cross country back to Arizona, where Mike would continue his probation. Neither of them wanted to stay longer.

First, they visited his grandparents. There was a stop at the cemetery. They stood by the graves, hand in hand. There was nothing left to say. They went back to the house for the night—just long enough time to pack keepsakes and clothes. Everything they wanted fit in a small trailer. The house was already on the market, furnished.

While Mom packed up a few last things that evening, Mike went back to the treehouse. He'd made plans to meet Eric there after his landscaping shift, to say goodbye. Back in the hospital, he'd found the letter to Eric in his notebook and added the whole story. Well, almost the whole story. What had to remain secret, would. That was a solemn promise he and Mom had made to each other. He'd mailed the letter. So when Mike climbed up the treehouse—the old rope ladder straining to hold him—Eric was there waiting with a hug instead of questions. They talked late into the evening.

Mom and Uncle Dave had cleared out Andrew's room weeks ago, leaving just the big furniture and a bare mattress. Mike brought his pillow and blanket in. He wept as he lay in his little brother's bed, looking up at the glow-in-the-dark stars they'd stuck on the ceiling together.

He and Mom left early the following morning, just before sunrise. They both cried as they closed the door for the last time, arms around each other as they walked down the porch steps.

*

Mike snapped back to the present. "What are you doing today?"

She paused for a moment, searching his eyes. "Me? Oh. I have an interview this morning at that marketing firm, then I'll be looking at a couple more houses. The one I showed you online, and another in Oak Creek. We'll have a home here soon, Mike."

They finished their coffee and headed to school. Mom drove into the wide turnaround. Around them, outside, was the familiar commotion of school busses, and kids filed into the wide glass doors.

"You have practice after school, right?"

"Yeah. Usual time. Pick me up after?"

"Sure thing. What time is your appointment with Liz tomorrow? Eleven?"

"Yep."

"We'll leave by eight or so. Morning traffic."

"Right."

"I know. Love you." He leaned over and gave her a quick kiss.

"Wait." She brushed a few strands of his hair and straightened his collar. She touched the silver cross she'd given him. Her eyes were wet. "We're home, Mike."

*

After school, he finished his run ahead of most of the other guys, just a couple of the faster ones keeping up with him and trading some small talk. He hadn't really gotten to know anyone yet. He was keeping his distance, maybe more than he should. There were two or three guys on the team who were pretty nice, and he figured they'd eventually become friends. *Give it time.* That's what Mom said. And Liz. So he was giving it time. They knew he was from back east. They knew he'd had a rough year, that he'd lost his dad and his brother. He'd shared that much in their conversations at lunch and at practice. But they didn't know about everything else. He wasn't sure when—or if—he'd talk about all that.

And there was a girl. Haley, from his history class. Haley with the tan, the green eyes, and freckles. She was cute, and she'd been trying to get to know him. He hadn't told Mom about her yet, but he had mentioned her to Eric. And to Liz, at last week's session down in Phoenix. He thought Liz would tell him to back off—not to get involved with any girls yet. But it was just the opposite. He had lunch with her in the cafeteria today (not alone, of course; not like a date), and he came close to asking her out for coffee. *Close.* He was pretty sure he would soon, though. And the truth was, she'd made her way into his thoughts more than a few times recently. Which felt good. Because…because *maybe you're sort of getting back to normal.*

He pulled open the heavy doors leading to the athletics wing, and got a drink of water from the fountain outside the locker room. Stepping in, he heard loud banter and laughter, locker doors slamming and voices raised above the noise of showers. It was a familiar sound, and he found it put him at ease in a way. He opened his locker and looked at his phone. There was a string of texts from Mom. "Gonna be a little late. Showing got delayed. Probably can't pick u up til 6:30. Make it up to u w/dinner out. Don't be smelly! C u soon."

And one from Liz: "Call me ASAP."

It was five-fifteen. He closed the locker, went back outside, and called Liz back.

She picked up on the first ring. "Mike."

"Hi there."

"Mike, they found him."

"What? Where?"

She cut him off again. Her voice was oddly calm. "He's dead. He must have fallen. Hunters found him. Animals had been at the body. Wolves or something."

"Oh." It's all he could manage to say.

"I have to go. A few calls I have to make. I just wanted you to know first. It's gonna hit the papers soon. I don't want you to talk to any reporters or cops in the meantime, got it? Lawyers will handle all of that. I'll see you tomorrow. Eleven, at my office, right?"

"Right. Eleven."

She ended the call. He looked at the phone, like he was expecting it to tell him something. The sun was hot on his neck, and the t-shirt was drying quickly. He pictured Liam, broken, sprawled on the scree of a ravine.

He expected a stronger feeling. Something. Shock, maybe? He'd felt so, so many things. But now…there was almost nothing. Just…

Peace.

John, one of the guys on the team, clapped him on the back as he walked by, startling him. "Hey, Mike. Everything okay, man?"

"Oh. Yeah, fine. Just tired."

"Yeah. It was a long run. You did good."

"Thanks."

"See you tomorrow?"

"Nah, I have to miss Saturdays, remember?"

"Oh yeah. Cool. Well, see you on Monday at school, then." John kept walking toward his car, waving his keys by a lanyard. He stopped and turned back to Mike. "Hey, you need a ride home or something?"

"Nah. My mom's coming in a while and we're going out to dinner. I gotta get cleaned up. Thanks, though."

"See ya. Oh—yo! I almost forgot!" John jogged back to him, a grin on his face. He squinted into the sun.

"Huh?"

John looked around, and lowered his voice. "Haley's all over you." He laughed. "She's friends with my girlfriend."

"Oh."

"Yeah, well, listen. It's your move, as they say. Got her number?" John reached for his phone.

"I've got it."

"So message her, man. Oh—one more thing."

"Sup?"

"Some of us are meeting up to play pool tomorrow night. That place downtown. It's next to a dry cleaner on Saddle Road. Around eight. Lemme know if you can't find it."

"Yeah. Okay. I probably will. Thanks, John."

John gave Mike a thumbs-up as he walked away. "Later."

He should have been excited. About texting Haley. About meeting up to play pool tomorrow night. But as Mike made his way back to the locker room, he kept seeing Liam's face. Liam smirking after one of his one-liners, Liam's narrow-eyed glare, and the cold, emotionless way he'd looked at him up on the mountain pass, when he'd pointed the shotgun at him.

He almost ran flat into someone when he came around the corner, muttered an apology, and kept walking to his locker. He did the combination, opened it, and set the phone down. He was about to undress, but stopped. Instead, he closed up the locker and went back outside again. Most of the kids had left, and the parking lot was pretty quiet. He bent down and re-laced his shoes, stretching his hamstrings a bit.

And ran.

He followed the driveway out, turning out onto one of the residential streets, moving at an easy pace. Physically, he felt good. Loose. He had already run seven miles at practice, and his footfalls felt light as he padded up the quiet road, breathing easy even as it started to climb. It was a gentle, gradual slope as the road bent, heading toward the massive red sandstone mesas about a mile away. The sun was behind him, and his shadow jogged in front of him. The red rocks seemed to glow, contrasting with the deep blue, cloudless sky. The dry air made him feel fresh when he ran, even though it was hot. The houses became more spaced out the further he went. The air was tinged with sage and juniper. And it was quiet. Really quiet. In fact, all he could hear was the sound of his own shoes on the blacktop.

Would she tell the others?

Taylor and Manny were both home. Mike had only talked to them once in the past couple weeks, but they sounded okay. They had arrangements similar to his—probation officers, counseling, restricted travel. But they'd all been given a second chance, thanks to Liz's recommendation. Taylor was home. His father had moved out—some court-mandated inpatient clinic or something like that. As for Manny, his brother was still locked up, but he was living with his aunt and uncle back in Queens.

And Aidan. He'd just gone home from Montana a couple days ago. Well, no, not home. His parents couldn't hang around that town after everything that happened. They'd flown out to Denver, where he'd been transferred for emergency surgery and intensive care. From what little Aidan was able to tell him through the haze of pain medications, they'd decided to move out there instead.

He wondered if he'd see them again. *What, like a survival reunion? Maybe go back up to Camp Freedom and do some catching up, just to relive some memories?* He smiled at the thought. Although…oddly, a part of him did want to go back. He'd talked about it with Liz. She'd nodded, but hadn't said much. She'd had Jim's body exhumed and buried next to their son. Mike had asked about attending. But Liz wanted a private service.

Liam. He wasn't happy to hear he'd been killed, or unhappy. It was confusing. *Did you want him to get away? No. Not that.*

You wanted him to disappear. But Mike couldn't find himself angry about almost anything these days. He was too tired. Exhausted.

I'm running out of anger, maybe.

Ha! Running out! He pictured Andrew laughing at the pun. And he smiled. He laughed out loud, in fact.

He picked up speed as the hill grew steeper, and soon he was accelerating more, going even faster, maybe pacing six-minute miles, stretching out his stride, using his entire core, feeling the road beneath his toes as he pushed off with each step. His breathing fell into a new rhythm, everything working together, the dry air whooshing in his ears now, the sound of his own breathing drowning out his footsteps. He felt strong. Fast, and healthy, and good. The road curved around a switchback, still climbing, and he leaned into the turn, speeding up, pushing even harder. Sweat poured down his face, and he sprinted. He kept going for a full minute, then gradually slowed, coming to a halt at the top of another switchback. He stopped, lifted off his t-shirt, and paced for a bit as he caught his breath. He sat down on the side of the road, leaning against a sandstone rock, breathing hard, looking out at the town stretched out below him and the mountainous desert beyond. He felt the cross dangling around his neck, the way it slid on his chest as he breathed, the sweat trickling off of him.

Sitting up there, his heart beating strong with the cool rock against his back, he realized Liam held nothing over him anymore. Whatever cosmic force of justice existed had held Liam accountable for what he did, and maybe, just maybe, that sort of made up for the DeAngelos not having to face what they'd done.

But that wasn't really why he found himself smiling.

It was because he was here in this new place, this new home, with Mom. And because she'd stopped drinking. And because there was money in the bank for the first time in their lives. Because his little brother wouldn't ever hurt anymore, and because Dad would be so happy for them. He was talking to Eric again, and a new friend offered him a ride home from his new school today, and a pretty girl with green eyes wanted to go out with him. Everything was clean and dry out here. There was not a single bleeding cut on his body.

And now he was going to run back, clean up, and go out for enchiladas with his mom. He stood up and jogged back down the hill toward school, taking it easy now, embraced by the warmth of the late afternoon sun.

BOARDING PASS
A NOVEL BY PAUL CUMBO

A hotel burns in a small Wyoming town, and uncanny coincidence reunites a young firefighter with his father amidst the smoke and flames. Hearing the news from across the country, a boyhood schoolmate travels west both to visit his friend and escape his own troubles at college. This seemingly impulsive journey becomes nothing less than a pilgrimage that revisits the past, illuminates the present, and defines the future for all three men. A coming-of-age novel for all generations.

A 2014 *Shelf Unbound* "Notable Indie"
A *ForeWord* Clarion 5-Star Review
ISBN: 978-0988208605
Visit www.paulcumbo.com

TEN STORIES
A SHORT FICTION COLLECTION
BY PAUL CUMBO

Set in varied landscapes, these ten short stories provide glimpses of humanity from a multitude of angles. They tell of men, women, children, and families at different stages of life's journey: beginnings, endings, and stops along the way.

A 2014 *Shelf Unbound* "Notable Indie"
ISBN: 978–0988208629
Visit www.paulcumbo.com

ACKNOWLEDGMENTS

This book is dedicated to my grandfather on my mom's side, Norman Gannon Sr., who moved on from this life a few years ago. He was a man of honor, faith, and immense love. He would have helped Mike figure things out, and I think he'd be proud of this book. Sometimes, when I hear the crunch of gravel as I walk on Irish Hill Road, or sit quietly and listen to the rushing water flow through the 'crick' behind the cabin he built, I'm sure he's there with me.

Kiele Raymond, my developmental editor, helped me immensely. Her insight into narrative structure, character-building, and nuanced language vastly improved the initial draft. I have a tendency to overwrite descriptions, which end up groaning under the weight of excess language—much of it in the form of silly adverbs. Kiele helped me see this and address it.

Stephen Parolini, aka "The Novel Doctor," provided a superb late-stage editing pass and helped me pull off some important detail work. Dr. Tom Cumbo (my dad) caught a handful of typos that somehow eluded four rounds of professional editing.

Early test readers, including Anne Cumbo (my mother), Scott Flaherty, and the entire Sardinia family (Tim, Margaret, Timmy, Jack, Ben, and Harry), gave vital feedback that helped me smooth some rough edges and filter out some overwrought melodrama early on in the process.

My brother David, a remarkably talented artist, has done all four of my book covers. It's hard to explain the level of careful attention that goes into Dave's work. He really pulled off something special with this one—it captures the emotional depth of Mike's struggle in an understated but spot-on way.

I have to thank all the people who wrote and produced *Dungeons & Dragons*, because playing it as a kid served as the foundation for my understanding and love of storytelling. Thanks to Dave Goehrig, who played *D&D* with me the most.

Indie publishing is not without expenses, and a few people helped get my venture off the ground financially back when I released my first novel. They include Paul Paterson, Michelle Capizzi, Jana Amelingmeier, Alberto Sevilla-Sacasa, Jane Buck, Tim Sardinia Jr., Joe Bielecki, Johnny Murray, Ben Schmid, Juan Estrada, and Morgan Cook.

The guys I've taught and coached for the past twenty-two years, at both Canisius High School and Georgetown Prep, have really been the ones who have enabled me to understand the teenage male psyche (inasmuch as anyone does, that is).

Dr. Leonard Sax, Michael Gurian, Dr. Michael Reichert, Dr. Ann Holmquist, and Dr. Jim Power, all experts in adolescent male development, have been influential. Each read the novel, reviewed it, and offered generous praise.

I owe gratitude to my four brothers, Tom, John, Peter, and David. Because, well, they're my brothers. And because they provided a first-hand experience of brotherhood—which kind of matters in this story.

My wife, Megan, who is a fine lawyer and wonderful mother, helped me work out the legal aspects of the story, lending it credibility. She also puts up with me, and keeps smiling, and that's really something.

Finally, I owe thanks to my kids. Matt, Kate, and Ben, I love you more than the sun and the moon and the stars in the sky and all the chocolate chip cookies in the whole wide world.

ABOUT THE AUTHOR

Photo by Erin Townsend

Paul Cumbo is a high school English teacher. He coached rowing for twelve years, during which his crews earned multiple U.S. and Canadian national championship titles. He has also served as a swimming coach, retreat director, and service-learning coordinator. Paul's books include *Boarding Pass*, a novel; *Ten Stories*, a short fiction collection; and *Blue Doors*, an institutional history. His articles have appeared in *U.S. News & World Report*, *The Buffalo News*, and *Independent Ideas*, a publication of the National Association of Independent Schools (NAIS). As an editorial consultant and freelance writer, Paul's clients include professionals and small businesses as well as some of the world's most prominent names in the corporate, academic, and nonprofit sectors. He co-founded the Camino Institute, which offers immersive, service-oriented retreats in the rural Dominican Republic. Paul lives near Buffalo, New York, with his wife and children.

www.paulcumbo.com
@paulcumbo

www.ingramcontent.com/pod-product-compliance
Lightning Source LLC
Chambersburg PA
CBHW021403110726
47901CB00008B/2037